Melba's Wash

ESSENTIAL PROSE SERIES 166

Guernica Editions Inc. acknowledges the support
of the Canada Council for the Arts and the Ontario Arts Council.
The Ontario Arts Council is an agency of the Government of Ontario.
We acknowledge the financial support of the Government of Canada.

Reesa Steinman Brotherton

Best Wishes Dr. Alam

Melba's Wash

Reesa Steinman Brotherton

GUERNICA EDITIONS

TORONTO • BUFFALO • LANCASTER (U.K.)
2019

Copyright © 2019, Reesa Steinman Brotherton and Guernica Editions Inc.
All rights reserved. The use of any part of this publication,
reproduced, transmitted in any form or by any means, electronic,
mechanical, photocopying, recording or otherwise stored
in a retrieval system, without the prior consent
of the publisher is an infringement of the copyright law.

Michael Mirolla, general editor
Julie Roorda, editor
Interior and cover design: Rafael Chimicatti
Guernica Editions Inc.
1569 Heritage Way, Oakville, (ON), Canada L6M 2Z7
2250 Military Road, Tonawanda, N.Y. 14150-6000 U.S.A.
www.guernicaeditions.com

Distributors:
University of Toronto Press Distribution,
5201 Dufferin Street, Toronto (ON), Canada M3H 5T8
Gazelle Book Services, White Cross Mills
High Town, Lancaster LA1 4XS U.K.

First edition.
Printed in Canada.

Legal Deposit—Third Quarter
Library of Congress Catalog Card Number: 2019930420
Library and Archives Canada Cataloguing in Publication
Title: Melba's wash / Reesa Steinman Brotherton.
Names: Brotherton, Reesa Steinman, author.
Series: Essential prose series ; 166.
Description: First edition. | Series statement: Essential prose series ; 166
Identifiers: Canadiana (print) 20190049022 |
Canadiana (ebook) 20190049049 | ISBN 9781771834001
(softcover) | ISBN 9781771834018 (EPUB) | ISBN 9781771834025 (Kindle)
Classification: LCC PS8603.R6715 M45 2019 | DDC C813/.6—dc23

To my father, Samuel Steinman

*"It doesn't matter who my father was;
it matters who I remember he was."*
— Anne Sexton

Contents

Prologue, XIII

Part I

CHAPTER 1, The Island, 2

CHAPTER 2, Deer Curve, 5

CHAPTER 3, Birth Day, 8

CHAPTER 4, The Naming, 11

CHAPTER 5, Frieda's Baby, 14

CHAPTER 6, Just Like a Woman, eh?, 22

CHAPTER 7, Queen For A Day, 24

Part II

CHAPTER 8, Good Beginnings, 28

CHAPTER 9, Trying On Boys, 35

CHAPTER 10, Good and Oak and Two Pregnant, 38

CHAPTER 11, Your Sorry Looking Face, 40

CHAPTER 12, Montreal 1945, 42

CHAPTER 13, Melba's Tune, 50

CHAPTER 14, Life's Just Not Fair, 56

CHAPTER 15, Esther Girling, 58

Part III

CHAPTER 16, Esther Weinstein, 64

CHAPTER 17, 1962, 68

CHAPTER 18, The Little Brown Coat, 73

CHAPTER 19, The Counting Room, 75

CHAPTER 20, Over My Dead Body, 78

CHAPTER 21, Birthing a Bathroom, 84

CHAPTER 22, No Kleenex on Deer Curve, 88

Part IV

CHAPTER 23, Out the Kitchen Door, 94

CHAPTER 24, Summer, 98

CHAPTER 25, The Washcloth, 101

CHAPTER 26, Making Believe, 103

CHAPTER 27, Minced Meat, 105

CHAPTER 28, Esther is a Television, 109

CHAPTER 29, Getting to Know You, 111

CHAPTER 30, Miller's Font, 116

CHAPTER 31, Liar Liar, 119

Part V

CHAPTER 32, End of Summer, 124

CHAPTER 33, Fall, 126

CHAPTER 34, Winter, 130

CHAPTER 35, Some Spring, 135

CHAPTER 36, Another Summer, 138

CHAPTER 37, Victor Woods, 142

CHAPTER 38, Willa Cather's Cottage, 149

Part VI

CHAPTER 39, Saint John, 162

CHAPTER 40, Arriving Halifax, 165

CHAPTER 41, The Prat Family, 171

Part VII

CHAPTER 42, Glass Walls, 178

Part VIII

CHAPTER 43, High River Flood, 186

CHAPTER 44, Squatting, 194

CHAPTER 45, Grand Manan Island, 197

CHAPTER 46, Good Riddance, 201

CHAPTER 47, Dark Harbour, 207

Epilogue, 210,
Acknowledgements, 211
About the Author, 212

Prologue

I AM THE TEN-MONTH-OLD BABY that Melba and Russell Girling traded to her sister Flora and Sammy Weinstein for a black and white floor model RCA Victor television set, on Grand Manan Island, New Brunswick, back in 1954. I am also the young Jewish Princess who grew up in Côte Saint-Luc in Montreal, Quebec. This is a story remembered, not remembered.

Sometimes I light two short white candles for the Sabbath eighteen minutes before sundown on Friday. I sing the prayer and gently wave my hands. I leave the candles to burn down, flicker, and go out.

> "Baruch atah Adonai, Eloheinu Melech ha-olam, asher kidshanu b'mitzvotav, v'tzivanu l'hadlik ner shel Shabbat."
> "Blessed are You, Adonai our God, Ruler of the universe, who has sanctified us with commandments and commanded us to light the Shabbat candles."

Today, even after seventeen years living in Calgary, watch my baby finger delicately pierce the air while I sip tea with freshly squeezed lemon, from a fine bone china teacup, then smear thick cream cheese, followed by thin folds of fresh lox from Abe's Deli, onto a boiled and wood-fire baked bagel like the ones from Montreal. Or I might just as easily decide to make a toasted ham and mayonnaise sandwich like Mummy and I used to have at Kresge's lunch counter on Fridays after she got her hair done. We didn't tell Daddy about that.

After more than forty years, the princess and the goy still squabble. We have a hell of a time making decisions, especially about food. In the grocery store, only I hear the kibitzing back and forth that goes on in my head. While one hand holds Manischewitz broad egg noodles, and the other holds the cheaper generic brand, I think: "You really want to spend the extra dollar?" Soundlessly I answer: "Damn it, yes I do. I'm making chicken and luchen kugel."

With a tiny huff, I drop the egg noodles into the shopping cart, where I imagine crackling cellophane bags and cardboard boxes and jars will argue their inherent privilege to be there. I pile the Kosher food at the back, separated with a family-sized box of rice-type cereal from the bacon and dairy products I've stacked in front, where they won't be close to the sweet marbled halva and the watchful Manischewitz matzo.

The checkout clerk quickly scans soup, vegetables, bacon, syrup, slowing as she slides a box of matzo meal over the scanner while giving me her "shame on you" face. This is the first time she has looked at me. I smile at her and think: *You don't know the half it*. And frankly, I don't know if I do either.

We Weinsteins occasionally ate bacon, sprinkled with brown sugar, and broiled in the oven like the Queen of England has hers prepared. Yes, nothing less than the Queen's bacon on the occasional Sunday morning for our own self-declared royal family.

Some mornings, just for the hell of it, I toss a poppy seed bagel in the air, right in the middle of my kitchen. If I catch it seed side up, I head to the refrigerator for lox and cream cheese. If it lands, well you know, the other way, the day is up for grabs. Either way, I follow breakfast with my anti-depressants and anti-anxiety medication.

I look at a portrait of the three of us taken in the lobby of the Catskills Hotel in New York State. I'm wearing a short-sleeve aqua print dress with a crinoline and belted at the waist, and over it, a new white angora cardigan trimmed on the cuffs and up the front with sequins. I talked Mummy into buying it for me a few minutes before we posed for our photograph. She didn't think I needed it, so that's why her smile isn't real. I'm standing in front of Daddy with my hands joined loosely in front of me, and my feet in ballet style second position. He's wearing a white shirt, striped tie, and a monogrammed white hankie barely sticks up from his jacket pocket. His suit is charcoal grey and his matching shoes have just been shined.

Mummy is wearing a stunning bronze cocktail dress and her sable mink stole. Her coloured auburn hair is perfectly teased and backcombed, stiff with hairspray. She is standing shoe to shiny shoe beside Daddy, leaning into his right shoulder; her arms wrap his at the elbow. Her diamond necklace and wedding rings sparkle. Daddy's hand hangs at his side between us, with nowhere to go. His left hand is solid and warm on my shoulder.

Written on the back of the photograph in Mummy's handwriting is:

"the royal family" 1959
Flora, Sammy, and Esther

Melba's Wash

This portrait now hangs on my dining room wall behind an empty chair. But when I was growing up in Montreal, it hung on the dining room wall behind Daddy's chair. As a child, I didn't know that a photograph doesn't always capture the truth, that sometimes a photograph cements a lie to history. Or many lies.

Part I

CHAPTER 1

The Island

GRAND MANAN ISLAND WAS A SLOW, one-and-a-half hour ferry ride from Blacks Harbour, New Brunswick, Canada, south and east into the frigid waters of the Bay of Fundy.

From the air, the island appeared to slosh back and forth between New Brunswick and Nova Scotia, side to side, as if it were swaying in an old tin pail held by long fingers of the moon and the sun. The cliffs and coves and people and sand were baptized every twelve hours by the pushing and pulling of merciless fifty-foot tides.

North Head was the largest village, where the ferry docked, beside Fisherman's Wharf, where generations of respectable churchgoing men had their mother's or wife's or daughter's name painted on the bow of their fishing boats.

Eighteen churches anchored the island along the twenty-one miles of paved road that coursed the eastern shoreline.

The Grand Manan Hospital, the Nursing Home, the drugstore, the abandoned movie theatre and record store, the wool shop, and the inns and hotel – for those who were from *away* – were all at the Head. The hotel had a liquor licence. The bar, with after-hours off sales, opened for business in 1978, the year after the drugstore began to sell condoms.

Farther down Island Highway 776 was the Whistle lighthouse, the North Head dump, and Pearl's restaurant where you could get a hamburger, French fries and soda, and either drop off or take out the latest gossip.

The western shoreline was steep rock walls, with the exception of Dark Harbour, which was accessible by car and boat, where dulse was harvested at low tide. Men, mostly, picked and stuffed fifty-pound sacks with the purple sea vegetable, loaded them into dories and rowed back to the natural breakwater. The wet sacks were dragged above the high tide line where the dulse was thinly spread over black fishing nets that covered the beach rocks. Here it dried in the sun and the wind.

Melba's Wash

Heading down island, villages were snuggled around coves bitten from the coastline. Each cove was a harbour, with a settlement of white clapboard houses that were either painted with traditional black window trim and matching black roof, or red or green trim and shingles. They surrounded white painted churches with peaked, red rolled asbestos roofs, and praying steeples. You could hear bells chime on Sunday mornings.

Melba and Russell Girling lived in his mother's house, almost halfway between Grand Harbour and Seal Cove on what was known as Deer Curve, where there were four houses and no church.

There were no cars parked in their dooryard, no bicycles lying on the gravel and grass driveway where children might have carelessly dropped them, and the last flakes of white paint desperately clung to the greying exterior of the small one-and-a-half storey clapboard house. The Girlings had a one-seater outhouse, a trout in the well, pigs in the barn, a cow tied to a rope, attached to an iron peg hammered in the ground where the septic field should have been, and they had children. Lots of children. But they lived in a house, on a hill with a name, and not simply out the dump road, or out the back road, like some families who lived in shacks with no running water or electricity. Places where a few two-fours of beer might hold up a front stoop, and rusted out cars, or just their seats or engines might be planted in the dooryard, and wild purple and pink and white lupines blossomed undisturbed among them in the spring.

The Girlings couldn't hear any church bells, only the deafening silence of the earless and the blind, with their condescending tongues in the graveyard around the corner. Shame on you Baptists, and Catholics and Anglicans and Pentecostals. Didn't you know that you can tell a lot about a family by looking at the laundry hanging out on their clothesline? Didn't any of you see Melba Girling's wash? Diapers flying in the salt breeze, greying and thinning season after season, blue and red, blood stained polka dot handkerchiefs hanging wrung out of square, patched knees on pants, mended dog-ears on shirts, and darned, and darned again, work socks that either blew dry in the summer or froze dry in winter.

As Esther's two brothers Paul and Luke grew, they fought their old man, defended their mother. Sometimes shirts ripped and buttons were lost. If you listened beneath the yelling, you could hear each crack and split as buttons flew into the air and dropped quickly, *ping*, onto the iron heat grate in the front room, then tipped slowly and sank like a drowning dory into the furnace down below in the cellar. Meanwhile a man-boy tried to nail his old man against a dark green plastered wall, and his smooth hairless fingers dug into the throat of a drooling Russell Skunk.

Young blood pumped and Luke tightened his grip. The round whiskered face of the old man turned red. Yes, Russell was drunk, and had Lloyd Slader's voice in his head saying, "How's that TV of yours working?" and laughing from a table over in the corner of the bar.

"You broke her friggin arm!" Luke wanted to kill his father.

The oldest brother Paul pulled young Luke's fingers, one by one like rotten teeth, from the smocked layers of skin that wrapped their old man's red neck.

Russell Girling was usually drunk as a skunk, so Russell Skunk is what most people called him. He wasn't always this way; Melba knows when he started drinking heavily, but she won't admit it was when she gave Esther away.

He was also a deckhand on a dragger, and when he worked, more often than not, he drank most of his pay on the other side of the Grand Banks, usually in the first bar in the first port that the Betty-Jo docked.

On Monday, even with a broken arm, Melba washed the smell of hatred from size fourteen and sixteen boy's shirts and hung them on the clothes-line. There were traces of blood from Melba's hands on the wooden clothes pegs. Her knuckles were red and cracked with eczema, and her fingers were split with stinging cuts from slips of her knife when she was boning salt herring on Saturdays at Thomas' smoke shed down in Seal Cove.

CHAPTER 2

Deer Curve

NOT YET SUNRISE, Russell Skunk sat on the edge of the bed in yesterday's underwear and pulled on grey work socks with red wool ringing the top, and darned heels. His green pants were outlined with salt stains from fish scales that had dried and rubbed off underneath his hip waders. He pushed his feet into the waiting pants, stood, buttoned the waist underneath his hairy stomach, and pulled on a white undershirt. His fingers fumbled with the buttons on his green work shirt, as he looked at his eight-month-old son Luke, sleeping in the same old crib the rest of the kids had slept in, the same crib he had slept in, in the same house, his mother's house, that was originally over on Wood Island.

Around 1920, there was better fishing, wrinkling, clamming, and dulsing on Grand Manan, and a school for the kids. Best of all was talk of a sardine factory being built in North Head. All but a few Wood Island families moved to the Big Island, as they called it, and most had their houses barged over, like Russell's father Percy did. The house was skidded down the dooryard to be placed on a wood foundation, but before dinnertime, Percy had a heart attack and died right where he fell. He never slept a night on Deer Curve. Russell was five, and watched his father crumple to the ground.

LUKE WAS SICK AFTER HE WAS BORN, and didn't take to Melba's milk, or cow's milk, or Carnation milk either. Poor little fellow screamed with cramps and just couldn't keep anything from coming back up, or out the other end. Melba called her sister Flora like she always did when she needed help, and Flora's husband Sammy arranged for Melba and Luke to arrive in Montreal within a few days to see a doctor. Doctors cost money. Melba and Russell didn't have any.

Flora didn't work anymore, and she didn't drive, so she and Melba usually took taxi cabs to and from the hospital, or Sammy gave Melba a lift on his way to work, and picked her up on his way home in the evening. Melba still dreamed of shopping for makeup and nylons and expensive clothes in the big city, and going to the movie theatre, and nightclubs, and to dinner parties at fancy restaurants. Flora had that life. Melba wanted it. Had always wanted it. *All* of it, and the more time that passed, the less Melba thought about going back to Grand Manan.

The doctor suggested several different milk formulas and finally with the introduction of the third one, Luke stopped crying, and began sleeping for longer periods. By nine weeks old, Luke's colour turned a healthy pink; he smiled and gained one pound. Over coffee and Danish one morning after Sammy went to work, Flora asked Melba when she was going back. Melba said she wasn't going back.

"Have you lost your mind, Melba?"

"No. You must've lost yours. You said you'd send for me after you got settled in Montreal."

"Melba! You sound like a child. That was almost ten years ago. It didn't work out."

"Didn't work out for me on Grand Manan either! You have no bloody idea what it's like for me down there."

"I didn't force you to move to that little Peyton Place and marry a fisherman, a poor fisherman yet."

"Like I had so many choices. I had two kids! One of them yours, remember?"

"I remember. I'll always remember. And if I didn't remember, I have you to remind me, don't I? This is about you, Melba. You have three other kids back there. Just who do you think is going to bring them up? Russell? He's called five times for you to come home. Collect!"

"I don't care how many times he calls, I just don't care."

"Well, I care. I'm going out to play canasta with the girls tonight, and while I'm gone, you are packing. I'm calling Sammy at work to make the arrangements, and you're going back! Do you hear me?"

Melba heard her, and turned and ran to the den where she and Luke were staying. She threw herself onto the bed like a disappointed and desperate child. Luke napped while his mother thought about killing herself, or killing her sister. *No, instead I'll seduce Sammy. Maybe tonight*, Melba thought.

MONTHS LATER, back on Grand Manan, Russell looked from Luke to Melba, then turned and slapped her playfully on the ass, as if she loved him, and he loved her, and everyone in every corner of his mother's house was happy, and he hadn't raped her pregnant body. *Whoremaster*, she thought.

I'll fix him. Without rolling over, Melba raised her arm and swung at him, batting only air. Russell had gone.

His large frame and short legs scuffed up the gravel driveway to catch a ride with his boss, Cyril. If Russell wasn't waiting at the top of the driveway, Cyril drove right past Deer Curve and hired someone else down at the wharf. This was how it would be when Russell started drinking.

When Melba heard the snap of the screen door on the porch, she rolled over. Her face turned into Russell's pillow breathing in the foul odour of greasy hair and fish. Her stomach became sloppy as a hogshead of fresh herring slapping and flapping around down in the belly of a boat. She was eight and a half months pregnant; this was not morning sickness. She threw up the smell of Russell Skunk into a lime green plastic bowl, the bowl she used for popcorn for the kids on Saturday nights, the one the kids had teethed on, and beat right silly with wooden spoons. And tomorrow Luke would probably sit cross-legged on the kitchen floor wearing it as a hat.

On the dresser, little Ben read six-fifteen. With her index finger, Melba traced the faint baby line from underneath her breasts to her pubic hair. This one was only eleven months younger than Luke.

Melba pushed herself up out of bed and caught her reflection in the small oval mirror on the dresser. Her mother's mirror. One of the few things she brought with her to Grand Manan from Janeville, New Brunswick, after her mother died. *I was never beautiful like Flora*, she thought.

She put on slippers and a housecoat, left Luke sleeping in his crib, and headed downstairs to the kitchen to wash up and brush her teeth before the other kids woke up. As she walked past the barn to the outhouse, she thought: *I just can't do this anymore.*

CHAPTER 3

Birth Day

IT WAS SUCH AN ORDINARY DAY on Grand Manan when Esther was born, with early morning fog hanging in the harbours, and low-lying areas. Out from the Seal Cove breakwater, the bell buoy rang loud and deep, swaying side to side in the wake of another herring carrier weighted low with eighty hogsheads of fish. The Betty-Jo was one of several pumpers idling in the harbour waiting to pump the herring.

If you had walked through a hundred unlocked kitchen doors at exactly the same time, you'd probably see shortwave radios on top of fridges, and hear the familiar static and squeal of marine bands quivering in and out: "Ssss, got a load on. Fours and sixes, ssss." On those days, islanders who lived close to Seal Cove and North Head often woke to the sound of the sardine factory whistle.

Esther was born a week early, late in August. She would continue to call her mother Melba, until she made up her mind whether or not she was giving Esther away to her Aunt Flora and Uncle Sammy. Melba didn't seem to want her.

They'd been together for eight and a half months, their weight stretching out pie dough with a rolling pin, or pushing and folding and punching down bread dough on the kitchen table every three days. Mondays were wash days, and Esther wouldn't miss being squeezed against and over the washing machine, as Melba pulled heavy wet clothes from the cold water to put them through the wringer into the rinse tub and back again, only to have to pick them up one more time to hang on the clothesline. Esther's oldest sister Frieda usually brought the dried clothes in and did the ironing too. Melba and Esther planted the garden, weeded the garden, and for two months they'd been picking vegetables for supper. So much bending. Esther was tired thinking about all that they did: scrubbing floors, emptying commodes every morning, feeding the pigs, keeping the woodstove going, and washing her brothers' and sisters' faces and tushies.

8

Melba didn't have a name picked out for Esther, or for a boy either, if she happened to be a boy. She had two brothers. Luke wasn't one year old yet, and Paul was almost four. She also had two sisters. Liona was six, and Frieda was almost thirteen. Frieda thought there was another child somewhere. She swore she heard a baby crying when she was little, and living up in Janeville. When Melba told Frieda there was no baby, and not to talk such foolishness again, Esther felt Melba's heart pound faster, and they became warm and tired. She was remembering leaving that baby with the minister at the church.

Being born was disgusting, not to mention the difficulty of holding on during contractions. Just when Esther figured, okay, that's it, I'm out of here, someone yelled: "Don't push." It was the doctor!

The final wave came maybe one minute later. Memories of Melba began to squeeze out of Esther's body like she was being fed through those washing machine wringers. Frantic and confused, she tried to fight leaving her, but Melba pushed down and started yelling, her voice becoming louder and more clear, then Esther was out, and she was cold, and memories and fragments of memories, and words and fragments of words rushed out of her and off her into a pail on the floor. Someone cut and tied her umbilical cord. Melba's intense sadness and jealousy, the lies and anger, were gone from Esther. She was alone.

Nurse Kitty, the pale one with the nicotine stained fingers, gave her a warm sponge bath, wetly familiar. She prayed for a warm blanket. Such a small request. Kitty pinned Esther into a gauze diaper, which caused her legs to splay like a dead chicken, and after dressing her in a backless nightie tied at her neck, Kitty laid her down on a flannelette receiving blanket, tucked in all limbs, rolled her up like a holishke, and placed her face down on a scratchy sheet with a boiled clean smell. Thankfully, Kitty moved Esther's head to the side before she left. That's when Esther saw a pink card taped to the side of her bassinette. In blue ink was printed: Girling, girl. She wondered why she had no name.

Exhausted, her body sore, Esther drifted in and out of sleep until she heard Nurse Right, the tall one with the husky voice, say that "none of them knew anything about birth control, and the only difference between these two babies is three and half hours, and three quarters of an inch in length." Esther opened her eyes and saw the name Francine Slader, printed on a pink card on the bassinette next to her. Francine had blonde hair and brown eyes. They had plenty in common besides their birthdays, and would have lots to talk about the next time they met.

But tonight, on the day of their birth, they looked at each other and listened to the nurses. Like there was anything better to do?

"Sure is queer, these two born within hours of each other, wouldn't surprise me if …"

"Nurse Right! That's just talk."

"Talk? Maybe. But at least Lloyd Slader has his own boat and can look after his, not like Russell Skunk. I know for a fact that Irving Oil's got them on C.O.D., and I know for another fact that they're buried deep into Mason's store."

"I don't know about all that, but Melba says she's too tired to feed hers, and would we give her a bottle."

"She's too tired, is she? Well, I'm too busy! Take the baby to her. Melba can sleep when the baby sleeps."

CHAPTER 4

The Naming

L UKE WAS ONLY ELEVEN MONTHS OLD when Melba brought home the new baby.

Frieda called her new sister "my baby." At times she was also called shit-pants, piss-ass, and a whole array of colourful names, until one day Flora telephoned. She wanted to know the baby's name.

"She's got lots of names around here, but not one I can put on her birth certificate," Melba said, chuckling.

"She doesn't have a name yet? Melba, she's almost a month old, for crying out loud!"

"Well, you think of a name for her then if you're so smart!"

"Just a minute." Flora held her hand over the receiver and talked to Sammy.

"What about Esther? Sammy loves that name."

"Oh why's that, Flora?"

"He says it comes from the Old Testament," Flora said.

"Okay, she can be Esther then!"

"My God, you don't even care what her name is?"

"Not right now I don't, Flora. I'm too tired."

"You better stop having babies, Melba," Flora said sternly.

FLORA WAS RIGHT, she didn't want another baby. Melba tended to Luke in the mornings, and Frieda tended to Esther.

"How's my baby this morning? Oh, you're some wet. Let's get you washed up and we'll have breakfast." Frieda adored her baby sister, and Esther loved Frieda's young face with the soft voice.

"How about we dress you in some blue clothes today, Esther?" Frieda laughed. All there were, were blue clothes from Luke and Paul. Frieda fussed with her baby until the very last minute when she had to catch the bus for school. When she came back in the afternoon and dropped her books, she didn't go for the fridge like the others. She went straight to get Esther and give her a bath.

11

One afternoon, Esther sat propped in her playpen, shaking the rails and hollering, "a-ba a-bab a-bababa" at her mother while she called Flora.

"Collect call from Melba Girling.

"Do you accept the charges?

"Go ahead please."

"Melba, it's the middle of the day! Is everything all right? Is Esther all right?" Flora asked.

"Yes, she's fine."

"What about Luke?"

"The kids are okay. It's me, Flora."

"You sound awful. Did that bastard hit you again?"

"No. He's been not too bad. It's me. I'm so tired. I need a break."

"You should have thought about that before you got pregnant again!"

"That's not fair. I did get pregnant. Now I'm tired, I tell you!"

"Maybe you should go to the doctor? You weren't this tired after Luke was born."

"I wasn't?"

"No, you weren't. When you brought Luke up to the specialist, the three of us played cards until late almost every night, remember? And we went shopping downtown almost all day!"

"Well when his milk got changed he started to sleep through the night, that's why."

"Esther must be sleeping through the night for God's sake."

"It doesn't matter. I just can't do it, Flora. They're only eleven months apart; it's too much."

"Doesn't Frieda help you?"

"Yes, but she's in school all day."

"Can't you lie down and nap when Luke and Esther do?"

"Never seems to be the same time, Flora, and you forget, Paul's up all day."

"Well, what can I do?"

"I want you to take Esther," Melba stated flatly.

"Oh for God's sake. Esther's just a baby, Melba."

"Right, she won't know any different whether she's here or with you."

"Melba, I don't want a baby to look after."

"Well, I didn't plan on tending your daughter Amy for all those years either, Flora. You owe me."

Melba's Wash 13

"You weren't going anywhere. You had Frieda to look after anyway. Besides, Mama looked after Amy. It's not the same – Sammy and I don't have any kids."

"Mama looked after Amy, my ass. And what about when Mama died? Where were you but off gallivanting around Montreal with your boyfriend?"

"I'm going to hang up if you keep this up."

"You hang up and I'll show up on your doorstep with all of them, not just Esther."

"You're talking crazy, Melba!"

"You left me and Mama. You said you'd come back to get Amy and me and Frieda. You never came back, Flora. You never came back. When's it my turn? Tell me when's it my turn?"

"Your turn to what?"

"Have a break from kids."

"Okay. Okay, I'll talk to Sammy and see if we can bring her up for a couple of months in the spring."

THAT WINTER IN THE BRIGHT SNOW OUTSIDE the bedroom window, Esther's sisters and brother chopped down a beautiful, alive and breathing spruce tree from way in the back of the yard. They dragged it to the front room and cut off its flawlessly symmetrical top, replaced it with a nest of coloured tinfoil, and put a fake candle in its centre. The tree was wrapped so tightly with strings of popcorn that the branches appeared to be hugging each other and could no longer move with the breeze of bodies walking by. The family hung apples, pinecones, ribbons, and curled hardtack candy and round popcorn balls on the tree. Underneath were a few scattered presents wrapped in newspaper, and several wrapped in thick, bright, colourful Christmas paper with foil bows from Flora and Sammy.

CHAPTER 5

Frieda's Baby

B Y SPRING, ESTHER HAD BABY MUSCLES, and could, and did, shake her playpen up close to the bedroom window. She saw that same spruce tree lying half propped against another tree along the edge of the woods, now with yellow and brown needles, some branches naked, and even some strings of half-eaten popcorn that attracted the squirrels and birds.

Needle-nose hummingbirds darted past the window too quickly to focus on, but Esther heard chickadee songs, and those awful summer gulls laughing in excitement on their way to Fisherman's Wharf. She smelled moist fiddleheads that rose like apostrophes from the damp ground along the low edge of the yard, and boat-gas fumes from chain saws working back in the woods where the smell of gas overpowered the woody scent of newly sawed lumber. At night she saw the Little Dipper hanging in the sky and it poured sleep dust into the corners of her bright brown eyes, bending tiny pink lips into a wonderful crescent moon shape.

Other times, when it wasn't clear enough to see the Little Dipper and the northeast wind was blowing hard, the boats either came in or didn't put out at all. Then Russell Skunk, smelling like whiskey, would hang around, like the flu, making everyone miserable. The steps sighed under his weight when he climbed the stairs to go to bed with Melba.

He'd snap down the faded, moth eaten, dark green blind over the bedroom window, and then move the playpen into the hallway. Esther felt like the cat that got kicked out of the house at night because it was a nuisance wanting in and out at all hours. Her playpen blocked the hallway that was cool and draughty as if the northeast wind drifted through there. But spring and mud and gravel were not far away. There was only scant snow down the garden path where her brothers used to toboggan.

If her sisters had to pee in the night, they peed noisily in a tin pot kept under their beds. The boys peed in a mason jar. On mornings when Russell Skunk was in bed with Melba, Esther woke to look up at dark green plaster walls, and dust balls as big as her head. Sometimes bigger. Toys were lost inside of them, and none of the kids had the guts to reach in and grab for a hairy matchbox car.

No one swept the linoleum floors upstairs. Perhaps they were waiting for the dust balls to get big enough, and strong enough to gather the momentum to travel on their own down the hall and come to a dead stop on the top landing, where they would grow, like snowballs being rolled around the dooryard, until it eventually fell from stair to stair during months of soft breezes from small quick feet running up and down past the ever growing dust monster. It might be winter when the ball finally reached the bottom landing, twice their original size.

"Frieda, did you throw dust balls in the wood stove again? I smell hair burning," Melba hollered.

"No Mam," Frieda said.

"Did you put your dirty pads in the fire, because I smell something right awful."

"No, I said. I put them in the burnin' barrel!"

Russell Skunk made a fire in the wood stove in the middle of the night before he left on the boat fishing, and the water in the side tank was already hot enough for washing up. Dry warm heat radiated from the stove. The smell of a large pot of porridge and raisins spiced with a hint of cinnamon filled the air. Steam rose from a large tin kettle off to the side.

"Mam, am I hearing you right?" Frieda hollered. "Where's your head at? You can't just give away my sister, for Heaven sake!"

"You hold onto your horses, missy. Aunt Flora and Uncle Sammy are only taking her for a couple of months. You know right well I have to go stringing herring as soon as the fish start running or I won't have enough stamps for next winter. I can take Luke down to the boning shed with me, but land sakes, I can't take two of them – I wouldn't make any money."

Melba, wearing a faded green paisley house dress and black bristle rollers in her thinning hair, sat sideways on her chrome chair across the kitchen table from Frieda waiting for the next comeback.

"What if I stay home from school and keep house? Please Mam. I love her."

"I know you love her, but don't start in with me again. My mind's made up and I've arranged everything with Aunt Flora. Her and Sammy are taking Esther up to Montreal to stay with them for a while." Melba spoke quickly in a nervous voice.

Frieda was angry and left the table.

Holy dying! What was Melba thinking of? Frieda thought. She already had Esther, and four more kids. Frieda and Liona did all the work anyhow, but mostly Frieda. She was the oldest; Liona would only turn seven in the fall. And what Frieda didn't do, she helped out with. Like the wash. Frieda was always on the other side of that wringer washer. She was always on the rinse side. Though most times that tub was so foamy you couldn't tell wash from rinse anyhow, except rinse was in the tin washtub.

Winter was the worst. Melba and Frieda dragged that washer into the kitchen from the porch, always getting jarred something mighty when the feet hit the broken threshold. Washing and rinsing wasn't too bad compared to having to go outside and peg them on the line in the winter. That was Frieda's job. Sometimes the clothes were stiff before she could even get them pegged. Like the old man's fishing clothes. Once in a while, if it was blowing real hard, and cold enough, the pants and shirts would freeze up just as if he was still wearing them. Then if Melba wasn't around, Frieda giggled some hard hurrying into the house with those frozen work clothes. She knew she could scare the bejeezus out of the little ones! She would tuck the stiff shirttails inside the fat waist of the frozen pants and balance that green fool on a pair of gum rubbers against the wall at the bottom of the stairs. Then she'd call the kids to come downstairs. They would start screeching when they saw him.

The stupid dummy didn't timber over for a good fifteen. And the kids were too scared to come down until the fat thing melted into the cracked linoleum, and they were sure it wasn't the old man. Frieda loved funning those kids.

All Melba had to do was tend Esther for a bit while Frieda was in school. She did the rest: bathing, changing, feeding, dressing. The only thing she didn't do was get up with her during the night, but she was up tending to her first off in the morning while Melba lay in bed yelling for all the kids to get going to school. She was the one that should have gotten up and got going. Imagine, she was still brown as a bear from lying out in the dooryard in her underpants and bra all summer.

It was true the fish would be running right quick, and Melba said she was going boning herring because Russell Skunk wasn't making any money again, and Mason's store wouldn't give them any more credit. Melba said Frieda could go with her on Saturdays stringing herring and could make as much as two dollars in one day if she learned right quick.

Frieda supposed it wouldn't matter too much if Esther went up to Montreal with Uncle Sammy and Aunt Flora for a while. In any case, Esther

Melba's Wash 17

didn't know from nothing, No one would be asking her if she'd mind leaving her mother, and would she mind just packing up her bottles, and diapers, and all her blue clothes, and getting herself on the train to Montreal.

Rumour had it this wasn't the first time Melba had had a mind to give that kid away. Frieda had heard tell up at Pearl's restaurant that she left Esther up to the hospital after she was born, and Russell Skunk took Melba right back up to North Head in Grew's taxi to get her. He probably still owed for that fare. Frieda wondered how those old biddies up at Pearl's knew all this; of course one of them, Mabel, was the half-sister to Ted Grew's wife.

Poor Esther. Frieda remembered her screaming blue murder from the day they brought her into the house. Screaming like she didn't know where her mother was, even when Melba was sitting right there. Esther didn't eat well either, then woke up bawling all hours of the night. Melba said she hadn't had a good night's sleep since that kid was born and she had to find some rest somewhere. Somewhere? *Like she could get it up to Mason's store*, Frieda thought. Every day she said this, like no one had ever heard her before.

FRIEDA WAS STILL ANGRY. She went back downstairs and asked her mother: "How long is she going for, Mam?"

"Six months at most."

Frieda watched Melba push stale butts from one side of the round ashtray to the other with her lit cigarette, and remembered when Aunt Flora put her cousin Amy up for adoption. Frieda still missed her, and that fuelled her smart mouth.

"Does the old man know what you're doing?"

"Don't you concern yourself about your fath' r. I'll take care of him."

"He's not my fath'r, as you put it!"

Frieda picked dried pieces of food off the wide ribbed chrome edge of the heavy Arborite table.

"Well, he's the only one you've got."

Frieda pushed her chair from the table and walked over beside the wood stove. Some father. She knew what he was really like! And her intestines started crawling around like snakes in a pit until they tied themselves in knots like sausages. That's when Frieda's abdomen became hard, and the pain began. It showed on her face, but Melba didn't notice.

"What about the other kids, Mam? Luke's just a baby, but what about Liona and Paul, do they know what's going on?"

"Not yet. And don't you be saying anything either. There's no point in them making a fuss too. I'll tell your sister and brother when I'm ready."

Frieda laid down on her old brown iron framed bed that night, in the foetal position, hugging her thin pillow into her stomach and thinking about her cousin Amy.

Years before, Flora had left Janeville, New Brunswick and moved to Montreal to find a job. She left her daughter Amy for Melba and their mother Victoria to look after. At the time, Melba had three-year-old Frieda as well.

The two little girls played house, and store, and school, bathed together in a porcelain claw foot tub, and slept in a three-quarter bed together in the dormer bedroom above their grandmother Victoria's bedroom, just as their mothers had.

Victoria died when Frieda was five. Shortly after, Melba took Frieda and Amy and moved to Grand Manan where she had found a job as a housekeeper for Mrs. Girling – Russell Skunk's mother.

A year later Amy was adopted by an older, childless couple that quickly moved away to the mainland after the adoption papers were signed.

Frieda remembered praying that the Sheppards would adopt her too. She missed her cousin, and had tried to keep in contact with her on the telephone, but her new mother, Mrs. Sheppard, told her not to call again. "Amy has a new life now and isn't allowed to see any of her old relatives."

TWO WEEKS PASSED and Frieda stopped by the post office every day after school.

"Good gracious, Frieda, you back again?" Mrs. Stamp said, who knew full well that what the Girlings were waiting for had arrived, and thought, money again probably. Mostly all that came were bills wearing red stickers blabbing Final Notice on the front of the envelopes. Mrs. Stamp and Frieda had figured it out long ago – an envelope from Montreal would arrive, and the next day Melba would be in to the Post Office cashing a money order from Mr. Sammy Weinstein.

"Yes. Mam's waiting for something."

"Well, there's something today from your aunt Flora, mighty big envelope for just a letter, I dare say, eh Frieda?"

"Wouldn't know, Mrs. Stamp," Frieda said through curled lips.

Frieda knew the routine too. And knew that Mrs. Stamp was betting on Melba showing up the next day to cash a money order from Uncle Sammy. He had been sending money orders as long as Frieda could remember.

Frieda stepped outside. It seemed cold to her; she had just taken a shower in the locker room after gym class.

From Grand Harbour to Deer Curve was more than a mile, and Frieda could practically walk the distance blindfolded because she'd done it so many times. And good thing because, by the time Frieda reached the Grand Harbour bridge, a northeast wind had started blowing a spring storm inland off the Bay of Fundy. Suddenly, the fat wet snow began to fall so heavily she could barely make out the edge of the road and where the ditch began.

She knew she was carrying her baby sister's ticket *away*. Frieda clasped and squeezed at the envelope in her pocket with angry mitts. She knew she carried her sister's future in her mittens that day, mittens sticking to the damp paper envelope. She wanted to walk slowly, but it was some awful cold. The wet, slapping wind was stinging her face and she cried along the way. She didn't tell anyone that. She almost stopped in at old Donald's house to warm up but knew a damned sight better. Mam would be some mad if she was late. Frieda pictured her standing at the broken taped-up front window staring out into the snow covered dooryard, watching like a hawk for her to get home.

Frieda had been praying for her own baby since Amy left. She just had to have a baby because the end of the world was coming. The Pentecostal minister who lived across the road had told her that, if she prayed hard enough, the Lord would provide her needs. She never forgot this, so Frieda went back to see the minister when Melba got pregnant with Esther. He told her she wasn't old enough to have her own baby yet, so God sent a baby to Melba.

Frieda approached the house and hollered from the top of the driveway at the figure watching out the front door from behind broken panes of glass. "She's my baby too!"

Inside the back porch, Frieda stomped wet snow from her boots. Melba pulled the kitchen door open.

"Did anything come?"

"'A mighty big envelope,' as Mrs. Stamp put it."

Frieda unbuttoned her coat and handed Melba the mail.

"That nosy old bitty."

At least she hasn't given any of her kids away, Frieda thought, standing still as a melting block of ice on the mat at the back door. Melba tore into the manila envelope and shook the contents onto the kitchen table. A few small bluish-white envelopes slid out. A letter. A train schedule. Train tickets. And another envelope with cash.

Melba read, and sorted papers, and pocketed the cash in her apron. She didn't see Frieda's tears, or the short blonde hair on her forehead and cheeks thawing into perfect pin curls.

"Well, don't just stand there like a ninny, get those wet clothes off why don't cha? You're dripping all over the place."

It's only water, Frieda thought. *Why don't you go to hell?*

"When's the ol'man coming home?"

"I don't know. I've been listening to the radio, reception's in and out, but from what I can make out, they pumped ninety hogshead of herring today way over on the south shore, and there's a whole mess of boats that are full and waiting. They'll be out a few days, I imagine."

Later that night Frieda heard the attic trap door opening and the folding ladder release. Melba had been on the hunt in the attic for a grip. Frieda's last thought before she drifted into an uneasy sleep was that her mother didn't look sick and tired tonight; in fact, Melba looked, well, happy, excited even.

The next morning Esther opened her eyes to see Melba staring at her. She changed her pissy pants and carried her downstairs to the kitchen. By the time Frieda padded down the stairs, Paul and Luke were playing on the floor building a corral around the heat register with the set of Lincoln Logs that Aunt Flora had sent them the year before. Melba was mixing the milk and Esther sat in her highchair with an old tie of Sammy's wrapped around her waist, gnawing on a Grissol stick. The ingredients for molasses cookies were sitting on the kitchen table.

FRIEDA WOKE TO THE SMELL OF FRESH BAKING, and she got to mix the margarine. The kids all fought to burst the orange egg yolk-looking blob in the bag of margarine. Though usually they quickly tired of the mixing, leaving Melba to finish blending the colour evenly.

"I slept in," Frieda said. "I'm late for school, Mam."

"Oh fiddlesticks, so you are. Well, I thought we might spend the day together."

Oh fiddlesticks? Haven't heard that one in a while, Frieda thought.

"Why's that? We never spend the day together."

"Day after tomorrow Esther is going up to Montreal with Aunt Flora and Uncle Sammy," Melba said.

"So she's really going?"

"I told you my mind was made up, Frieda."

"Who's taking her?"

"Do you want to, Frieda?"

"I might just as well. Either I go with Esther or stay back and keep house, right?"

I'd rather be the one away just in case the old man comes in off the boat and gets it in his head to get in my bed, Frieda thought.

"Well, I wouldn't put it quite that way."

"What way would you put it?"

"Don't you back talk me, missy. You don't have to take her."

"If she's going, I'd rather be the one to go with her. As long as she's coming back."

"Okay. That's settled then," Melba said. "I'll put the boys and Liona next door to Woodman's early Wednesday morning, and we'll get the first boat over to the mainland. We'll grab a cab to the train station and get you settled on it. I should be able to catch the last boat back to the island."

"How long will I be staying in Montreal?"

"I suppose until Aunt Flora doesn't need you anymore. But don't fret, Frieda. Aunt Flora and Uncle Sammy will use you right good while you're there."

CHAPTER 6

Just Like a Woman, eh?

FRIEDA HELD ESTHER ON HER LAP for the whole trip. Occasionally she whispered in her ear; her close breath tickled.

"I wonder if you're going to remember this trip, Esther. I sure will. You're my little Esther blue. You know that, don't you? First off I'll be telling Aunt Flora and Uncle Sammy that you'll be needing white walking boots, your own dolly, some pink jodhpurs, a pink dress, and I'll tell them you like the hall light on at night. No more blue for you, baby girl. Can you hear me, Esther?"

Esther couldn't ask her sister to stay with her, but she reached for her hand.

"Only four more hours and we'll be in Montreal. I'm missing school. Did'ja know that? Oh boo-hoo! I wonder if Aunt Flora and Uncle Sammy will take me shopping in one of the big department stores downtown."

Rattles and knocks and squeals and sparks let them know they were close to Montreal. Gradually the train slowed down to almost nothing, but Frieda felt like they were skidding down the track just the same, leaving her stomach on the seat behind them.

"I see them, Esther. There's Aunt Flora and Uncle Sammy. I know that's them. Look. They're standing on the platform. Land sakes, Esther, we're finally here, Windsor Station."

Esther was curled in a foetal position, with her head tucked under Frieda's chin. Her eyes were wide open, staring blankly into Frieda's damp shoulder.

"Oh my soul, you must be scared of all the noise, aren't cha?"

Frieda wished she could clamp her own hands over her ears and stop the god-awful sound of metal scraping on metal. But she couldn't loosen her grip on Esther, seeming suddenly so heavy, like a twenty-pound package of that white margarine with the orange belly button centre.

On the station platform, Sammy lifted Esther out of Frieda's stiff arms. She looked up at him and said: "Da da, penny."

She opened her tiny perspiring hand, and there it was, a shiny penny covered with blanket fuzz and baby dirt that filled her small lifeline cracks.

22

They all wondered where that lucky penny came from, and how long she'd been holding onto it.

Sammy grinned, and gave her a big smooch on the cheek. "Just like a woman, eh honey!" Flora seemed perturbed, but smiled and offered her arms to take Esther.

"No!" Esther yelled.

She wrapped her short arms tight around his stout neck and hung on for dear life; her fingernails pinched his skin.

"Sheesh! Look what she's done, Sammy."

"Gott in Himmel! It's only a scratch, Flora. She's just scared."

CHAPTER 7

Queen For A Day

I T WAS ABOUT THREE WEEKS after Frieda got back to the Island from Montreal that she walked into the front room after school and saw Melba set down in that scratchy, gold rocker. Luke was asleep across her lap, and the chair was pushed right up close to the television. She was watching *Queen for a Day*.

I'd like to slap you, Frieda thought.

"When did that come?" she exclaimed, looking at the television.

"Looks like it came today, now don't it?"

"Well, don't you look some smart sitting in front of Esther's TV," Frieda said. "Where's your crown?"

"You little bitch! It's my TV. It was a gift from Aunt Flora and Uncle Sammy."

"What did you do to deserve that? Give them my baby sister?"

"By the jeezus, if Luke weren't on my lap I'd slap you right into tomorrow. You're going to be some sorry you crossed me, Frieda."

"No. You're the one who's going to be sorry. Kids were talking about you today at school, you and Aunt Flora. Aunt Flora never came back to get Amy, did she? No. And they're saying I'll never see Esther again! That's what they're saying. And by tomorrow, half of them will know we have a TV because Angie Wicker sits behind me and her ol'man works the freight on the boat."

Frieda was sorry, she said, a TV would help out down home, keeping those boys busy. Sammy had said he wanted to send something nice back for the family while Frieda was there. When she said a television, she was kind of joking, because who's going to go and buy someone else a television set? No one even had one on the Island yet, except maybe the Mountie. She should have said a bathtub. Now wouldn't that look comical coming off the boat with Girling labels stuck all over it! At least folks would understand that. Lord knows they could all use a good wash. But they just won't

24

Melba's Wash 25

let it rest that Girlings had one of the first TVs on the Island. The way news travelled, most of the Island knew they had an RCA television before Russell Skunk did.

"Lands sake, don't you carry on making mountains out of molehills. All this has happened and it isn't even tomorrow yet. If anybody says anything to you just tell them it's a present from my sister. If they're talking about us then they're giving someone else a break. People will always find something to talk about."

Streams of tears cascaded over Frieda's cheeks; she tasted the salt on her lips.

"Mercy sakes, what now?"

"I miss Esther. I want her to come home."

"Frieda, look, what's done is done."

"What's done is done? What do you mean what's done is done? She's coming back, right?" Frieda screeched, and moved toward Melba.

Melba didn't flinch.

"Yes, she's coming back. I just don't know when."

"I don't believe you."

"Believe whatever you want, Frieda."

"You better not be forgetting about Esther like everyone's forgotten about Amy. I can't even talk to her on the telephone! She's not allowed to talk to, or even see me."

"Amy's got a new life, Frieda."

"What, like Esther?"

Silence.

"You just wait till the old man gets home off the boat and finds out what you've done," Frieda said. "I hope he beats the bejeezus right out of you."

"Did you think that your fath'r didn't know?"

"He's not my fath'r. But if he did know, I'll bet he thinks she's comin' back soon."

"Shut your trap! You're the one who was wanting to go on the train. You're the one who took her up there. And it seemed just fine then, now didn't it? Well, didn't it?"

"I'm only thirteen. I'm not supposed to know what's fine. You are!"

"Well you're old enough to be rolling around up in the hay loft with Stretch Richards, now aren't you? You didn't think I knew that, did you?"

"We weren't doing anything!" Frieda shouted.

"You get off your high assed horse, missy, and go peel the potatoes for supper. And while you're at it, you'd better start praying one of us doesn't go and have another baby that needs tending."

FRIEDA WATCHED MELBA AND RUSSELL over the next few months. They were some sickening, the pair of them, carrying on like they'd won a bingo cash pot. Mason's store had gotten paid off, and they could charge the groceries again, so Friday nights the kids got a ream of suckers or nut bars or some other sweet. Frieda knew where the money came from. The boys were young; they didn't much remember that Esther was gone anymore even though it had only been a few months. Liona mentioned her once in a while, mostly when she was looking for a baby doll to play house.

They were all told never to mention Esther again.

Melba announced: "Esther has a new life. And Aunt Flora and Uncle Sammy don't want any of you kids butting in on it. You forget about her. And if it ever happens you run into her years from now, don't you dare let on who you are."

MONTHS TURNED INTO YEARS, and the kids took for granted that there'd be two or three big boxes of new clothes and toys at Christmas time from Aunt Flora and Uncle Sammy. But Frieda still felt something mighty when she saw her name on a gift tag. Her head would drop, and tears would fall onto her Christmas package. She had seen through it all, and had known her baby sister wouldn't ever be coming back.

And all the Girling kids worried just a little bit, because they heard Melba and the old man talking late one night:

"Com'ere, Melba, wanna try for another TV set? We'd be the only ones on the island with two TVs."

None of them heard her answer, but they heard the whack of Melba's dead feather pillow and knew it landed on Russell Skunk's head. They all knew what she'd be thinking – that hell would freeze before she'd spend nine months being pregnant with another television set. She'd go for the flush next time.

Part II

CHAPTER 8

Good Beginnings

I N ANOTHER BEGINNING, before Esther, Luke, Liona, Paul and Frieda were born, you could travel up by Bathurst, New Brunswick where you'd find the Tracadie River. Close by, on the east side of the river, about a mile from Nepisquit Bay, was Janeville, and the Goods' store, where Flora and Melba were born to Victoria and Ray Oak.

From the wide front veranda, and from the attic rooms with their dormers peeking out over the wooden sidewalk, you could see down most of Main Street to the telegraph office, the post office, and the big general store owned by the Eddy mill. Way off in the shadows were the lights from the train station platform, and farther down, the roof of the Janeville Inn. The blacksmith's shop was across the hard gravel road from the post office, and not far from there was Trinity Church, standing pure and white and tall. You couldn't walk down the steps of the Goods' store and not look at that white church, reminding you to feel thankful about something. And you'd better think of something to be thankful for, because on Sunday that church bell would ring to remind you where you should be, relentlessly beckoning all the good people, and some high and mighty ones too.

A GREY SHINGLE SWAYED IN THE WIND from a short chain above your head as you walked up the steps to the covered veranda. Stencilled on that shingle was the name "Good," faded, yet local people knew whose store this really was: It belonged to Victoria. Flora and Melba's mother. It could be considered that Victoria was ahead of her time keeping her maiden name hanging outside on the shingle, but more likely, she was just plain ornery about what was hers.

Most days, either fine and sunny, or drizzling and overcast, you'd see people standing on the veranda chewing the fat, or resting on the wooden garden swing. Often youngsters would be propped up there, with small pieces of hard candy to suck on while their parents did their business in the store. Some families from back up in the woods only came into town every two weeks and had little time to waste when they bought or bartered for the little extras and the odd supplies at Goods' grocery store; they had livestock and chores to get back to.

Victoria Good had worked in the store as far back as she could remember. Melba and Flora grew up doing the same, under her expert, strict supervision.

May, Esther's great-grandmother, died of influenza when Victoria was only eight years old, and Esther's grandfather Ray Oak raised his daughter.

But Victoria never learned to knit anything together, including her own family. She grew up working in the store with her father; she was a businesswoman, and she was a yeller and a teller. If she wasn't yelling at you, she was telling you just the same thing. Didn't matter who you were. She'd get at Esther's grandfather Ray Oak for just about everything she could think of: "Can't you do anything right? Do I have to do everything myself? Dear God, just do it, never mind why. I'm the one who went to school and learned my sums, and took the fourth reader, I know the right way to do things around here."

However, Victoria hadn't gone to high school. She never wanted to; she wanted to stay working in the store alongside her father. Eventually she kept the books for the Goods' store. Harley boasted that she was mighty smart with figures. It was no surprise that, after her father died, Victoria kept the store for another thirty years.

Much of the stock was taken in trade, like eggs and butter, maple syrup, and sometimes split wood. Some people paid their accounts with lobster. Lobsters were so plentiful at that time that any caught and uneaten or unsold were used in the fields as fertilizer. But the Oaks had a taste for lobster, and would never say no to someone needing supplies and paying with lobster. Lobster filled their stomachs, but not their bank account. And lobsters didn't pay the mortgage on the store and house, which over the years kept getting extended and extended until it was impossible to pay off in their lifetime. The Goods' store shingle should have come down when Harley passed away; only Victoria's stubbornness, and bank credit kept it open.

Some families bartered labour for essentials, especially in the winter. There wasn't much cash around, and for most of those thirty years, the store barely made enough money to pay suppliers for stock such as coal and kerosene and canned goods.

Life was hard for people in the villages. There was drought and even a plague of grasshoppers. The Great Depression and WWII left farms almost unattended. When the Riordon sawmill and the Buttimer mill burned down, families struggled just to eat. Ray Oak left his job in the woods working for Gloucester Company at Little Landing to help Victoria with the store. He had been a woodcutter from the time he was twelve, "making fifty cents a day, and all the grub I could pack away," he always said proudly.

Ray was a patient man, but not patient enough to be ordered around all day and all night by Victoria, or any other woman for that matter. But he wasn't a fighter. He was accustomed to the daunting hours of pulling the heavy crosscut saw it took him and his mate to fell the tall jack pine up river, sometimes working twelve hours a day, but he wasn't accustomed to being ordered around day and night by his wife.

For a year he put up with her mouth, listened to her rant and shout orders. Move this, pack this, unpack that, strap this, and twine that. Then one day Ray took a job at the sawmill down at Teague's Lake, cutting railroad ties, leaving Victoria to run her jeezley Goods' store.

That got him away from her, and back among the men, at least for ten hours a day. Such disappointment. He remembers when they met: Victoria, tall, poised, and clever and naïve of life beyond the store; and him, lonely. A widower.

Down at the sawmill, Ray and his partner Bucky complained over the silver lids of their tin lunch cans about their bossy wives who were too big for their britches. The two men couldn't figure how they never saw it in the beginning. When did their wives change? They didn't know how things had gotten this way, but to keep peace, the men thought they would be better off allowing their women to think they did know everything.

Ray and Bucky were men stuck, like peas in a pod, but zipped in for life, by choice. They were stuck on the side of the smoking edger during the daytime and around their wives' smoking skirts at night.

RAY AND VICTORIA HAD BEEN MARRIED fourteen years and had no babies, until 1918, the year of an earthquake down shore. That cold and blowing December brought them their first daughter, Flora, followed by five years' bad luck. Ray says this because Victoria had two miscarriages during that time.

And then, the next time, during the earthquake in February of 1923, with the floor shaking underneath her chair like a train was steaming right into the front room, Victoria went into labour with their last child, Melba.

People came into the store for many years teasing that it took an earthquake for Victoria and Ray Oak to have a baby.

Melba's Wash 31

It may have been that Victoria never wanted kids, that she'd been sure after being married fourteen years, and having no babies, she was barren. How could she not be after all that time?

She'd been independent as far back as she could remember, but Ray's right arm at the same time. She missed her father something awful, even though she could run the store and the house by herself.

Victoria was quite happy when Ray went to work all day down at the sawmill. She only needed him around when Flora was small, and required tending to, and to do some bull work out in the storeroom in the evenings. She didn't trust him with much else.

"Why can't you stack things over there the way my father did? You're just about useless around here, Ray Oak."

Eventually, Flora, who was five, took care of little Melba. Flora had attended her little sister's birth. She knew the baby was coming that day. Victoria had told her. Even still, she was terrified to leave her mother alone to fetch Mrs. Lydia the midwife, who lived above the post office, or to get her father down at the sawmill.

Instead, Flora ran sobbing up the back stairs after her mother to the living quarters. "Are you all right, Mama?"

"What are you bawling for? You're not having a baby."

Victoria walked slowly and awkwardly across the front room and sat down in her father's old burgundy horsehair chair. She braced her hands on the low wide arms for what she knew was soon coming. She slid her hips to the edge of the chair.

Together that day, Flora and her mother heard cups and saucers clink against each other on the open shelves in the kitchen. The big old house moaned and groaned like it was going to give birth as well. Victoria knew right away what was happening outside, but Flora didn't remember the earthquake five years earlier. That one came a few months before she was born. She shook like the silverware in the kitchen drawer.

"Flora, run upstairs to my bedroom and bring down the clean sheets from the second drawer in my bureau. Go Flora, go and get the sheets."

Flora ran up the stairs as if carried by the howling wind that pounded the walls and windows trying to break into the house. One, two – second drawer. She ran back to the top landing and called out: "No sheets in the second drawer, Mama."

She counted again from the bottom drawer – one, two. Flora was just five years old. "No sheets, Mama." Distracted by branches blowing and slapping the house, she looked out the tall bedroom window. All hell was breaking loose outside.

Then Flora faintly heard the echo of her name from below and snapped to attention. She ran to the kitchen and tore down the curtains from above the sink; she didn't know why she did this. The cream-coloured curtains had pictures of red kettles of steaming water on them. She stared at them in her arms, suddenly proud of herself, her breath became more even.

"FLORA! Bring the sheets."

"I'm coming, Mama."

Standing in front of her mother Flora offered up a nest of starched cotton curtains. She stared between Victoria's open legs. "Mama, there's hair down there." And very soon Melba was down there, not caring if there were sheets or curtains underneath her.

There was rumour that, later that afternoon, Oliver Labelle, a labourer from the mill, happened into Goods' store. Flora remembered hearing the tinkle of the bell on the store door, and heard the latch slap back into place. Victoria had gone down those thirteen stairs and filled an order for Oliver. She told him to follow her in the storeroom and get the sack of salt himself. Oliver rounded the counter heading for the back room and noticed Victoria was shaking. He lowered his eyes and near fainted when he saw blood drippings on her legs. He left his sack of salt sitting on the floor, right where it was in the storeroom, turned and headed quickly to the sawmill to fetch Ray.

Ray wasn't too surprised when Labelle came bursting into the trimming shed. Victoria had never made any bones about needing him, and he briefly considered working the rest of his shift before going home. But those were just thoughts. He had other not so nice thoughts about his wife, but at that moment he was excited about the baby, and brushed himself of sawdust and spite and sprinted home up the hill. Home, to find Flora sitting cross-legged on the hardwood floor in the front room holding a curly-haired, round-faced Melba wrapped in an armful of kitchen curtains.

Soon, above the clicking of bone knitting needles in warm kitchens, and behind starched hats at the Catholic Women's League meeting, this story passed from lips to ears. Some said Victoria Oak was so tough she could deliver her own baby in the morning and be back working in Goods' store after lunch.

Melba's Wash

WHEN FLORA WASN'T IN SCHOOL she looked after Melba, but a piercing holler always sent her flying down the stairs to help in the store. Growing up in the Goods' store, Flora and Melba learned quickly to follow their father's lead and stay out of their mother's way.

The girls grew up sharing the attic. From there they could hear people coming and going all day, taking the wide wooden plank veranda steps, and the store bell tinkling and the spring snapping the wood fly screen door back into place.

Flora and Melba climbed a ladder, one rung at a time up to their little tower that overlooked Main Street. Closing their bedroom door they pretended to shut out the store below.

"Flora, let me see, let me see."

Flora had swiped magazines from the store and carefully turned pages of high fashion so she'd be able to put them back on the shelf.

"Let's go shopping, Flora. Can we go shopping?"

"No! We are prisoners."

"What's prisoner, Flora?"

"It's us, Melba."

They pretended they were captive in their tower and could see far beyond the town. Flora spent many hours dreaming and telling stories of how they would escape the tower of Good one day, and go to live in the land of the other people.

Sometimes Oliver Labelle's daughter Effy came to play. The three girls would skip round and round the rough brown framed bed. Faster and faster and faster, twisting the cold iron with all their muscles as they sang, "round and round and round she goes, and where she stops, nobody knows." The bed sculpted into a stylish black carriage. White fabric embroidered with dainty crimson flowers and tiny green leaves covered the bench seat. Melba, Flora, and Effy climbed onto the seat and held tight the reins as they drove the carriage down Main Street all the way to Bathurst, to William's Dress Shop. They tried on new spectacular evening dresses of gold and purple brocade, with shiny satin piping and tiny satin covered buttons, and front pockets for titties that they stuffed with stockings. And white wedding dresses, some with sequins. Effy insisted that it was bad luck to try on wedding gowns if they weren't getting married. Flora and Melba didn't listen.

Hours later, with a yell from Victoria that travelled two floors, "SUPPER," they brushed rusty iron filings off their hands onto their skirts and climbed down the ladder backwards one rung at a time.

Over the years though, the jack pine in front of the Goods' store grew tall, close up to the dormer window in their bedroom, while inside the house, the attic ladder grew into a narrow staircase that Flora and Melba's maturing bodies could leap two steps at a time.

CHAPTER 9

Trying On Boys

SATURDAY NIGHT THE YOUNG PEOPLE in town looked forward to the dance at the Odd Fellows Hall across the Bass River Bridge at Salmon Beach. There you could meet boys you'd never dare look at in church. The ones that made you blush and stutter, and tell lies about how old you were, and some boys that didn't go to school, or church either. Boys that had tailor-made cigarettes tucked under their white, short shirtsleeves and a mickey of rum under their belts.

Toward the end of the night, after hours of dancing over the sawdust floor, and teasing each other with intentional, accidental touching and brushing together of thighs and breasts, young girls and boys recognized each other's building sweat as something that needed exploring.

Anxious eyes sparkled at one another as they left the hall, weaving a path through people on the dance floor that they no longer saw, on their way out behind the hall where the outside yard light didn't quite reach. There, a man-boy would push a confused young girl against the whitewashed wood siding. His knee rubbed hard, then softer, back and forth between her legs while his hands felt inside her blouse.

Later walking back inside, they paused long enough for the boy to pull the girl close, very close to his body and they leaned into the wall just around the corner from the door, and he'd cover her lips with his and push his young hard groin against her, leaving her with a dewy feeling between her legs, and wondering what this boy had in his pants.

It was at one of these dances Melba first got close to Lucky, a boy who used to go to school. This was when Melba's girl body got so close to Lucky's boy body that he pushed his tongue in between her nervous small lips to distract her while he pulled the crotch of her cotton panties aside, rubbing the tip of his young slender inexperienced third finger over and over a stiffening little nub of pulsing flesh, followed by a surprise slip back and up and into her vagina.

Later that night under the bedcovers, Melba slid her own hand down to her furry part to see what it felt like herself, to see if the little hard nubble was still there.

Victoria, disgusted with Melba and Flora when they came home giggling and carrying on like fools, would poke Ray in the ribs with her elbow trying to rile him out of his sleep and into her rage. "Those two just came in the door!"

In winter the young crowd went skating on Miller's Brook, or sliding down the hills over at the Clifton Quarry, and on many moonlit nights you could see young people coasting four or five on a sled down the hill into the shadows, with only their own hot breath to warm themselves.

Snow and fog and freezing rain usually left in early spring, giving way for salty spring breezes to dry up the fields for planting and baseball. After long hot days, young people from around the countryside would meet in an empty field to play a ball game without rules, then dip into Nepisquit Bay to cool off. When the sun disappeared and the evening fog rose from the sea, slithering inland between the black spruce trees, they would have a bonfire on the beach. But before lighting it, they circled the spot three times. Folklore said this would keep them hidden from the lanterns of any snoopy townsfolk.

Older kids smoked and shared rum or whisky from a flask that was passed around. The younger ones puffed their first cigarettes and tasted whiskey as it went by.

Flora met Scot Baker on one of those nights.

"Haven't I seen you over at the Goods' store?"

"My parents own it. I'm Flora."

"I'm Scot."

"Everyone knows who you are. You're the one telling the men what to do over at the mill. At least that's what some of the men complain to Papa."

"Well someone has to! They don't like it much, I know that."

Scot was a young engineer hired from a Montreal company to help troubleshoot the electrical system at the Eddy mill during the winter shutdown. The Eddy mill originally commissioned Scot for three months, but they kept him right through to the summer.

Flora and Scot took Melba with them when they went with wagonloads of other people to the blueberry barrens at Burnsville, south of Black Rock or down to Salmon Beach to dive off the wharf.

"I hope you don't mind that I always bring Melba along."

Melba's Wash   37

"I don't mind, it's fun for her – she's a kid."

"She's more like my child than my sister."

"Why's that?"

"I was there with Mama the day she was born, and we've hardly been apart since."

Melba stood at the edge of the wharf and shrieked whenever someone ran beside her and jumped, holding one knee in their arms and the other leg straight, splashing into the black water.

"Look at me, Flora," Melba yelled.

"I'm watching. I see you."

"If I tried to go somewhere without Melba, Mama would be suspicious. She's like that."

"Let's forget about Mama for now."

Scot put his arm around Flora and kissed her full on the lips while Melba was swimming.

At home, Flora never breathed a word that she was spending time with a man; she knew better. And as long as she brought Melba with her, she figured her secret would stop there. Flora had heard the old biddies in the store say how "Mr. Bruce, the foreman down at the mill, said there was someone from Montreal to teach the men the workings of the new relays and switches."

CHAPTER 10

Good and Oak and Two Pregnant

FLORA SAT ON THE EDGE OF HER BED and read the love note Lucky had given Melba that day.

Melba I love saying your name, it's like putting a piece of candy in my mouth. Meet me after school down at the crick, there's something I want to give you. LL

"Melba, this is corny."
"I think I'm having a baby, Flora."
"What?"
"I haven't bled in a while."
"How long has it been?"
While Melba thought about it, she undid the front buttons of her frock, and pulled the dress to her sides. "Look, I have tits, Flora. Took five months to get them, but see …"

VICTORIA WAS TOO EMBARRASSED to take Melba to the hospital to have her baby, so she called in Mrs. Cross, the midwife. Just as well. Melba's young pelvic bones spread wide; she'd be spitting out babies like some people spit out cherry pits. Late one spring night, Mrs. Cross left Melba and Victoria with a small, squalling, healthy baby girl. Her name would be Frieda. Frieda's skin was loose and stretched like a dead chicken, but plastered with blonde fuzz like a new chick. Melba was only fourteen years old but she and Lucky sure made one cute baby. Things changed for Melba once she had Frieda. At the dance hall, Lucky was heard calling her a slut.

FLORA'S BOYFRIEND SCOT finished his contract fixing the electrical systems at the Eddy mill that fall and went back to Montreal. But before he hopped the train, he helped fix it so Flora didn't bleed again for nine months.

38

Melba's Wash 39

During the first couple of months of Flora's pregnancy, the attention at home, good or bad, was still on Melba and little Frieda. Flora spent much time sprawled out on her bed, legs bent at the knees hanging over the iron bed frame gnawing on bitty size pieces of crackers, disappearing for hours inside magazines that she still swiped from downstairs in the store.

Scot said he would write as soon as he got back to Montreal, and Flora waited for him inside those magazine pages, dreaming of the life she wanted. Flora's eyes held a picture of a mink stole and her imagination petted it like a cat. She sat on pages of large dinner parties, tables elegantly laid out with three sets of silverware framing each place setting. Water goblets and wineglasses sat on finely crocheted lace tablecloths. She licked her third finger with her tongue and turned page after page memorizing where to buy an equally elegant suit with matching purse and hat to wear to such a party.

But by Flora's fourth month of pregnancy she couldn't hide the truth any longer. Flora, with the tall large-boned frame of her mother, had grown breasts that no one could miss.

Victoria was beside herself with the embarrassment of yet another pregnant daughter under her roof, and Ray, who was now quite weak with emphysema, sat mute in his rocking chair listening to Victoria rant, but concentrating on his breathing.

Flora also gave birth to a baby girl, Amy, a cousin for Frieda, and Amy looked as much like her mother as it is possible for a newborn to look. Her eyes were brown as dark coffee and round as begged coins, with extra long thick eyelashes. Like Flora, she had brown straight hair and wore a precious pout on her full lips.

Amy was a sweet, happy baby, calm and content, as if she knew that her parents had really loved each other the night they made her, together, in the dark.

CHAPTER 11

Your Sorry Looking Face

VICTORIA AND RAY WERE READY FOR THE EXPECTED. For morning, for nighttime, for opening the store, for closing the store, and for getting the meals built. Victoria's long strong arms were quick to sweep tell of it away with the corn broom into the trash and out to the burning barrel at the end of a day. She wasn't, however, prepared to hear Flora's announcement that she was leaving not only the house, but Janeville.

"Mama, I have something to show you."

"What is it? I haven't got all day. I have to get that order together for the Riordon mill's family picnic."

"It's an advertisement I clipped out of the newspaper. It's an ad for sewers and cutters and pressers needed at Mastly's factory in Montreal."

"Scot Baker's bunch came from Montreal."

"Yes, but that's not why I'm going."

"Going where?"

"I'm going to Montreal to look for a job."

"You can't leave well enough alone, can you? You're going looking for that Baker fellow, aren't you?"

"I'm not going there because of him. There's work in Montreal. I have to get away from Janeville – there's nothing for me here."

"He's probably married, you know. That's why you haven't heard from him. You mark my words, Flora."

"I'm going there to apply for a job making hats, like this ad says."

"Making hats? You think you want to make hats, do you? Ray, did you hear that?"

"Yeah, I heard, Victoria."

Ray wasn't working at the sawmill anymore, and was only able to do the small lists of chores Victoria gave him. He dusted shelves and filled the penny candy jars, and was a friendly face to greet folks who came into the store.

"Effy and I are going by bus to Montreal to apply for jobs."

40

Melba's Wash 41

"You and Effy? Effy whose mother died when she was just a pup, Oliver Labelle's Effy who's spent half her life under my roof? I should have known you two have been up to something. Makes sense now. All that visiting back and forth and both of you giggling like fools. Well, good riddance is all I can say."

"Now Victoria, you don't really mean that," Ray said.

"Oh yes I do."

"Mama, I'm not a fool. We're leaving in the morning, and Melba's going to take care of Amy for me until I get settled."

"What! You're running off to Montreal and leaving Melba to take care of Amy. Did you hear that Ray? Melba can't take care of Frieda. Melba can't take care of Melba half the time. What you really mean is that I'm going to be taking care of Amy."

"I never said that."

"Maybe you didn't sound out the words with your lips, but that's what's going to happen. Lord above Melba, what in God's name are you bawling for?"

"You hate me, that's why. You've always hated me. Just listen to yourself how you talk about me."

"There ain't enough of you to hate, strong wind would blow you over silly girl. But I swear, all the two of you think about is yourselves. Yes, the both of you. You're a selfish pair. A right selfish pair you are. Have either of you thought about me for one tiny minute? Have either of you noticed my swollen legs and ankles, or the headache band creased permanently around my grey hairline? Yes, grey hairline. I've never asked for those. And neither did I ask for you girls to go and get pregnant. You little bitches have been some lucky. I know other girls around town that got themselves pregnant; they went to Montreal or Toronto to have their babies and put them up for adoption. One of them, the Harp girl, was disowned by her family. You two know the Harp girl.

"Dear Lord, you've been planning this for some time, haven't you, Flora? No, I don't want any answers; they'd just be a pack of lies anyhow. I'll be dead when you finally come back for little Amy. Go and make your hats, and find Scot Baker too – you'll find him married. And you mark my words Flora, you'll be lucky if Amy remembers your sorry looking face when you do come back."

CHAPTER 12

Montreal 1945

D URING WWII, Montreal factories retooled to supply massive amounts of ammunition for the war. As a result, many people moved to the city to work. Although war raged in Europe, it wasn't felt on Montreal doorsteps. The atmosphere of the city was almost party-like; business was booming – the war business. Dinner parties were still catered with caviar, Cuban cigars, and Seagram's Crown Royal whiskey. In the evenings, the one small difference was that curtains and drapes were drawn all over the city, and many people ate by candlelight.

Montreal is the largest inland port in Canada, and after the war, for shipping and manufacturing. It was not business as usual, but better than ever. Textiles were made to outfit millions of people in matching hats and handbags, and gloves, shoes, nylons, suits, and fedoras. Modern appliances sprang seemingly out of the blue from assembly lines in factories left dormant during the war. Abandoned blueprints lying dusty in drawers surfaced to become Hoover vacuum cleaners, Frigidaire refrigerators, hair dryers, and high speed Mixmasters. Men circled ads for real estate in *The Montreal Star*, and soon bought brand new houses.

Young single girls, especially attractive ones like Flora and Effy, had no trouble finding work after the married women gave up their factory jobs to keep fancy kitchens and bathrooms sparkling.

AFTER THEY SETTLED INTO AN APARTMENT, the first call Flora made was to Dorval Electrical. She introduced herself to the male voice on the other end of the line as a friend of Scot's, from Janeville, New Brunswick, and that she had met him while he was working down there at the Eddy mill.

"What a coincidence you should call today. Scot has never missed a day of work since he started with the company, except today. He phoned this morning that he's not coming – his wife's having her baby. He took her over to the Montreal General."

"How wonderful."

Melba's Wash 43

"Do you want to leave your name, ma'am?"

"No. That's not necessary. Thank you."

Flora heard the echo of Mama's voice. "He's probably married. You mark my words."

That afternoon the two young women went to Mastly's factory to apply for jobs.

"Put your name on this application and take it upstairs, first door to your left. Hey! Wait a sec. Say Maurie sent you. You're on the cutting line, dolls."

Flora and Effy climbed the narrow grey wooden stairs to see Maurie's boss.

"Eyesight good, health good, you know how to sew, yes, natch, yes, you both start on Monday. Seven o'clock. Maurie won't put up with tardiness from his girls. If you miss your streetcar on your first day, don't bother coming in."

Flora and Effy worked on the same table cutting felt for men's fedoras. They giggled and twittered like fool canaries while they clipped the soft shaven felt. Oh, they loved the feel of the material between their fingers when they first started working. But it didn't take long to find out the dye came off on their sweaty hands, and that's where it stayed for quite a while.

When Flora had read the ad in the Bathurst newspaper for sewers and cutters, she didn't have the image of a dreary factory, one with dim light bulbs hanging on wires from rafters, and a furnace that probably only kept the boss's feet warm upstairs.

Flora and Effy had never thought about how they would cut out those soft fedoras. Who would have thought that you'd stamp the pattern on the material with a heavy press and then a big pouf of chalk would fly up in your face? And each time Flora marked the felt, Victoria's "mark my words" settled invisibly onto the work table and she had to wait for the dust to settle to find her scissors to cut the pattern pieces.

Back in Janeville, making hats had sounded like a clean job, even a fun job. But after three months of working in the factory, Flora went home on the streetcar at night with dusty auburn hair, white shadowed nostrils, and black tipped fingers. She looked nothing at all like women in the magazines she had spent years dreaming about. Flora and Effy had blisters on the sides of their thumbs and the inside of three fingers from squeezing the heavy scissor handles. Eventually they got smart and wrapped their fingers with bandage tape.

For the first month, at night in the small, furnished apartment they shared on Sherbrooke Street, Flora and Effy sat cross-legged on the couch cleaning their fingernails, and yacking, until there wasn't even the sound of traffic below.

Soon Effy met a man named Rick Allen, and they began going out on the weekends, to nightclubs, and drive-in fast food joints like Miss Montreal. Sometimes they took Flora with them.

Nights when Effy was out, Flora sat alone by the window in the tiny kitchenette of their fourth floor apartment. She stared at the city street lamps hanging like bunches of grapes, and listened to the city sounds. The traffic below seemed to scream "your sorry looking face ..."

Sometimes she wished she could forget about the whole lot of them back in Janeville, and forget she ever heard Victoria say: "I'll be dead when ..." But she couldn't put off searching for a second job any longer.

Compared to the accidental meeting of Effy and Rick in the apartment building elevator, Flora and Sammy's meeting had the makings of a first rate B movie of the period. To Flora, meeting Sammy was the fate she deserved. Not the magazine life she had dreamed of for years back in Janeville, not yet, but it would be. It was too bad she went to Sammy wrapped in her pale skin scarred with secrets and lies. Not that it would have made any difference to him – he was head over heels in love with her. But it might have prevented the hairline cracks in his big heart from exploding one day.

In the beginning, life was an orange julep ...

"My God, Effy, you should see this guy at the delicatessen. Is he a doll or is he a doll? He looks like Clark Gable. That's it, Clark Gable slicing smoked meat and pastrami. I fell in love with him before I even knew who he was, before he even looked at me, Effy."

"Flora, were you buying cold cuts, or applying for a job?"

"Applying for a weekend job. Effy, I know this sounds a little crazy, but I was drawn to him from somewhere inside my gut. No, it was more like being pulled right inside him and I knew he'd been waiting for me all my life, like we both knew it and one of us just had to say something to make it so.

"Our eyes actually locked on each other, like a deer's eyes frozen in car headlights, for what seemed forever – though it was probably only a second or two – and then he asked me if I'd ever done this before. Done this before? I'm thinking, done what before? Fall in love? Or been a waitress?

"Effy, there I was trying not to laugh and at the same time trying to hide the blisters and the dye on my hands, and you know how I get when I'm excited, arms flying, elbows going, and I'm thinking: Done this before? I've been cooking up, serving up, and cleaning up since I was a kid. 'Flora do that. Flora do this.' There isn't anything I can't do."

"Flora, slow down. I haven't seen you this excited since you met Scot. Oh, sorry. You're talking too fast. Take a breath will you!"

"Scot is nothing. Scot is dirt. I managed to get it out that I worked the register in Mama's store back in New Brunswick. He tossed an apron over the counter and said: 'That's good enough for me. Job's Friday five to nine, and Saturdays ten to six. Friday is the only day anyone ever eats in, mostly it's a meat market and take-out, but my uncle Myer insists on keeping those four booths over there for the regulars, the guys that have been faithful to our smoked meat sandwiches for twenty years.'

"I start Saturday. The delicatessen is just over on Côte-des-Neiges. Effy, you've got to come in and meet him. Only one word of caution: When you do come, for God's sake, whatever you do, don't order a ham and cheese. It's a Kosher Deli."

"Does he know you're not Jewish?"

"He didn't ask. I don't want anything getting in my way. I want this man."

"Does the Kosher deli-man have a name, Flora?"

"Sammy Weinstein," she replied.

FLORA'S DAYS AT THE FACTORY flew right into Friday nights and Saturdays when she would work at the deli. But for the first month, she didn't see Sammy. Another fellow, Stanley Cohen, the full-time butcher, worked instead.

One Friday night, Stanley called Flora over to the counter. "Flora, he has a wife and two kids, you know."

"So why are you telling me? Sammy already told me."

"Do you think I'm so blind that I can't see? Because I like you, Flora, even if you're not Jewish." Flora and Stanley both laughed.

"He's got a rich man's family, a boy, and a girl. The wife might be a schlep, but that means nothing. Nothing. He'll never divorce her, Flora. It's just not done. I want you to know that. Sammy, well he's another story. Sammy would give you the shirt off his back. He's soft. He's too soft. If he knows you, he'll make you a loan with just a handshake. Just a handshake, in this city, oy vey, it makes me shiver. Sammy always says: 'Stanley, a handshake is as good as money in the bank.' But I'm not like Sammy, and I don't trust some of the shysters I've seen him with. He's too schmaltzy and someone's going to take him for a long ride one of these days. I try to watch out for him, me and that gold mezuzah he wears around his neck."

Flora went home from the deli that night, reeling with excitement and dread. He'll marry me, she thought. It's different with us.

She tried to sleep but woke up every hour until four o'clock in the morning when she gave up and wandered out to the living room in the dark. She went right for the telephone book and looked up Samuel Weinstein, and found that he lived six blocks away from her over on Clanranald Street. So what if it was the middle of the night? Flora put on her long coat over a short nightie, slipped on her shoes and strode confidently and elegantly to his apartment door like a model taking her runway.

There she froze, her gloved hand on the locked door handle, when she saw the doorman walk toward her from inside the building. She could hear her mother's voice: "Flora, what's wrong with you, how could you do such a thing? Tomcatting around in the middle of the night. You don't knock on men's doors in the middle of the night. You need a knock on the head instead." *Damned you, Mama,* she thought, but listened to the voice and turned around and walked back home.

Flora was twenty-four when she left Janeville, and those last years had been hell. Having to act so good and yes, by God, thankful too. Smile at the town gossips from behind the counter in the store. She hadn't been with a man in so long – not since Scot. Hadn't been anywhere in four years, except to see the doctor and Gold Rush days at the church.

"Serves you right."

Shut up, Mama.

THE NEXT DAY WAS SATURDAY and Sammy worked a few hours that afternoon at the deli. At the end of the day, he offered Flora a lift home, then changed his mind, and offered her a drink and some Perry Como at his apartment.

"I've been hoping you'd ask."

A month later Flora gave up her job at the millinery, and moved into Sammy's new apartment on Clanranald Street, many steps up from the place she'd been living in with Effy. Sculpted concrete columns lined a U-shaped turnaround, holding up a large canopy so the residents wouldn't experience the weather stepping out of their vehicles. The valet parked Sammy's Oldsmobile in the underground parkade, after he wished Mr. and Mrs. Weinstein a polite good night, or good morning, or good evening, and Shabbat Shalom. He was pleased to address the gentlemen's ladies however they wished to be addressed. He knew he would be tipped handsomely for his tasteful manners, quick discretion, and thoughtfulness.

During dinner, the evening of Flora's last day at the factory, Sammy gave her a tissue-wrapped glove box. Inside lay a pair of white, elbow-length evening gloves, trimmed with sequins. The fourth finger of the left hand glove wore a substantial diamond mounted on a wide band of white gold. Smaller diamonds curly-cued around and down each side of the setting.

Oh no, she thought. *You've got what you wished for. Now what are you going to do? How are you going to tell him about Amy?* She would have to tell him about Amy; she had to send money back home to Melba. A cloud of fear followed her every day that Melba might call or write and squeal about Amy before she had time to think of a way to tell Sammy.

Flora didn't have to wait too long. Melba did call. Their mother Victoria had passed away. Flora didn't tell Sammy she died until after Victoria was buried. She wasn't ready to talk about Amy. She didn't have her lies in order.

And Mama's words held her in fear: "Amy won't remember your sorry looking face." "I'll be dead when ..."

Soon, a letter came from Melba:

Dear Flora,
You should have come back for Mama's funeral. Did you even tell your Sammy that she was dead? He would have brought you down. Too late now, put her in the ground yesterday. Amy is some upset; she'd been calling her Mama, you know. You should've come down.
I have to move by the end of July. Bank owns the house, the store, the whole mess of it; lock, stock and barrel. I never knew. I thought there'd be money come out of this. I'm in a real jeezless pickle. What about Amy? Send telegram. Should I come to Montreal?
Melba

Flora stopped dead, dead as those jammed wringers on the washing machine. She tugged and pulled at her lies, and wrung and squeezed omissions into some almost ungodly shape. The lies and omissions had become so tangled, she could barely remember which was which, but she did, finally, hang the whole story out in the open and held her breath waiting to see if any of it would wash with Sammy.

"Flora, how could you not tell me such a thing? Your own mother! Your own daughter! What kind of a person are you?"

"A sorry one, Sammy."

"I should say so! We will go pick up the child immediately. Shame on you, Flora! You have disappointed me."

Sammy got up from the kitchen table, took his jacket from the closet, and left the apartment. Flora held her head with two hands and cried.

The next day Flora sent a telegram:

Melba, coming for Amy STOP be there in 2 days STOP Flora

Victoria had come down with pneumonia and never recovered. No wonder. She'd been tired her whole life. Tired of standing straight holding up the slouched reputations of her daughters. Tired of getting up before dawn to light the kitchen stove, getting breakfast for kids who either sat in high chairs or on a chair boosted with the Robert Simpson catalogue and an old leather belt cinched around their middles to keep them from falling over. First she raised her own daughters, then her granddaughters. And there was always the Goods' store.

POOR DISTRAUGHT AMY had not seen Flora in four years and didn't recognize her as her mother. There was only one way little Amy would have gotten into the black Oldsmobile for the drive to Montreal to live with Flora and Sammy. Her shrieking, jerking body would have had to be stunned, somewhat like a knock on the head to a feisty fish trying to break free of a fishing hook, and then packed in the backseat between their grips, like a sardine in a can.

On the drive back to Montreal, only a stuffed brown monkey called George, pronounced *en français*, sat between Flora and Sammy in the front seat of the car. Neither of them spoke, but the words in Flora's mind were her mother's: "Amy won't remember your sorry looking face." She was right. Amy remembered Victoria as her mother, and Victoria had just died. Amy's next familiar was Melba, and Amy would not be taken from her.

Flora thought: *Well, we couldn't put Amy screaming and kicking into the car and simply drive back to Montreal.* Besides, Flora didn't want Amy. She'd rather have the monkey in the middle.

Melba's Wash 49

Sammy drove back to the city, silence and George between them. Amy didn't want the damn thing. All she wanted was the woman she called Mama. She was only seven years old.

Flora held her left hand in her lap, her fingers turning her diamond ring around and around.

CHAPTER 13

Melba's Tune

A MONTH LATER, while Frieda and Amy sat at the kitchen table eating toast and homemade applesauce, Melba wrote a letter to Flora. And every once in a while she'd look aside in disbelief at the black print typed on the papers from the lawyer Buttimer that were lying next to her coffee cup.

Dear Flora,
I never would've guessed that Mama and Papa gave credit to so many families during the depression and during the war. It doesn't say that in the legal papers from Mr. Buttimer, but that's what he told me. The papers are mostly columns of figures with debits and credits, and the numbers don't look good. I've been trying to manage here these past months, but as Buttimer said, it's better to walk away than try to get the bank to carry the store.
It seems that when times were really bad and people ran out of credit at the Eddy mill general store, Mama and Papa gave out credit here, like the year of the grasshoppers. Remember the year of the grasshoppers, Flora? Remember how dark it was looking out over the cornfields when the grasshoppers swarmed in? I didn't know that they destroyed the crops that year. Did you know that?
There's no money, just bad debts. Some years they only made token payments to the bank. And other years they only paid the interest. I never had any idea, did you? Extra money that did come in was paid to suppliers to keep the store stocked.
Anyway, Mr. Buttimer went up and down and over the papers right in front of me. There isn't going to be any money, Flora. The place just isn't worth much right now cause no one has any money. He figures we'll only get what's owing on the house and store if we're lucky enough to sell it at all. Anyway, I can't run this place by myself, Flora, so I say we put it up for sale and hope for the best.

I need money, so I'm answering an ad in the *Maritime Journal* for a Housekeeper down on Grand Manan. Mrs. Cross's daughter Kaye married a fisherman from down there. Remember Kaye Cross, the midwife's daughter, Flora? I do. She's near my age. I'm gonna get ahold of her. It's supposed to be nice down there. And milder winters – it's close to the U.S. border.

Call me and tell me what you think.

Melba

When Flora got the letter she was mostly concerned about Amy. Would Melba take her too? She telephoned right away.

"Melba?"

"Thanks for calling right away. I don't know what to do. I need a job."

"I know. I know."

"What do you think about the housekeeper job on Grand Manan? Do you think it's a good idea? It's so far away from Janeville."

"Well, if the store is gone, there's not much left for you there. Maybe you'll meet someone on Grand Manan."

"I suppose."

"I think you should go. It might be good for you to start fresh somewhere else. You already know Kaye. She'll introduce you to people."

"That's true."

"What about Frieda and Amy?"

"The ad said one child was okay. So what am I going to do with Amy?"

"Maybe they'll let you keep her for a while, then put her into foster care. Maybe someone will adopt her."

"Oh, I can't. She and Frieda are like sisters, but I'll let you know if I hear tell of anyone."

"Frieda could still play with her, you know."

"I suppose."

"Why don't you phone and get the job? It'll all work out, Melba. Sammy and I will still help you out."

"Okay, I'll call."

"Everything will be all right."

THE PAY FOR THE HOUSEKEEPER JOB was room and board and a monthly allowance. Melba rang up the number in the newspaper and told the woman she was interested in the job, and had one daughter. Which was true. Amy was Flora's daughter. And she'd been keeping house her whole life, which was also mostly true.

She didn't bother to explain that she'd had another baby, a son, three years after Frieda was born. Victoria had talked her into leaving him with the nuns at the church. He was adopted and no one saw that boy again.

The woman was Mrs. Velda Girling. There was no Mr. Girling – he had been dead some time. Velda was anxious about hiring Melba, and made arrangements for her to set out by bus to Saint John to catch the ferry over to Grand Manan Island in three weeks' time.

Velda Girling was a tough old broad. And maybe smart too. By letting it be known in her ad that a child would be okay, she let the world, or at least the Maritimes, know that she was desperate, and knew it was likely the person who answered the advertisement would be as well, and more likely to stay on for a while if she already had a kid of her own to look after.

She advertised for a housekeeper, but maybe what she really wanted was a wife for that lazy, stupid son of hers – Russell, who didn't have a pot to piss in.

When Melba accepted the job, she didn't mention she'd be showing up with two young girls. She figured if two kids turned out to be a problem, well, she'd work something out. Maybe Kaye could keep Amy for a while. People always needed money, and Flora was still sending money orders to take care of Amy. Surely she could find someone who would look after her.

Melba, Frieda, and Amy waited, nervous and alone, on the wharf for Velda Girling. The other walk-on passengers had already left. Finally an old car arrived with a young man at the wheel and an older female passenger. Velda got out first and walked over to the three of them. She spoke first.

"Are you Melba?"

"Yes I am. And this is my daughter Frieda, and her cousin Amy. Amy is my niece. If it's all right with you, she'll only be staying with me for a short time until I can make other arrangements. I hope you don't mind, Mrs. Girling."

"A short time? Okay, that will be fine. Come along. My son Russell is waiting in the car."

They climbed into Russell's father's car. His father may have been dead a long while, but his car still had a few miles left in it. They drove three quarters of the way down island, mostly in silence, past Grand Harbour to Deer Curve. There were only four houses on Deer Curve. Woodmans' right next door, Stucky Girling up the hill, that big old abandoned house of the Crockers just up and across the road, and the preacher's house.

Melba's Wash   53

Melba thought she'd be keeping house for someone's kids, but it turned out the kid she'd be cooking and washing and cleaning for was twenty-five-year-old Russell. Velda was getting on in years and didn't see and hear too well, or so she had told Melba when she first arrived.

Russell was short for a man, not even five and a half feet tall, but like Melba, he was cute, and wore a short light brown brush cut. Melba was a horny little thing and hadn't been with a man in years. It didn't take long before she and Russell were trying out the three quarter bed upstairs she'd been sleeping in and Melba became pregnant with another daughter, Liona. It would be many years before Melba heard the rumour that Russell slept with his mother until he was eighteen.

Velda recognized the sound of bedsprings coming directly from the bed in the front bedroom, the one that used to belong to her. And she didn't take too kindly to the sneaking and creaking around the house after dark.

"It's not right," she said to herself, not too ferociously. Finally one morning Velda called Melba and Russell into the kitchen and told them quite firmly to sit down at the table because there was something she had to say.

Suppressing a grin, she said that she'd known from the start about the sneaking around they did at night and she knew that Melba was pregnant whether Melba knew it yet or not. Velda had gotten what she had wanted from her eighty-cent advertisement in the *Maritime Journal*. *Deaf all right,* Melba thought.

"This is my house. But, I'm getting old, and if you two will get married, you can have the house for a wedding present, so long as I can live with you for a few more years."

Which they did. Velda stayed with them on Deer Curve until Liona was seven, then spent her last years living with her sister in Grand Harbour.

The house wasn't any prize. It was a six hundred square foot storey-and-a-half clapboard house on wood foundations. The ditch fronting the property was a prickly one: blackberry bushes, thistles, and alders. There were no steps up to the front door. You entered through the porch around the back. Electrical and telephone lines clamped to a hydro pole connected the house to the community, like a hook on the end of a fishing pole. Down by the woods was an old pig barn, and a one-seater outhouse was off to the side where there was always an audience for you. You couldn't go for a b.m. without the pigs knowing. One or another would snort to let you know they knew you were there, which resembled the whole island actually. Some said you couldn't fart in a windstorm without everyone knowing who did it.

MELBA KEPT AMY WITH HER for a couple of months at Girlings, but then let word get around that she would pay to foster her out. After all, Flora was still sending money, more money now that Sammy was dishing it out. So when that opportunity arose, Melba fostered her out before Flora had a chance to try to get Amy again. She'd had seven years in all to do that.

Amy moved in with the Sheppard family in the Cove and lived with them for six months before Flora came down to the Island to try and woo her with the same George monkey that Amy had refused eight months earlier. But the Sheppards were a good family, a churchgoing family, a family with money and a piano. They loved Amy right away; they'd been praying for years for God to send them someone to play that piano. They had no children of their own.

Amy hadn't seen Flora since before Victoria died, and screeched in Flora's face when Flora finally showed up at Sheppard's to pick her up just after her eighth birthday.

"I hate you, you can't take me, I want to be adopted, you're not my mother," echoed from where Amy stood on the stairway, to the foyer below.

The Sheppards didn't want to lose Amy and were ready for Flora with adoption papers just waiting to be signed. Flora put up a fuss in the beginning, or perhaps a show. She said she couldn't understand why Amy hated her. What kind of things had the Sheppards put into her head she wondered? Not that she really wanted Amy. She was set in her ways now. But it would make her look bad to Sammy. Amy held her small hands against the sides of her head and screamed until Mr. Sheppard finally ushered Flora outside.

The second day, a second try, the same scene. This time more vehemently. "I hate you, I don't ever want to see you again, I want to be adopted." Flora gave up and signed the adoption papers and told Amy she hoped that she was happy now.

Amy was, as they say, nobody's fool. The Sheppards weren't either, and it wasn't long before they packed up, including that piano, and moved away to the mainland. Frieda, who had been spending almost every day playing with Amy at the Sheppard's, cried and screeched and begged to be adopted too. But Frieda would never see her cousin after she moved away. No one in the family ever heard tell of her again, which was too bad because Frieda and Amy had been as close as any real sisters could be, like their mothers.

Melba's Wash

After spending a week with Melba on the Island, Flora went back to Montreal where she became cinched in her new life, just as tightly as the kids back home in Janeville, in Goods' store, had been cinched in their chairs at mealtimes. And Flora had no intention of falling from the grace she'd been given.

CHAPTER 14

Life's Just Not Fair

FLORA KEPT BUSY FOR MANY YEARS travelling with Sammy all over Quebec and northern New Brunswick selling his brother Myer's men's clothing line. They spent time at Sammy's cottage, and drove to Maine, New York and New Hampshire for occasional weekends. Flora no longer worked at the deli. She played canasta once a week with the girls, had her hair done, and cooked thick steaks and prime rib roasts for dinner. Sammy generously and gladly handed over money for everything; Flora's magazine life was building. All except for the one thing Flora wanted – and Stanley had warned her. He was a good judge of Sammy, had known him all his life. Stanley told Flora that Sammy would never divorce his wife – it just wasn't done. "It's just not done Flora. You can be happy with what you've got, or you can take a walk."

Sammy's wife Ethel had kept the house in the city, and Sammy kept the cottage up in Petite Lac Long, a privileged summer vacation spot just outside of Ste. Agathe. Flora and Sammy spent weekends there when he could, and Flora stayed up there for most of the summers. Some of the neighbours were pretty cold fish to Flora, especially the Smiths next door. But then why not, Bessie Smith had been friendly with Ethel for years and years. Saltzmans, Rhoda and Maisie, in the cottage behind them, were good to Flora, but only because they loved Sammy. He was such a nice man.

One morning Flora was repotting the big philodendron plant that stood in the foyer. It had been five years since Amy had gone. The telephone rang, collect and person to person.

Stupid stupid Melba, Flora thought, leaning into the Arborite counter. She'd married that good for nothing herring choker with the nickname Russell Skunk. He had that name before she arrived on the island; that should've warned her. Who in hell has a name like Russell Skunk? All he was good for was making babies. She had five of them now, and couldn't afford any one of them. Well, now she was sick. Is it any wonder? And she wanted Flora to take the youngest, Esther, just for a while, she said, a couple of months so she could get some rest.

Flora wondered if she had a choice.

"She wants us to take the baby? The baby girl she couldn't think of a name for, *Gott in Himmel*, I chose the name for that child. We should take her Flora," Sammy said with a smile on his face.

Sammy was a sucker for Melba and those kids. He felt so damned bad for them. They had nothing. Not even proper medical treatment. There was one general practitioner on the island and if you came down with anything he couldn't treat, set or stitch, he sent you away to the mainland. Well, that wasn't so easy if you had a brood of kids, no money, and nowhere to stay up in Saint John. Sammy supposed people could die on that island, just because they couldn't afford to go away to the mainland.

So when Melba called and asked Flora to keep Esther for a while so she could rest, Sammy was thrilled, and went to Ogilvy's and ordered baby furniture and toys to be delivered to the apartment.

He was excited like a little boy at Christmas, not that he'd ever had a Christmas, but it seemed like it in their apartment on Clanranald Street when Ogilvy's delivered Esther's baby furniture. Even the doorman wished Sammy Mazel Tov on the future arrival. Of course, the doorman had no idea the arrival would be in full form, already six months old. A high chair, dresser, crib, a lamb lamp, blankets, diapers, plastic dishes and a little boy doll with raised wavy red hair and brown eyes, who resembled a baby Red Buttons, were delivered and the doorman helped take them up the elevator.

"Why are you spending so much money on a baby who's just coming to visit for a few months?" Flora wanted to know. It seemed like a waste to her. What would they do with the baby furniture when Esther went back?

"We'll send everything with her when she goes back, so what's the big schmiel, Flora? It's not like they can't use the extra things. It's only money, honey!"

Sammy was having fun. It had been twenty years since he did this for his own son and daughter. He was forty-four now and the gifts he bought them now were much bigger; next year he'd buy Aaron a house when he got married. And before long, Riva would be graduating from McGill University and getting married.

Flora had no idea that Sammy met his kids regularly, on campus when they had time, or for lunch at Schwartz's Delicatessen on the Main, or for dinner at his mother's.

CHAPTER 15

Esther Girling

ESTHER WAS STILL WITH FLORA and Sammy the summer she turned two, when Melba and Russell showed up at the cottage in Petite Lac Long on a sweltering Thursday night. They pulled in the gravel driveway like they had been out for a Sunday drive up to North Head, not a six hundred mile trip from New Brunswick to Montreal in a borrowed station wagon. They'd come to get Esther and take her back to the Island. At least that's what fell out of Russell's wet mouth when Flora asked them what they were doing there. Russell had the kind of mouth that bubbled with hangover spit or drunk's drool from the corners or foamed in spaces where teeth used to be.

Melba had been close-mouthed much of the trip, which was unlike her. But what could she say, really? That she didn't want Esther back? That she had enough kids to look after already? That Esther wouldn't know who the hell she was any more?

She knew only too well what was going to happen – just what had happened with Amy and Flora. Esther wouldn't remember her sorry-looking face either. Besides, Melba figured Esther was better off with Flora and Sammy. She would probably be the only one of her kids to have anything of their own that was new; she'd travel and go to camp. She would have a better chance to make something of herself. Esther would never want for anything – anything except her mother, and her sisters and brothers.

Russell Skunk had never told Melba about all the jeezly bullshit he'd been getting from some of the men, strangers even, from the other side of the Grand Banks. A few weeks back, before their trip to Petite Lac Long, the crew docked the Betty-Jo for the night in Lubec. They had pumped ninety hogshead of herring from the Kate-Lynn that night, and then headed, sure as fog, over to the Lost Anchor to get full. The Lost Anchor stunk of leathery, red-faced men, all wearing matching green gumboots speckled with old fish scales, and similar quilted plaid hunting jackets in either red and black or green and black.

Late into the night, Russell moved from the bar to a table and chair along a wall that was easier to balance on and against. He sat there, shoulders hunched, head hanging forward, bloodshot eyes half-mast. A dirty hand held a shot of rye whiskey and he heard a voice from somewhere in the smoky, dimly lit room.

"Hey, how's the reception on that tee-vee of yours?"

Son of a whore, Russell thought, without lifting his head.

"Yeah, mister Skunk, ya got bunny ears for her yet?"

"Son of a f-ing whore," Russell muttered into his shot glass without looking up, right before he threw the watered-down whiskey deep into the back of his throat, and swallowed hard, as if the whiskey were solid.

"Son of a whore," is all he said.

And then he thought he remembered smashing her lying mouth, trying to make her stop lying, trying to make her say why she didn't want that baby back, and hearing all the useless excuses about her back being sore, and how the kid would have a better life with her sister. She carried the rest of 'em around, didn't she? Things were good enough for the rest of 'em, weren't they? Esther's no different.

She has a sore back does she? Well, by the jeezus, he thought, *when I get in off the boat at the end of the week, I'll mount her and break her jeezless back.*

RUSSELL SKUNK TURNED BLOOD RED in the face when he heard Esther call Flora and Sammy, Mummy and Daddy, suddenly realizing she wasn't calling for him and Melba. What did he really expect? He probably never thought much about it. He had simply got it into his head that they were coming up to Ste-Agathe, the lot of them, and getting the girl. Enough was enough; Melba couldn't play sick forever. They showed up with Frieda and Liona and the two boys. It looked like an exhibition had pulled into the small side yard. An oatmeal-coloured canvas tent was set up outside for the kids to sleep in.

Daytime had been quiet at the cottage, but now there was the sound of play and tearing around and yelling and chasing and tagging of young agile bodies. "One, two, three on Liona."

Sammy arrived Friday night as usual from the city loaded with black bread, bagels, Cott's nectar, and Seagram's whiskey in its navy and gold trimmed bag that Esther would use for her marbles, change, or doll's clothes, a new beach ball from those huge wire cages at the gas station, and a shiny silver dollar. That was pretty well what most of the fathers drove in with Friday nights, give or take the nectar and the silver dollar.

He drove up to find all the lights on in the cottage, and a station wagon with New Brunswick licence plates parked in his driveway. *Oy vey*, he thought, *I wonder how long they're staying?*

They stayed three days. The older kids swam in the lake during the day, and Sammy gave them nickels to play pinball next door at the dance hall in the evening. Russell emptied a bottle of whiskey each night and when he was full he'd slur: "By-de-jeezus, loadin' yous-all up in the mornin' and headin' down home, all-of-you by-jeezus." Melba stood behind his chair making hand and mouth signs for Sammy and Flora to ignore him, then she pulled Russell Skunk off to bed.

The fourth morning Russell woke up early, ousting the kids from their sleeping bags. He took the canvas tent down, and even folded Flora's plaid, fringed horse blankets. They were leaving.

Melba sat in the kitchen on a Dutch blue wooden chair, hands folded in her lap, trembling with nervousness like a schoolgirl, her small feet curled around the rungs of the chair. She had pulled it away from the table and placed herself in front of the wood stove so she could watch Flora give Esther a bath in the oversized porcelain kitchen sink. An occasional tear from the corner of one eye or the other might have fallen on her folded hands as she sat there staring at Esther and Flora. Maybe she was figuring out how she was going to leave without Esther. Maybe she was practising her lines, or her lies, over and over in her head.

Esther poured warm water over herself with a brown plastic coffee mug and giggled when her curls tickled, straightening down her back with the weight of the water.

It was Monday, ice day. Sammy told the ice man to just go right in, he'd been there a hundred times before. His sudden entrance cracked Melba's tension into perspective, making her jump at the sight of him carrying his ice pick holding a dripping block of ice through the kitchen. He pushed the ice into the icebox like he usually did, then straightened up, taller and· loftier than when he came in.

"Good day to you, Flora. Wee one having a bath, is she?"

"More like she's washing the floor, Richard."

"Ice Mummy. Ice." Her small hands wagged in the air like a happy dog's tail. Flora gave her some ice chips, and Esther shook them in a cup. "Oh, cold."

Flora wrapped Esther in a checkerboard towel from Old Orchard Beach and dried her off. Melba cried as she watched.

Esther giggled when Flora sprinkled baby powder under her arms, between her toes, and under her two chins.

Melba walked over to the kitchen table thinking she might dress Esther. "NO, Mummy do it!"

Melba turned, dried her eyes on the sleeve of her blouse and went outside. Flora heard her talking to Russell.

"I'm not going."

"What do mean you're not going? Get Esther and get in the goddamned car."

"I said I'm not going. Only one of us is going with you, either me, or Esther, but not both. By jeezus, I mean it, Russell. If you want that kid so bad, you take her, and all the rest of them. But you're not having me too. She's better off where she is. She thinks that Flora and Sammy are her parents. For God almighty sakes I can't even get near her, and neither can you, you fool. She clings onto Sammy with her life. At least one of my kids will have something. We have enough kids to look after."

Their voices faded into the tall swaying cutgrass over by the side of the dance hall. Flora had long ago stopped thinking about how long she and Sammy would keep Esther. Sammy walked around the corner; he'd heard the conversation. His eyes flowed with tears. Flora had never seen Sammy cry.

"Flora, you know they can't give her what we can. She's ours now. Flora, I beg you. I want to keep her."

Flora looked out the kitchen window. The Girlings were all in the car except for Melba who was walking up to the screen door.

"Flora, Sammy, can you keep Esther for a while longer?" Melba mumbled through the black mesh.

Esther sat in Sammy's strong arms, his free hand gently squeezed Flora's shoulder.

Sammy said: "Don't ever worry about this little girl, Melba. We'll give her everything money can buy."

Melba turned around and headed back to the borrowed station wagon idling in the driveway. She must have been crying in great huge gulps; her chest was heaving, she was perspiring and felt nauseous. There must have been so many tears in her eyes that, as she waved good-bye to Esther, she was probably seeing double, no triple, and maybe even more than that – Esther can only imagine.

Probably all their eyes, Esther's, Flora's and Sammy's, were blurred with tears of relief as they saw double green screen doors, and heard them bang shut at the exact same time, and watched double clouds of Girling dust travel by the dance hall and down the lake road.

In the backseat of the borrowed station wagon, Luke sat sideways on Frieda's lap. He cried and snivelled and wiped his nose on the back of his hand until it was so wet he used his shirt. Luke was three. He didn't really know why he was crying except that Frieda was, and it's difficult to snuggle into a chest that's crying or laughing without doing the same yourself.

Frieda wasn't sure why she was crying either – whether it was because she knew that Esther would never be coming back, or because she started thinking of Amy, or because she knew she was pregnant and would soon have her own baby to tend to. All she knew was that she felt like someone had just cut off her arm. In her mind she kept thinking, I have to do something, I just have to do something. But I don't know what.

Poor Liona was confused – Frieda usually didn't cry. And Liona had been thinking that if school in the Harbour weren't starting in a couple weeks she would've liked to stay up there at the cottage with Uncle Sammy and Aunt Flora. Paul reached for Liona's hand and squeezed. He looked scared, like he was wondering whether each time the car slowed down a bit if he was going to be left at the side of the highway. Liona reached for his hand, squeezed it into hers and stared out the window while anger moved in and settled permanently in her jaw.

And Russell Skunk never had another sober day for the rest of his life.

Part III

CHAPTER 16

Esther Weinstein

ESTHER WEINSTEIN WAS BORN AUGUST 29, 1954, the adorable, chubby, curly-haired brunette and bright brown-eyed daughter of Samuel and Flora Weinstein, who presented themselves as a respectable, wealthy, married couple. Flora and Sammy both wore wedding rings, were called Mr. and Mrs. Samuel Weinstein, and Esther was introduced as their daughter. These were the lies they lived.

"The royal family," as Flora referred to them, lived on Wolseley Street in a newer part of Côte Saint-Luc, where houses were not mirror images of one another. But most of them did have attached garages that opened by remote control around five o'clock on weekdays. The men returned home in the evening, removed their rubbers, fedoras and overcoats, and sat down to dinner with wives and children who waited for them before taking one bite.

The dead-end street was quiet, with yellow and red maple, elm, and horse-chestnut trees scattered in yards and lining the boulevard. In the front yards, hedges grew between most houses, forming property lines. Backyards were back to back with the houses on the next street. Fences separated them. From the air you would see checkerboards of concrete patios made with different coloured stone.

In the spring and summer, landscape gardeners came weekly to trim the hedges, cut grass, and plant flowers. They raked yellow, red, and scarlet leaves in the fall, and wrapped rose bushes in burlap for the winter.

North of Côte Saint-Luc was Hampstead and the Blue Bonnet Racetrack, Westmount was to the east. The Kahnawake Reserve was south across the Mercier Bridge, and Dorval Airport was to the west.

Although Esther often drove on bridges over the St. Lawrence River with Flora and Sammy, she didn't know that she had left one island to live on another. They spent the summers at the cottage, where the Weinstein princess played with Robbie Katz. Little Robbie's father owned Katz's grocery stores, the stores that gave away pink elephant stamps as incentive for buying their groceries. Children begged to lick and paste the stamps onto pages in the small booklets that were used to save for things like padded lawn furniture and bicycles.

Robbie and Esther could easily have passed for twins; they were a yard-stick tall, each with a fine mop of dark brown soft pin curls framing their round faces.

They would sometimes sit on the steps of the dance hall, tush to tush, short legs crossed at white ankle socks. Little tanned arms waved to the side, then pulled a chocolate Camel or Lucky Strike or Winston candy cigarette held between two fingers, into their mouths.

"Ah, Winston tastes good, eh?"

Tear off a bit more paper, have a little suck, a little bite maybe, then a small hand pulled the cigarette away again, and they blew chocolate smoke into the air from their chocolate lips.

"Like a cigarette should!"

"Yes, shall we have another puff, honey?"

"Tell me when you're ready, dah-ling."

"Ready Freddy."

Little mimics, that's what Flora called them. To the rest of the small lake community Robbie and Esther were irresistibly adorable and were never without chocolate cigarettes or ice cream Fudgsicles.

On pleasant warm mornings, they sat in the yard cross-legged playing marbles on a horse blanket that covered a wild looking lawn. The lawn didn't resemble the evenly manicured and clipped grass, and pruned hedges of Côte Saint-Luc where, every Thursday, like a cartoon, half a dozen deeply tanned, foreign speaking, short men with curly dark hair wearing white undershirts, would unload tools, wheelbarrows, lawnmowers and hoses from backs of rust-scarred green trucks that had their radios blaring. All morning the men would whistle, and mow most of the lawns from one end of the block and back again on the other side.

Flora watched Esther and Robbie scour the yard for stones to weight the corners of the blanket.

They picked purple and white clover, buttercups, red and yellow paint-brushes, wild coneflowers, tiger buttons, and shafts of tall wheat grass to make fricassee for lunch. After mixing the ingredients in their pails, they added a touch of water from the outside tap and took turns stirring the concoctions with wooden kitchen spoons. The fricassee simmered in the sunshine on pretend stove elements they had built putting their favourite marbles around the base of the pails.

Suddenly Esther screeched: "Oh, noooo!"

Esther and Robbie watched as a garter snake slithered onto the blanket, heading, they thought, for the fricassee. But no, it was really snaking its way to the sparkling peridot marble at the edge of the blanket. And right before their eyes – gulp went the snake, and there was one less marble.

Esther screamed, dumped the fricassee and slammed the pail over the little garter snake all in one movement. She held it there, firmly to the ground. Flora heard the commotion. It sounded like Esther just had her leg ripped off by a grizzly bear. She ran out from the kitchen, heart pounding. And there they were, the two of them, all in one piece. Flora looked down at Esther.

"He's ... he's ... (wipe nose on arm) got ... got ... my (sniff, sniff) mah'ble."

"Who has your marble?"

"The snake has it. In the pail, Mrs. Weinstein."

Flora picked up the pail, and the snake.

"For God Almighty sake Esther, I thought you were dying. Stop that crying."

"He ate my peridot. You said it was my birthstone. Now I don't have any birthstone. I'll never have a birthstone again, never." Esther ran into the cottage, the screen door slapped shut behind her.

"Oy vey," Flora muttered as she walked across the road to the wild rose hedge and sent the garter snake, and Esther's birthstone for a ride in the air over the top of the hedge. *Friday can't come soon enough*, she thought.

Fridays the dust kicked up on the Lake Road with the arrival of fathers and husbands who had been working in the city all week. As always, backseats and trunks of cars were loaded with fresh produce and one inch thick T-bone steaks to grill on the barbecue. Esther looked forward to getting another shiny silver dollar, and a huge noisy beach ball filled with tiny pebbles from the gas station where Sammy filled up.

Saturdays, Sammy would often take her next door to the dance hall to play the pinball machines. Esther stood on a chair and played the right flippers; Sammy stood behind her playing the left. Both father and daughter's brown eyes lit up as bright as the small islands exploding with lights and ringing when the silver balls hit them. Flippers sent the balls crashing into the islands making them blink on and off, and ding and ring, and then deflect onto other islands until eventually the balls, one by one, found their way into the gutter. Before they left, they'd sit at the long soda counter and have a Cott's nectar. Then Esther would stand up on the red vinyl covered barstool and climb onto Sammy's shoulders for a piggyback ride home.

Esther loved going to the cottage in the summers. Hanging out at the hall, swimming in the lake, and later going to camp. There weren't as many rules at the cottage.

CHAPTER 17

1962

"WHY CAN'T I GO IN the living room, Mummy?"

"Because I don't want any footprints on the carpet until everyone arrives for dinner."

Esther didn't want to look into the living room at the new furniture like she was looking at a magazine; she wanted to be on the page. She remembered the night the royal family went to pick out the living and dining-room furniture. It was dark outside by the time they got to the furniture showroom, and Flora wore her mink stole. The showroom was big enough to ride a bicycle through and around the furniture displays, and they were the only people there besides the well-dressed gentleman who showed Flora the furniture.

A few days later, a five-tonne truck backed into the driveway and deliverymen unloaded a complete French provincial dining room suite, a sectional couch with wide stripes of pale blue and off-white and thin strips of gold, and a large coffee table with matching end tables. Later, Flora arranged matching brass cigarette case, lighter, and crown-shaped ashtray on the new kidney shaped coffee table.

For weeks, Flora stood on the threshold of the champagne-coloured carpet, between the saloon doors from the kitchen, and simply stared at the dining room and the living room, as if it were a painting.

Esther didn't understand the relevance of footprints in Flora's picture because Mrs. Cranshaw, the charlady, came every Friday to vacuum them up.

AS AN ONLY CHILD, Esther spent a lot of time with her adult family, and learned from and about them by listening. If Flora and Sammy had talked about Melba, and Russell Skunk, and their kids, Esther would have heard. What she did hear was how Aunt Mina drove everyone crazy with her high-pitched Brooklyn accent, even her husband, Uncle Howard, Sammy's brother. "Vant, vant. Buy, buy." More than Howard could afford at the time. Howard admired his wife's thin body and long dyed-blonde hair and her

68

dancer's svelte legs as she kibitzed around with the men, wagging her longer than life cigarette holder in the air. The women loved her, but thought she was just too much. "Too much of everything except hair maybe."

At a Saturday night dinner party, Mina and Howard arrived at the Weinsteins' late, as usual. As they emerged from the foyer, Sammy's sister, Aunt Libby, said, trying not to laugh: "Mina. Your hair. It's nice eh?"

With that acknowledged, the dinner party could continue.

"LIBBY. YOU LIKE MY NEW SHIIIT?" Flora giggled over the altered "shift." Brazen enough to mention a dirty word among the other women.

Libby laughed. "Oy vey, have you seen such a muumuu like the one Ethel has on tonight? Where is she anyway?"

Flora answered: "Maybe she took her muumuu to the bathroom!"

They stood in the kitchen yackety-yacking, tasting the hors d'oeuvres – all of them overweight, except for Mina. She was in the living room with the men who told their more manly, money, business jokes between Mina's trips to the liquor cart for "just a bit more vine honey, please."

At the end of the belly jouncing in the kitchen Mina joined the rest of the ladies.

"You know vhat?"

"No, what?"

"My Harvey. You should hear him recite the Torah. He's a natch. Maybe he'll be a Rabbi."

Howard and Sammy sputtered into their glasses. They were in the living room but they heard that remark. Sammy told Howard that maybe those boys spend too much time with their mother.

"You're right. But what can I do?"

"Maybe you should send them to camp."

"Every year I ask them. They don't want."

"Well this summer maybe you shouldn't ask. You should just send!"

The women finally brought the hors d'oeuvres into the dining room and laid them out on the buffet. Esther danced in and around their bodies offering plates of finger food to the men.

More shushed now. "And Sadie, where's Sadie?"

Sadie was Esther's grandmother.

"Down in Boston. Vacationing."

"She spends more time in Boston than in Montreal."

"Aha aha. I vunder vhat's in Boston?"

"Maybe you should ask one of her sons?"

"Ah. But maybe her sons don't want to know!"

Libby said: "Sadie always was a little strange. Can you imagine anyone marrying your father's brother? That's vhat she did."

"I know. I know. But always I vunder vhy. Vhy she married her family. And now, now she doesn't spend time with her own family. She's either in New York, or Miami, or Boston."

"Well. As long as her boys are bankrolling her, she'll be vacationing."

"And can you blame them? She's their mother."

Libby changed the subject.

"My Beverley, maybe she's too thin, eh? Too thin, too tall, too much on the telephone. And Ellen. Ellen never comes out of her room. Plays her clarinet and studies. Night and day. Day and night. Tell me. How's she going to have a life?"

"And you think that's something, Libby? My Sammy's Esther, the mimic, she went into the bathroom a few weeks ago and came out with barely an eyebrow. She said it hurt too much to pluck them like I do so she cut them off with my cuticle scissors. And I told her, now she's going to have bushy eyebrows for the rest of her life. But does she believe me? Does she believe a word I say? She thinks they'll look just like mine!"

"You should be flattered she wants to look like you, Flora. Actually if she looks like anyone, she looks like Sammy. Funny eh? And where is Esther?"

"The little lush is probably going around slurping up the red bottoms of the wine glasses."

"Oh Flora, how you talk! Seven years old and you think she likes the wine?"

"You don't believe me. Call her. Listen to her, look at her cheeks. You watch!"

Esther raced up from the den where she, Beverley and Ellen were dancing and singing to the record player. "She wore an itsy bitsy teeny weenie yellow polka dot bikini and in the water she wanted to stay. Hi Aunt Libby!"

"Come here and let me feel you." Libby pulled Esther close with her smooth fat arms, smooched one cheek and pinched the other.

"You're varm, my beauty. Feel Flora. Maybe you should put her outside for some fresh air?"

"I'll take Gigi with me, Mummy!"

"Oh. I don't know, Esther."

Melba's Wash   71

"Oh Flora. Let her go. To the end of the block and back."

"All right. But put Gigi's coat on her. It's cold out there."

She didn't need to tell Esther to put her coat on. She wasn't stupid. Esther buttoned her red fur coat and pulled on white angora gloves and bonnet. She put Gigi's brown fur coat on her, clipped the red diamond studded leash to her matching collar, and vamoosed out the double door, down the six steps to the walk.

Between the streetlights, it was dark and difficult to see the cracks in the sidewalk. Step on a crack, break your mother's back. She was scared to step on them so she took big steps and then a little one to skip across the crack when it appeared. Gigi ran ahead, wandering side to side, sniffing, and when she stopped suddenly, and Esther saw she was on a crack – she fell right over her. Gigi was all right, but Esther tore her leotards. A hole in the knee where she always fell and tore her leotards. Flora would be furious.

She could already hear what was to come. "Esther. You can't walk over the cracks in the sidewalk without falling? When are you going to learn to walk? Put your shoulders back. You're going to grow up and have a big hump on your back. My God, do I have to get you a back brace?"

Esther didn't go to the corner of the block, only to her friend Wendy's. Flora didn't like Esther going to Wendy's. They ate white bread, bread so soft you could pull the fleshy moist centre out of its jacket, roll it into a marshmallow size ball and pop it into your mouth.

As Esther picked Gigi up to go home, she thought: *Well, no more white bread, Mummy.* Wendy and her family had moved back to Antigua where she was born. Suddenly Esther heard a cracking noise, probably a tree branch moving in the shadows between the streetlights. Fear sent her into a run, bursting in the door like hurricane Hazel.

"I fell, Mummy. I fell."

"My God Esther. Another pair of leotards! When are you going to learn to walk?"

"Gigi made me fall. She ran in front of me."

"Oh, shhhure."

"My Sammy. Bless his heart. He works to keep Esther in leotards!"

"Flora," Libby said. "Maybe you should take her to the doctor?"

"Ahah ahah. I'll take her to the doctor all right. I'll take her to the doctor on the bottom of my hand."

"Flora. That's not nice. You shouldn't talk like that when you don't mean it."

But Flora meant it all right, only not the bottom of her hand, as she had bad eczema and her hands cracked and bled. At night, she smothered them with hydrocortisone cream and wore thin white cotton gloves to bed.

Flora used the yardstick. And there were always two or three extra ones standing in the corner of the garage, because once in a while the yardstick would break. Esther would laugh. Flora would be furious.

CHAPTER 18

The Little Brown Coat

ONE NIGHT ESTHER HEARD HER MOTHER CRYING and slipped out of bed, down the few stairs to the main floor to see into the den. Lying on the carpet, Esther slid head first from the stairs around the door-frame like a fallen question mark. Flora was standing in front of Sammy, sobbing, and holding each side of her head with her hands as if to keep it from exploding. Esther had never heard her mother cry before. Scared, she backed up a stair on her hands and knees. She heard Flora say "send her back," and wondered, as those words hit the air in the den, and drifted up the stairs: *Send who back? Gigi maybe?* She'd been making in the house lately.

What Esther didn't hear was:

"Okay Flora, I admit she's a little spoiled. So she wants a hundred dollar coat, so buy her a hundred dollar coat for crying out loud."

"She embarrassed me in the store."

"What store?"

"The Lad and Lassie store on Somerled, where she picked out the coat she wants."

"And did you tell her to pick out a coat?"

"Yes, but you're missing my point. She asked me to buy her the brown coat, and I told her no. Then, in front of the saleslady she said to me: 'How much is the coat, Mummy?' And I told her it cost a hundred dollars and that was too much money to spend on a winter coat that she'd outgrow. Then she announced that Daddy said she was worth a million dollars, so she'd just ask him. I could have died of embarrassment. So she asked you, and what do you say?"

"I didn't know she'd asked you already. What's the big schmiel anyway? It's only a coat, a little brown coat."

"The big schmiel is that she's coming between us."

"Ey yey yey, why do I have the feeling this isn't about the coat? What's the real problem here Flora?"

73

"I want to send her back."

"You could send her back? You would do such a thing? You would break my heart?"

Silence thickened in the space between them.

"I'll answer for you – I don't think so. You should go lie down, finish your cry. You'll feel different in the morning."

"Don't patronize me, Sammy."

"Well, let me put it another way then – over my dead body – I'll send you back first."

That night, Esther had nightmares again. Night after night, the same nightmare. A grey-haired woman with a large head and feet sat in a grey carriage on the light fixture out in the hall outside her room. She made choo, choo, choo noises like a train, and then she said: "I'm coming to get you, blue girl."

The hall light had always been left on so Esther wouldn't be afraid. When she went to bed at night, she tried not to look at the light fixture, thinking to herself: *She can't possibly be there again.* But sure thing, when Esther glanced up to see, the hall witch was there. Her tanned face grew bigger and her skin stretched thinner and thinner until she slid out of her carriage turning into a ball of dust. The dust ball attached itself to the base-board and moved like a train on a train track, scraping metal, from the hall into Esther's room. Choo choo, choo choo. Esther took an enormous deep breath and pulled the dark brown fitted bedspread over her head. She stayed under the covers until she felt like there was no more oxygen to breathe and then, in desperation, reached behind her for the chain to turn on the reading light. Esther would sit up in bed and take a book from her bookcase headboard. She read the same story on those nights, over and over again, the one about a poor little boy who had no home.

CHAPTER 19

The Counting Room

O N SATURDAY MORNINGS Sammy took Esther with him downtown
to the club on Saint Catherine Street. Identical brick walk-ups with
matching outside iron staircases lined the cement sidewalks. Upstairs was
the dance studio and downstairs was the club. Dozens of pigeons hung their
heads over the edge of the pebble roofs watching people come and go. Some
men entered the building through the basement, and left in the early hours
of the morning from the dance studio. Inside the building, doorways and
hallways and staircases were cleverly designed with a maze of possible exits
in case of a police raid.

Flora would have died to see the cigarette burns on the floor and on the
tables, but Esther didn't notice those scars. She thought the ceiling seemed
very high, or the floor seemed low. Large round dim lights hung over each
of the maybe dozen tables from long dusty cables.

Stanley, Sammy's right hand man, and Uncle Stanley to Esther, helped
teach her how to shuffle and deal like a card shark before she was five
years old.

Those mornings at the club, Esther would wait for Sammy in the office,
the back room. She'd nose around, opening, inspecting and closing tiny
drawers in his massive blonde oak desk, or play poker with Stanley, and
help herself to soda from the fridge.

Or occasionally, Sammy might say: "Esther, want to count some money,
honey?"

And Stanley might say: "Do you think Flora would like that Sammy?"

And Sammy might reply: "What's it gonna hurt if she counts a little
money? It's mathematics. Right Stanley?"

"Right boss."

AT HOME, ON SUNDAY MORNING from downstairs in the den, Esther would
call out:

"Daddy, I'm waiting for you!"

75

"Where are you, honey?"

"I'm in the counting room."

"Set up two TV trays for me, will you, baby?"

Sammy and Esther sorted hundreds of Canadian bills from the weekend at the club. She sat next to Sammy on the couch while he sorted bills by denomination. Esther arranged stacks of paper money at first by colour when she was young, starting with the brown ones, counting one million, two million ...

From up in the kitchen, Flora heard Esther singing: "The King was in the counting house counting out the money ..."

Then Esther heard the Queen yell from the top of the stairs: "I wish you wouldn't let her handle that filthy money, Sammy. It's full of germs you know."

"I'll wash my hands before dinner, Mummy!"

"Honestly Flora, it's only money, honey."

But before they washed, they sneaked a couple of hands of poker or black jack. Flora would hear Esther giggle and yell: "Hit me!" And Sammy would slap down another card for her to draw.

"Sammy," Flora would yell again. "You're not teaching her to gamble, are you?"

"Of course not, we're just having a game of cards."

"Hit me, Esther!"

THE COUNTING ROOM, really the downstairs den, was where the Weinsteins spent most of their time at home. That's where the television set was and where Sammy watched the fights, and all the games: baseball, football, horse racing, and Hockey Night in Canada. Those were the days of Northern Dancer, Rocket and Pocket Richard, and Mickey Mantle. Lorne Greene talked on the radio in Montreal, and Flora had a crush on his voice.

It was where Esther watched *Dr. Kildare* and *Ben Casey* and *The Flying Doctor* and *Lassie* and *The Ed Sullivan Show* and *Walt Disney Presents*. Late Saturday nights after watching *The Untouchables* with Eliot Ness, sometimes the royal family, all in their pyjamas, would get in their blue and white Pontiac convertible and head to Miss Montreal drive-in restaurant on Decarie Boulevard. They did this for years, until the night Sammy's car got a flat tire.

Esther slept curled up in the backseat wrapped in a car blanket through hot dogs at Miss Montreal, the flat tire, and the cop stopping to check out the suspicious looking guy in pyjamas on Decarie Boulevard who was trying to figure out how to change a tire.

Melba's Wash   77

"I told you this would happen one day," Flora said once the cop left.

"Well, you're in your pyjamas too, Flora."

"Yes, well I didn't have to get out of the car to change the tire."

"The cop thought it was funny, after he saw that we were all in our pyjamas and slippers! So, who was to know it's against the law to drive in your slippers?"

The three of them cuddled together on the couch under blankets during the Cuban Missile Crisis watching reports on television.

And sometimes around Chanukah Flora pestered Sammy about Christmas, set up a small artificial spruce tree in the corner of the den by the television set and tried to convince him it was for Esther.

CHAPTER 20

Over My Dead Body

ESTHER TOOK BALLET LESSONS – first position, second position, third position. "Mummy my feet hurt Can I take piano lessons instead?"

Patient Mrs. Plomp had to show Esther the same lesson almost every week because she practised "Moon River" and other songs instead of Royal Conservatory music. She did her best to try to teach Esther scales and theory, and tolerated her ridiculous giggling during the lessons. But each Wednesday, about half way through, Mrs. Plomp would twist her large body on the bench and look Esther in the eyes.

"What's so funny, little girl? Oh, never mind, just play."

Mrs. Plomp's fingers were also short, and very fat. When she played, Esther's eyes would see ten all-beef sausage wieners bump up and down the keys.

Flora picked Esther up from school in a taxicab on Fridays to go to Côte-des-Neiges to get her hair done in a Jackie Kennedy style beehive and often their fingernails polished. On the way home they went to Steinberg's for groceries.

They spent summers at the cottage, winter vacations in Miami Beach, and early fall vacations in the Catskills and Old Orchard Beach.

On school days, if you stood on the corner of Guelph and McMurray Avenue and looked through the diamond wire of the Frost fence into the Westminster schoolyard, you would have spotted Esther playing the game MISSISSIPPI with her friends. She was one of the many uniformed girls dressed in a navy A-line tunic, navy socks, and a fresh white blouse. She usually had bandages on her knees. Step on a crack, break your mother's back.

TWICE A WEEK, BEFORE BED, Esther put a list for Larry, the milkman, and some one-dollar bills and loose change into the washed glass milk bottles and placed them on the doorstep. She always awoke excited the next morning to find more bottles of chocolate milk, cream and eggs, and sometimes butter as well. People knew each other's names then. The man who delivered the dry-cleaning was Luxor, and the mailman was Richard. Esther knew she was safe to open the front door to these people with names, and handed them envelopes with money from Sammy at Christmas time.

On Wednesday morning, April 30, 1965, Esther woke up and brought in a quart of chocolate milk, a quart of whole milk, and a pint of cream. Then she got ready for school, just like she had got ready for school on Monday the 28th, and Tuesday, the 29th. She put on her navy school tunic, knee socks and white blouse and went downstairs for breakfast. Esther remembered having a toasted poppy-seed bagel slathered with cream cheese, a small glass of orange juice and a large glass of chocolate milk.

Montreal was usually a city of April showers, but not that day, not that Wednesday. That day was dry and pleasantly warm. Esther wore her navy cardigan, and left her umbrella standing in the foyer. She knew when to leave; like every other kid in the city who had to walk or ride their bicycle roughly the same distance, she left after the children's march on CJAD radio, at 8:20. As far as Esther knew, every child in the whole world left at that exact time for school.

Esther kissed Flora and Sammy goodbye, and left them sitting at each end of the kitchen table reading *The Montreal Star* and having their second cup of coffee and more cigarettes. Flora wore a sleeveless mauve flowered housedress and high-heeled slippers. Sammy wore a suit and starched white shirt. A fresh stiff hankie lay neatly folded like a crown in the breast pocket of his jacket. He had as many matching suits and shoes and ties as Flora had dresses, shoes, and purses. Esther had pulled the skinny end of his tie earlier that morning. On Saturdays, when there was more time, she would build the whole tie into its knot. Flora had showed her how. Flora usually straightened Sammy's tie during the week. Both loved the softness of the smooth silk wrapping over and under and through their fingers.

But that day, Esther had stood on the edge of Sammy's bed, reached around his stout neck and tucked his tie neatly underneath the collar of his white shirt. Sammy smiled big and gave Esther a peck on the lips.

"Perfect, baby doll."

THAT AFTERNOON a nervous looking Uncle Abe, Libby's husband, drove up along the street curb beside Westminster School. He waited for Esther to walk her bicycle out of the schoolyard, which was the rule.

"Esther, honey, Aunt Libby wants you to come to our house after school today." This was strange because Aunt Libby called Esther honey, not Uncle Abe.

Abe got out of his car, moving a little quicker than he usually did, and Esther saw his long thin arms shaking as he lifted her bicycle into the trunk.

"Are you okay, Uncle Abe?"

"Sure, Esther. Ellen and Beverley are at home."

"Good. What about Aunt Libby?"

"She's not home right now, but she'll be back later."

Esther wondered how her aunt could be out without Uncle Abe; after all, she didn't know how to drive a car.

"Where is she?"

"She's at your house with your mother. Your mother's not feeling very well today."

"That's funny. She wasn't sick this morning. Are you sure I shouldn't go straight home?"

"No. She wants you to stay with us until she's feeling better."

Abe left Esther with her cousins, and drove away in the car. Esther went directly to Beverley's pink princess telephone and dialled her own phone number. An unfamiliar voice answered. In the background Esther heard pitiful noises, like an injured cat, although she'd never had a cat. The voice was quick, almost rude: "Who is this?"

"It's Esther. I want to speak to my mother, please."

"Who's your mother?"

"Flora's my mother. You're in my house. Don't you know who my mother is?"

"She's not feeling very well. She said she can't talk to you right now."

"My mother is too sick to talk to me on the phone?"

"Well, yes, right now she is."

Esther hung up the phone, turned and headed out of Beverley's bedroom, out the front door and onto her bicycle. She rode home down Guelph to Westminster Avenue, then cut through the park where she swam in the summer, skated in the winter, and stole tulips for her mother in the spring. Her thighs pumped dangerously fast, feet sometimes slipping off the pedals. The rainbow coloured streamers flew out from her handle grips all the way to Wolseley Street.

Esther walked in the house and saw Flora sitting sideways in Sammy's chair at the grey chrome kitchen table, her beautiful pouf of hair flattened to her head on one side where she was holding it with one hand. Her face was white and puffy, her eyeliner smudged. Mascara streaked messily down from her eyes where she had rubbed her tears. She was wearing the same mauve housedress as when Esther left for school that morning.

"MUMMY, what's wrong? What are you crying for?"

Flora lifted her head a bit and looked at Esther, but no words left her lips.

"WHERE'S MY DADDY?" Esther screamed.

Two men in the house picked her up and drove her back to Aunt Libby's house. She cried and lashed out, and screamed for them to let her out of the car. She remembered nothing more.

* * *

Deaths

April 30, 1965

Samuel Weinstein passed away unexpectedly at the age of forty-nine after suffering a heart attack. Family and friends will miss him. He is survived by his wife Ethel, a son Aaron, and a daughter Riva. In lieu of flowers, please make donations to the Heart Foundation.

The Montreal Gazette, May 1, 1965

Esther didn't read the newspaper.

There was a funeral for Samuel Weinstein. Esther was not in attendance. There were no young children at the funeral. Someone said: "It just wasn't done." For thirty years Esther would wonder where they put her Daddy.

* * *

ESTHER REMEMBERED having passport photos taken and going to Syracuse, New York to see Aunt Effy. Day after day they went to look at houses to buy. She began to get excited. Some of them were nice and they were close to Aunt Effy. Mummy smiled once in a while, until the day Esther was playing ball with Aunt Effy's son in the gravel driveway and fell down. Flora slapped her across the kisser to try to make her stop crying. Effy yelled at Flora and took Esther in the bathroom to clean her knee.

It was badly torn up and they had to take her to the doctor for fourteen stitches. She wasn't allowed to go to the beach for two weeks.

Flora screamed at Esther in the car on the way back to the house about how she'd ruined her summer, how they couldn't go to the lake now, how she couldn't take it anymore and was sending her back when they got back to Montreal, just like her psychiatrist told her to do in the beginning. Aunt Effy tried to comfort Esther's sobs, and calm Flora down.

Esther thought, if only she hadn't fallen again maybe Mummy wouldn't have been so angry with her. She wondered if she was going to live in an orphanage like the little boy in her book who had no home. Where was she sending her back to?

Besides the smell of burnt hot-dogs in a frying pan, the next thing Esther remembered was the smell of the train station and the squealing of the wheels, and sleeping in a berth on the train.

After that was a boat. Esther didn't know where she was going and was scared, short of breath, and needed some fresh air. She went door to door trying to get outside, but they were all locked. Esther pleaded with a man who worked on the boat to let her out, but he said the water was too rough, and pointed to the chairs that were chained to the floor so they wouldn't fly away.

Esther looked over and watched Flora in her mauve patterned shift and beige high heels, smoking her menthol cigarette. She was flipping through a magazine and as she turned the pages Esther saw that Flora had all her "going out" rings on, and her good watch that Daddy had just bought her. She had managed to do her hair all by herself and looked stylish and beautiful. She looked out of place compared to the other women on the boat. She belonged in a magazine; she was that beautiful.

Esther longingly walked to her table and sat down. Flora didn't say anything.

"I love you, Mummy," Esther said softly, choking back tears, desperately trying to remove the building anxiety that would last for the rest of her life.

After some silence Flora replied: "I love you too, Esther." But she seemed emotionless, as if she was missing. Esther watched her take a small round pill out of a silver case, and put it in her mouth.

"Where are we going, Mummy?"

"We're going to see your real family."

"You are my real family. What about Daddy?"

"Esther, Daddy is gone!"

"Gone where?"

"To Heaven."

"But Mummy, how can that be? I left the two of you in the kitchen and went to school. Everything was all right."

"Esther, you're too young to understand. Daddy went to work that morning and after a quarrel with a man, he had a heart attack and passed away. The family sat Shiva at Bubbe's house. You and I weren't allowed to be there. This is all I can tell you right now; I'll tell you more when you're older, Esther."

"Mummy, I feel sick."

"Let's go to the bathroom."

CHAPTER 21

Birthing a Bathroom

M ELBA READ THE LETTER FROM FLORA AGAIN. She was so worried about that damned flush; she had three bathrooms in Montreal.
Melba almost felt a bit bad that she'd had those cupboards put in, but … it
was only money, Flora would have more.

June 30, 1965
Dear Melba,
Like I told you on the telephone, you have to take Esther back. I am in
no state to handle her; she thinks I've done something with Sammy for
God's sake. He loved her so much; I can't bear looking at her. She even
looks like him.
I pulled her out of school three weeks ago, and took her with me down
to Effy's place in Syracuse thinking maybe we'd move down there. Had
passports made and everything. I even looked at buying a small house.
I just can't do it, Melba. I'm tired. I've got nothing left to give her. She's
cooking her own meals – fried hot-dogs, burned black. The smell
makes my stomach turn, but I can't make myself look after her.
I took her to the psychiatrist with me and he tried to talk to her. I don't
know if she even remembers going. She's too young to understand why
she couldn't see Sammy, that his family took his body and sat Shiva
at his mother's apartment. I never saw him again after breakfast the
morning he died either. The doctor told me I'm not in any shape to
look after Esther, and I should send her back to you. Did I tell you my
hair turned completely white when Sammy died?
I've sold the cottage up at the Lake, and it looks like I have a buyer for
the house. I'm sending you a money order to have that bathroom put
in the house before we get there.
We'll be down (I'm bringing Gigi too) about mid-August. At least
Esther will have Gigi. I'll stay for a few days and then I'm going to

84

Syracuse to stay with Effy and Rick for a while. Don't you let Russell drink away my money.
Love,
Flora

Girlings got the money all right.

"Well by damned, Melba, never seen a thousand dollars before. That's right, one zero, zero, zero, a thousand smackeroos."

"It's for the jeezus flush, Russell."

Flora had sent that money for a bathroom, what should have been a glorious modern bathroom.

That summer, the older boys Paul and Luke, helped their father partition a cubbyhole off from the south end of the front room. They put a small window in the wall above where the flush would sit so a man could stand proudly to take a piss and peer outdoors at the same time.

FRIEDA WAS AT THE HOUSE THAT DAY. It took quite a while and help from Roger, and cousin Stucky Girling from across the road, but they did build that bathroom. They took off the front door to get the bathtub into the house, mind you. That was the first time that door was opened. They pulled off what was left of a very dry sheet of polyethylene from the front door. Roger had always wondered whether that plastic was there to cover the door from letting the wind inside, or plain hold the door firm against the house. Cracked pieces broke off in banner size wedges, framing the opening like a broken window. Stevie and Floress scooped them up and ran around the dooryard pretending they were the cavalry waving their victory flags, or maybe their surrender flags, while the wooden door was coaxed off its paint-chipped hinges and set down to use as a ramp into the house. There never were any front steps to that house, and they had only ever needed two to begin with.

Like a funeral procession, a squat cardboard box was lowered and carried from the back of Stucky's half-tonne truck. Stevie and Floress claimed that cardboard coffin. They would be sliding down the dooryard on it come winter.

First off that tub looked big enough, compared to Stevie and Floress, but soon they all wondered, eyeing it, it was maybe 3/4, 2/3 size. It wasn't a real tub for Heaven's sake. If that fat bugger Russell Skunk were to sink his lumpy arse in there, the water wouldn't cover his legs.

Into the house those men marched, over the door ramp, proud as all get out, down the hall to the kitchen, turning carefully to the left. They set the tub on its end, and walked it into the bathroom. Luke carried in the tiny washbasin that would be bolted to the wall. Two hollow aluminum legs held up its frowning front lip.

When finally the heavenly white porcelain throne was being ushered into the house, and lowered onto its final resting place, Stevie and Floress stood to the side and sang: "God Save the Queen," each holding a dirty little hand over their heart. They supposed that was the highest honour they could bestow on the flush that day. Yes sir, someone should've taken a snap.

Weeks later, the bathroom was still there. There were even a few shiny spots left on the taps that small fingers had missed caressing. But if you had half a brain, and looked at the unfinished 2 x 4 walls, you would see there was not a copper pipe in sight, or an asbestos one, or a PVC one either for that matter.

Instead of plumbing, Melba had called Able Cutter down from Whale Cove and got fitted for kitchen cupboard doors, where there were just shelves before. The plywood counter was covered with a sheet of white and gold flecked Arborite. The chipped porcelain sink was moved into the dooryard as a new feeder for the cow, and a new aluminum double sink was installed. At the back of the sink was a black rubber hand sprayer that pulled up through for washing muddy potatoes and for rinsing bar soap off the back of their necks instead of using a dipper.

"Melba, what are you going to tell Flora when she gets here and the flush doesn't work?" Russell asked.

"I'll say I ran out of money, that's what. I sent her a line two weeks ago and told her it wasn't going to be enough to put that septic in. But you know Flora, she knows everything. Well she was wrong this time."

"She didn't send that money for you to go and get yourself a new kitchen."

"Flora won't know that those cupboards weren't here before. Good grief, anyone looking at all of us living here would think we have a proper kitchen, now wouldn't they? Besides, it's not like those doors are new. They came from the old McAdam place down East Point Road. Mr. Cutter sized them to fit in here.

"Oh, don't you worry, Russell. Before Flora gets here I'll run across the road and talk to Uncle Spud and see if Flora can have her b.m. over to his place. She won't be down that long. Esther can use the same crapper the rest of us use behind the barn."

"By the Jeezus, Flora's going to be some mad."

"Well then, she'll have to bring down some more of Sammy's do-re-me and have that septic put in herself if she's going to be that high and mighty. Don't you worry, she'll have a hell of a lot more thousands stuffed in her girdle when she leaves Montreal. You mark my words."

"Well, I hope you're right, Melba, because they'll be here tomorrow!" Russell said.

CHAPTER 22

No Kleenex on Deer Curve

"ESTHER, DO YOU REMEMBER THE DAY you went to the hospital?" Flora asked. Esther Girling had been admitted to the Montreal Sick Children's Hospital when the doctor thought she had tuberculosis.

"Of course, I remember. It was scary because Dr. Benjamin always came to the house whenever I was sick."

"Do you remember me talking to the nurse behind the desk?"

"I don't remember you talking to anyone."

"Don't you remember me telling the nurse how lucky you were that you have two mommies and two daddies?"

"Why would you say that, Mummy?"

"Because it is true, Esther."

"You're meshuggeneh!"

"Don't be fresh with me, little girl."

"I remember sitting on an ugly, horrid, orange vinyl bench playing with Daddy. He was trying to blow up his arm through his thumb like Popeye. You watched us! That's what I remember."

"Do you remember me bringing you cucumber sandwiches and chocolate milk because the hospital would telephone every day and say you weren't eating what you called crap, and me bringing you bagels and smoked meat sandwiches and nectar too?"

"I remember you brought me food, and Uncle Stanley sent me flowers."

Esther remembered many things: the awful smell of clean boiled gauze pads, and nurses coming into her room, even during the night. They wore white gowns that appeared too big for them. As they walked closer, they looked like ghosts wearing white masks, and hands covered with rubber gloves picked up the steaming pads with silver tongs and placed them carefully on her swollen neck. She remembered crying until she fell back to sleep, and then the quiet whoosh of air opened into her room again. She saw the shine of the silver kidney-shaped bowl come closer, and the light fade as the door closed by itself. Again Esther heard the tongs clank against

88

the side of the bowl reaching for the hot strips of cotton gauze. She finally gave in and lay still on the pillow, whimpering like a baby. She never did have tuberculosis, just swollen glands; Esther remembered that.

"Do you remember Daddy promising you a new bike, a blue one, with handlebar streamers, if you'd get better and be a good girl in the hospital?"

"Of course, I remember my bicycle. Daddy said he'd buy me a three-speed bicycle if I didn't cry anymore. Mummy, you can't make me remember what I don't remember. I was only six. I don't even know where I am. I don't remember how we came here. Now you're telling me that I'm someone else! And that you're not my real mother, and Daddy isn't my real Daddy! You're a liar. You're a big fat liar. You killed Daddy and now you're leaving me here alone. I don't know these people. I won't stay. I'll follow you. You can't make me stay here. You can't just give me away. I'll go back to Montreal and live with Aunt Libby and Uncle Al, or I can live with Uncle Stanley and Aunt Gloria."

"For God's sake blow your nose. It's in your mouth."

"There's no Kleenex!"

"Esther, would you please just use this toilet tissue?"

"It's toilet paper!" Esther yelled.

"Do you remember wrapping all those Christmas presents every year? They were for your family."

Esther thought for a moment, and remembered holding one finger on the ribbon so Mummy could tie the bow. After that, they wrapped all the boxes in brown paper, and she'd hold one finger on the string.

"You said they were for your sister's family who were poor and lived far away."

"Esther! My sister is Melba. She's your real mother."

"Liar! She is not. Maybe they're your family, but I don't know them. They don't even have a bathtub, or a toilet, or a car, or even a real telephone! What's the matter with you?"

Esther pulled hard on Flora's shift.

"What's the matter with you, Mummy?" Esther screamed, holding her own hands against the sides of her head.

Flora straightened her dress and went downstairs to get some Kleenex.

"What's all the hollering going on up there?" Melba asked.

"I can't make her remember she has another family," Flora said.

"Did you ever tell her?"

"Well, not directly, but I thought she heard me admitting her to Children's Hospital when the doctor thought she had tuberculosis."

"Look at you – you're a mess, Flora. From what I heard upstairs, you could spend a month here and she still won't accept you leaving her here. You should just leave when you planned. She'll be fine once you're gone."

"I suppose so, but it doesn't sound like it, Melba. I don't suppose you have any Kleenex?"

Melba laughed. "No, I don't suppose I do."

Some time later, Flora went back upstairs with more toilet paper and a warm face cloth. She found Esther in a foetal position asleep on the bed in her clothes.

In the morning, Esther continued her relentless arguing, but now more panicked because Flora said she was leaving soon.

"You can keep Gigi and take care of her."

Esther screamed loud and hysterically at her mother: "She's your dog! And she'll get dirty. It's filthy here. There's no dog salon; there aren't even any sidewalks! There isn't a fence. Gigi will run on the highway and get hit by a car."

"How can you say such a thing?"

"How can you leave me here? Wait till Daddy finds out what you've done. You're going to be sorry."

"For God's sake blow your nose. It's on your face and in your hair."

Esther didn't care about the snot and pulled on Flora's arm crying, choking and begging pitifully.

"Tell me when you're coming back to get me."

"I told you, Esther, as soon as I find a place to live, and a job."

"But when will that be?"

"Not too long, dear."

Later that night, Esther overheard Flora telling Melba: "I won't leave her here with no toilet."

"Well, you had three bathrooms, Flora, but what do you really know about the price of a bathroom? I told you that you didn't send enough money."

Esther lay down in bed, leaving room beside her for her mother. No, Flora wouldn't be leaving her; there was no toilet.

Flora had promised Esther that she would wake her up the next morning, but when Esther woke up, Flora was gone.

WITHIN A FEW DAYS a contractor was hired to install a septic field. And that was how the Girlings' got their first flush, ten years after they got their first television set.

Part IV

CHAPTER 23

Out the Kitchen Door

IN THE TEN YEARS that Esther was away in Montreal, things didn't get much better on Deer Curve for Melba. After four years she had Stevie and Floress, one right after the other. She loved Stevie as much as she could love anyone. There wasn't much left for Floress because she looked too much like Russell Skunk. A real shame, because she was the absolute sweetest baby born to the Girlings, both in looks and temperament. She had a smiling round face, ringlets, and long, dark, curled double sets of eyelashes, and Melba's dark curly hair and deep brown eyes. Still, everything about her reminded Melba of her hatred of Russell Skunk. Floress grew up wearing Esther's hand-me-downs that Flora had sent over the years, so she was usually dressed smartly, a few years behind the fashion of the big city, but ahead of any fashion to hit the Island.

Frieda had six kids of her own. She was fourteen when Clover was born, just like Melba was when she had Frieda. She had thought her mother would help her with the baby, seeing how there wasn't a baby in the house anymore. She thought Melba would understand; how could she not understand? Frieda was sure her mother would help her. Help all right. Help her get packed, married, and out the kitchen door. Melba was not about to have any more bawling babies around.

"You pissed in your bed, now you can sleep in it." That's what she told Frieda.

One Saturday morning, Pastor Timothy married fourteen-year-old Frieda and sixteen-year-old Roger in the Baptist church in Grand Harbour. Both sets of parents had consented to the marriage of the two children, and attended the ceremony.

Roger's parents found the pair a two-room shell of a house at a cheap rent out on the east side of Moses' property. The place hadn't been lived in for a while. Skip Moses didn't even live on that chunk of land any more; he had moved closer down into the village because he wasn't able to walk that Seal Cove hill any longer. The house was set up high and back off the road;

there was no one living nearby. The closest place to them was the graveyard, and there wasn't much noise coming from there. The next place up the road was Spicers' and it was closer to the Girlings and that was a good two-mile walk uphill.

The house was originally two pieces put together on posts and beams and covered on the outside with grey clapboard like Russell Skunk's. The original shell was one room, a combined kitchen and front room, with two large square windows looking down to the road.

A huge grandmother wood stove sat on cinder blocks jutting out just enough from the wall to allow for the stovepipe. Frieda always kept that stove going; winter and summer there'd be a tin kettle and a large pot of water always simmering off to the side. They figured they were some lucky because there was no shortage of wood. Roger helped the loggers some days out at Miller's Pond, and they let him take the deadfall and any wood that fell off the trucks. Yes, they were always snugly warm in the kitchen. In the wintertime, mind you, there was frost on the walls in the bedroom. That's where Frieda would store the powdered milk she'd mix up in the morning for the kids.

Across from the stove, under the window, was a plywood counter about five feet long. A heavy old white porcelain sink sat in the middle of it. There were no taps, and the grey water drained down below into a big old lard can. A clean, but faded orange gingham curtain hung from the counter to the floor; behind it was a shelf. The shelf was usually bare, except for a mousetrap and old catalogues.

The bedroom, another of Skip's outbuildings, was literally hauled up from the road and added on to the back of the house. They punched an entranceway into the living room and, in Girling tradition, a discarded bed sheet hung across the doorway.

By the time Frieda was twenty-four, she and Roger had divided the bedroom in half, or almost half, with another bed sheet. There was a set of bunk beds on each wall, holding six kids, and behind them was Frieda and Roger's three-quarter bed. There wasn't much fuss. You just untucked the bedcovers at the foot of the bed when another kid came along, then tucked them back in, feet to feet. Frieda loved her babies and was happy for each one. She pulled and hauled water from the well at the edge of the property and did laundry in her wringer washer every two days until it broke down. Everything in the house was spotless and clean, especially her babies.

The well water was tasty, probably because there were trout in there swimming around keeping it clean. At least, that's what Russell Skunk told them. And Frieda was thankful that it was a downhill walk lugging metal pails of water into the house because she made that walk every day for all their water for drinking, and bathing. But best of all, they had a two-seater outhouse, one more bottom seat than the Girlings!

Feeding all those growing kids was a problem, especially in the winter when the logging was shut down and there wasn't as much fish given away down at Fisherman's Wharf. During those times, Roger and his friend Ollie became experts at stealing loaves of bread from the bread truck when it came down to the island on Mondays. The two of them used to chuckle and tell Frieda they had a serious plan they'd been working on for picking which store they'd loot the delivery truck at. Yes, they thought they were quite clever so they did. But really, which store they'd hit before the bread route was finished depended on how early in the morning they would drag their tails out of bed. There were only five small stores scattered along the eighteen miles of road that stretched the island.

Leon Cooper drove the bread truck for Chemical Bread Company back then. Leon was slow-moving, awkward, and as wide as he was tall. Roger and Ollie had no problem swiping a few loaves of bread for the week. They were well practised, and real cocky too. Unfortunately, luck changed for Roger and Ollie after a few months of sneaking milk off the milk truck. The containers were glass bottles then, and one slip, one spilled milk, and that's how Roger ended up at the farm.

There was no jail on the island so the court sent him up to the Saint John Penitentiary for six months. Two weeks for stealing the milk and five and a half months for resisting arrest. No one knew if Frieda and Roger ever did get off welfare after that.

AFTER FRIEDA HAD MARRIED and moved to Seal Cove, the fighting and carrying on between Melba and Russell got worse, usually when he was drinking, and that was most of the time. The Girling boys grew old enough to get tangled right into it once in a while. There were only four years between Melba's giving Esther away and her having Stevie and Floress. During those years she had a few broken arms and fingers and a badly sprained back from falling. From falling? From giving Esther away is more likely the truth. She had no idea just how angry she'd made Russell Skunk when she left Esther at the lake that summer. Mad enough to damn near kill her, or at least want to when he came home off the boat all liquored up.

A couple of times, Melba took Stevie on the train up to Montreal to see a big city doctor. Although there was always a general practitioner on the island where everyone else went to be seen, instead, she'd leave Liona keeping house for a few weeks, and go to Montreal. Just eleven, she had to take over tending the kids after Frieda moved out. She missed Frieda, and couldn't stay down with her in Seal Cove as much as she wanted to, but when she did, they'd talk about their mother, smoke cigarettes, and play gin rummy till all hours.

Liona wasn't as obliging as Frieda used to be; she'd only listen up if she felt like it. Sometimes she would mouth back and slam out the door, leaving Melba to look after her own kids on a Saturday night.

She loved those kids and she was good to them, just figured they weren't hers to raise, so she tried to be out of the house as much as she could. Once in a while, Melba would just up and leave. She would get up early and take off for a few days to the mainland on the first ferry, leaving just a note on the kitchen counter. Liona would be some jeezus mad. As she got older, she figured getting married was the only way to get away from mothering Melba's kids. So that's exactly what she did a few months after Esther showed up back at the house. Liona eloped with Ross Mackie from Deep Cove, and moved into a nice house with a bathroom.

CHAPTER 24

Summer

A FTER ESTHER CAME BACK TO THE ISLAND, Melba and Russell
Skunk started going to dances up at the curling rink in Herring Cove
on Saturday nights again. It was timely, Esther's return, being ten and old
enough to keep house for Stevie and Floress.

They could hear Melba on those Saturday afternoons, singing in the
house, trying to make the world go away, and putting on Avon products she
bought from Thelma Green. On her dresser were jars with dust-covered lids
of morning cream, nighttime cream and vanishing cream, almost matching
nail polish and lipstick, and blush and face powder. Frieda bought mousy
brown hair colour for Melba from the drugstore. Melba was too embarrassed of her thin greying hair to go herself.

Melba and Russell Skunk had a wash at the kitchen sink and when it was
dark, their oldest son Paul drove them to the curling rink in his lime green
Acadian. They were all pretty proud of his lime green Acadian. Girlings had
never had a car except way back when Melba first arrived on the island and
Russell Skunk had his dead father's old car for a few years. Once that was
smashed up, well that was that.

Paul picked them up again past midnight, on his way home from wherever he had been hanging out. More than likely, he was at the Legion in
the Harbour. Not inside the Legion, but parked outside in the parking lot
along with seven or eight other teenagers sitting in their cars, combing their
greasy Elvis Presley styled hair, and crooning away to love music, hoping
that one of the girls about to come out of the Young People's meeting across
the road at the church would accept a ride home. (And doing their own
praying for a stopover at the gravel pit for some poon-tang.)

At the dance, Russell propped his ass on a barstool, and his upper body
on his one elbow, and got loaded. While he held up the bar, Melba slid and
dipped and followed feet of other women's husbands in step to the latest
lovesick songs of the likes of Engelbert Humperdinck and Johnny Cash.

After the last dance, Paul arrived to pick them up. He manoeuvred his old man into the back seat, his mother in the front with him, and drove them home. At that time of the morning it was tense driving the Island roads, winding back and forth like they did, passing other cars, and winding in and out of harbours, and around people's lives – other lives, just as imperfect as the Girlings.

Melba softly coaxed Russell Skunk up the stairs to their bedroom and into their bed, hoping he'd pass out till morning.

There were no sounds in the house except his loud snoring, until he sputtered awake enough to want to fuck someone. Then all hell let loose. He said loudly, through his drunken drool: "Pussy loves Daddy, don'cha? Don'cha? Betcha love me lots when I'm over to Lubec, eh cunt?"

He felt and pulled and rubbed at Melba until she started punching at him and calling him whoremaster and trying to get herself out of the bed.

"I love you all right, you bastard, I'd love you to stay over in Lubec with your whores and not come back."

They pushed and shoved and yanked until the bedcovers were no longer on the bed. Then she saw him scratching his balls like he had fleas.

"You pig, you've got it again. The only thing you're good for is picking up the dose. I'll kill you, you son-of-a-bitch, you son-of-a-bitch." Thin, dead feather pillows slapped his head until he managed to grab them from her, then cheap smelling Avon bottles crashed against the wall above his head. In time things quieted down, because the kids were, after all, pretending to sleep. Melba turned the tin bed lamp off.

Of course, the kids knew what was going on, except for Esther. And if they listened, really listened, through the paint blistered walls and through the pale yellow scabs of wallpaper backing that looked like scratched chicken pox scars receding into the dark green flatness of the walls to the other side, you could hear soft young hot voices muffled under bed sheets "shhh, shhh."

IN THE MORNING, Floress poked her index finger into Esther's upper arm. "Hey, wanna play dolls?" She poked Esther again. "Can you hear me? Can I use your dolls?"

"Go away. I wanna be alone."

"Are you crying, Esther?"

"LEAVE ME ALONE," she said.

"But it's my room too!"

Floress two-stepped down dusty stairs and skipped into the kitchen. "Mam, Mam, Esther's crying."

"Yeah, I'll just bet she's crying, not that she's got anything to cry about. Been nothing but a spoiled brat all her life. What any one of you kids would give to have had the past ten years of her life. Maybe she'll cry it outta her system."

"What's in her system, Mam? Mam, Mam, what's in her system?"

CHAPTER 25

The Washcloth

IN THE BATHROOM Esther stood on her tiptoes in front of a small, mirrored cabinet that was mounted high up the wall. She jumped in the air a couple of times trying to see herself on the way down. She wanted to wash her hair. Looking in the bathtub, spiders and hair had collected around the corners. There were no water taps, and no showerhead. The small curtain-less window above the toilet looked onto the new septic field behind the house, and Esther was afraid when she sat on the toilet. She was afraid someone might look through the window. And they did.

The Girling house was full of bodies, bodies covered in hair and bodies still hairless, and backs erupting with white pus filled pimples, chins and foreheads and noses that mapped out adolescent acne. She wondered how they had a bath. She had watched Melba wash her thinning hair in the new kitchen sink after Mummy left.

Bang, bang, bang. There was no lock on the bathroom door. She grabbed the handle and wondered what to do.

"What're you doin' in there, taking a bath?" a young male voice yelled. The hair on Esther's arms stood straight up. She turned the handle and tried to leave without being noticed, but her brother Paul pushed past her into the bathroom with a folded thin towel and face cloth held up against his bare chest.

"About time you're outta there. I wanna have a bath, little girl."

Esther sat down in a chair around the corner pulling her knees to her chest. Floress bounded into the room coming from the other direction.

"How can Paul have a bath with no shower and no bathtub taps?" Esther said this blankly, flat, expressionless, as if she was talking out loud to herself and not expecting an answer.

"Don't you know how to wash yourself, Esther?" Esther didn't answer, and that might be why Floress went straight into the kitchen and told Melba that Esther didn't know how to wash herself.

"Can you imagine, a great big girl like her. Tell her you wash with a washcloth."

"Es-ther, you wash with a washcloth."

Maybe Esther was listening – more than likely not.

She was likely daydreaming of having a shower in Daddy's blue bathroom on Saturday mornings. She stood behind a frosted mermaid on the shower door who was about the same size as she was. It was cool in the bathroom because the window was open. Daddy had been smoking. She could smell the spent match. She showered, and rinsed her hair with lemon juice to brighten it, singing all the while along with "Bobbies" on her transistor radio: Vinton, Curtola, Darin, she can't remember them all. She ends her shower with "if I had a hammer, I'd hammer in the morning, I'd hammer in the evening, all over this la-and. I'd hammer out free-dom. I'd hammer out justice. I'd hammer out …"

She belted out the words, and stepped onto a baby blue chenille mat. Her young body welcomed a safe, light breeze blowing down on her from the small window above. "… the love between my brothers and my sisters …" Esther wanted to be a singer when she grew up.

CHAPTER 26

Making Believe

ESTHER WASHED HER FACE with a very thin facecloth, and brushed her teeth. She sat on a chair at the kitchen table and stared at Melba. There was a bowl of porridge with powdered milk on the table in front of her.

"I don't like this. And I don't drink white milk."

"Oh you don't, do you?"

"Do you have pumpernickel toast and plum jam?"

"No. We have porridge."

"Do you have soda crackers?"

"Gonna live on crackers, are you? Well have at'er. When you're finished your crackers, you can go outdoors and get some fresh air. Your sister and brother are out playing in the dooryard."

Esther knew what a backyard was, but had never heard it called a dooryard. Esther went out near noon and sat on the back step. It was hot. Stevie and Floress were playing make believe. They pretended they were going grocery shopping at Mason's store. Stevie pulled a bleached wooden wagon slowly along the sloped yard, the wheels making a racket going over stones and indents where stones used to be. Floress carefully picked up imaginary tins of peaches and pears and Spam, and marshmallows for toasting and placed them in the wagon.

"Do we have enough food for the winter yet, Stevie?" Stevie was almost one year older than Floress so was obviously smarter about these things.

"Looks like it, don't it to you? Did you buy chocolate Quick?"

"Of course, I did."

Floress parked the wagon in front of where Esther was sitting on the steps and stood with her feet slightly apart, and knees slightly bent. She waved her open palms in front of Esther's eyes, like windshield wipers, swish, swish. Behind them her puppy dog brown eyes and long dark eyelashes reached out to her sister. "Wanna play store?" She waited. There was no answer.

103

"Stevie, do you think she's sleeping with her eyes open like you do sometimes?"

"Awe, just leave her. I don't think she knows how to play. She never had no one to play with in Montreal."

"How do you know that?"

"Cause we're all here on the island."

Esther didn't see or hear her dirty-faced brother and sister; she was back on Wolseley Street. It was an ordinary summer day; she was where she should be, running through the sprinkler on the soft thick lawn, or going to the Westminster Park swimming pool with Heather. Mummy should be back soon. Why aren't we up at the cottage? Was it just yesterday that she pulled the skinny end of Daddy's tie and coaxed the wide end flat and straight on his chest?

CHAPTER 27

Minced Meat

FRIEDA AND MELBA sat at the kitchen table the next morning, coffee mugs in one hand, lazily rolled lit cigarettes in the other. They looked at each other while smoke plumed above them into the sunlight.

"What are you going to do with her, Mam?"

"Maybe I'll send her up to Kaye and Melvin's for a few days. She can do my housekeeping up there."

"Housekeeping! Land sakes, will you look at her? She looks like she just walked off a page of a Robert Simpsons catalogue, complete with painted fingernails. She doesn't know anything about housekeeping."

"Well, she'll have to learn then, won't she? Just like you and Liona did. Just because she's been away doesn't mean she's any different from anyone else around here."

"Oh for pity sake, she is different, she's hopeless. I took her down home with me the other day, her and Stevie and Floress, while you were working down at the fish sheds. My soul, she didn't know a blessed thing. I asked her to fill the kettle and put it on the stove and she couldn't even do that – she didn't know what a dipper was. She's the youngest kid she's ever been around. She's never seen a dipper before, let alone a diaper. There wasn't one fool thing she could do by herself: clean a diaper out, help feed the kids, heat water, or even just get water from the well. She was too scared to fall in. Mam, she didn't know what we used the Simpson's catalogues for. Never seen anybody so mighty daft in all my life."

"Well, I'm still going to give Kaye a ring. See if she can use her housekeeping on the weekend instead of me going up. If I can scour Kaye's place in a morning, surely Esther can do it in two days."

"Aunt Flora had a charlady, Mam."

"Well, for Crissake, she's going to have to learn sometime, might as well be now."

Melba had cleaned house for Kaye, every two weeks, for twenty years. It gave Melba five extra dollars. Kaye and Melvin lived on one of the few high

105

points on the east side of the island. Their house was built on a windy point overlooking the Bay of Fundy to the east.

Esther hung Melvin's green work pants, long-sleeved shirts, and grey work socks on the clothesline. She stood on her tiptoes to reach the line, and occasionally the force of the wind off the Bay slapped the clothes back into her face so she couldn't see, and lost her balance. Kaye watched her for more than an hour through the kitchen window, wondering about this polite young girl who had been away all these years.

Kaye and Melvin's house was tidy and well cared for. In the bathroom upstairs was a white porcelain claw foot tub, but no toilet. There was a chamber pot underneath the bed she would sleep in, and an outside privy for the daytime.

At lunch, the three of them had grilled cheese sandwiches with a pickle on the side.

"Your table and chairs are like our wooden table in the country," Esther exclaimed. "They were painted this Dutch blue too."

Kaye and Melvin looked at each other, mutually deciding whether they would ask the girl questions. Kaye gave in first. "And who lived in this house in the country, Esther?"

"Oh, we only lived there in the summers."

"Who lived there?"

"Me and Mummy and Daddy, of course!"

"Yes, of course."

"Would you mind dusting my hair after lunch?"

Esther giggled for the first time in a week. "How do you dust hair, Mrs. Kaye?"

"Why, with a hairbrush, my dear." Kaye's face contorted as if her feelings were hurt at being asked such a question. Esther knew quickly she shouldn't have laughed.

An occasional ssss ssss sssss from the shortwave radio on top of the fridge broke the air, but otherwise, the house was silent. There was no television set.

Mrs. Kaye was a bit of a taskmaster, an orderly type person like her mother had been, and after all this was costing her five dollars and food for a girl who had never kept house before.

"Could you wash up the floors, Esther?"

This time Esther held back her laugh, but was thinking: *What am I Cinderella? Next the chimney? What is happening? Dear Gott in heaven, I want to go home. Where has home gone?*

Mrs. Kaye filled a metal bucket with soapy water, and gave Esther some rags. While Esther carried the bucket, the soapsuds swayed back and forth, picking up momentum until the final eruption of froth spilled over the edges settling in pools on the floor, which she wiped up with a rag. This was how she washed the floor in the kitchen, the hallway, up the stairs, two upstairs bedrooms, and the bathtub room.

Esther sang Cinderella's cleaning songs under her breath, and refused to cry about her knees, they were scraped red and burning. In the front room, she rested on the floor against the back of the couch on her tush, and raised her arms and neck muscles into a high stretch, and screamed blue murder.

"AAAAH, AAAAH."

Mrs. Kaye rushed toward the scream, and found Esther sitting staring up at Jesus on the cross, hanging on the wall.

The next sound to escape Esther's mouth was mixed with vomit.

"Lord above child, what is wrong with you?"

"His chest is ripped open, Mrs. Kaye."

"What in heaven's name are you talking about, dear?"

"Don't you see him? Up there bleeding all over the place. His heart's ripped out and there's just minced meat left."

"Don't you know who that is?" Esther shook her head left and then right.

"That is our Lord Jesus Christ who died for the sins of the world on the cross." Kaye knew blessed well that there wasn't much point saying anything else except: "I'll get some more rags so you can clean up that little mess you made."

For the rest of the day, Esther slid around the rooms on her tush instead of her knees, keeping an eye out. By the time she went to bed that night she had lost count of him, the Jesus man. There were so many pictures, weeping ones, bloody ones, ones with angels and candlelit halos, statues of him on crosses, made of wood, bronze and silver.

Esther figured she'd never sleep because she couldn't stop thinking about all the longhaired pictures of the Jesus man hanging or sitting everywhere. She was right; they followed her into nightmares along with the hall witch, and woke her up. Esther had to go to the bathroom, and somehow remembered there was a pot under the bed.

After several noisy attempts to make water, Esther filled the bottom of the pot with toilet paper, then let the rest of her pee rush out. Noisy yes, but not as noisy. Then, the big question: What should she do with this thing? She thought about the Concord Hotel in the Catskills, and the Fountaine Bleu in Miami. She held an image of Daddy clearing up things they no longer wanted, the iron and ironing board, dishes and cups from coffee in the morning, or the remains of smoked meat sandwiches and French fries brought by room service the night before. So, ever so quietly, Esther opened the bedroom door and placed the pot out in the hallway.

Early on Sunday Kaye and Melvin drove Esther back down the island. They had intended to take her to church and for an ice-cream cone, but after that episode about Jesus, they decided to drop her back at Girlings before church, and skip the ice cream.

Melba was a touch concerned to see them pull in the driveway so early Sunday morning. "They're early, I'll just bet something happened up there."

Esther came in the house and wanted to go up to bed. She was sore all over and still exhausted from all the work she did the day before, but she stood in the kitchen quietly.

"Well, there was one thing, Melba. It's queer in a way. Esther worked hard, but she didn't know that she was the maid. She put her chamber pot out at night for the other maid to empty."

"She didn't! That little Christer."

"And if you don't mind me telling you, the child is a heathen if there ever was one. You better send her to Sunday school, and I wouldn't wait one day on that."

Before Esther left the kitchen, Kaye thanked Melba for letting her use Esther for the weekend and handed her a five-dollar bill that Melba folded and put inside her bra. Esther would never see a blue five again without remembering that Sunday in Melba's kitchen.

"So, you're a little smartass are you? Well next Sunday you're going to church with the Wright girls.

"What about my five dollars?"

"You've got your nerve, missy. Any money I see that comes into this house is mine."

CHAPTER 28

Esther is a Television

"I CALLED THEIR MOTHER, they'll be out on the road looking out for you. You can't miss'em. Gail's a great tall thing, and the other one's next to the size of a peapod. They've got hair black as shoe polish."

Esther walked to Grand Harbour to look for girls who might be Wrights. She thought: *What do Wrights look like? The opposite of Wrongs, of course.*

Esther found tiny ripe strawberries along the side of the road; the plants grew with determination up through gravel. She hadn't tasted anything that sweet since ... she couldn't remember, and spent a few extra minutes crouched at the side of the road.

"Hey, wanna a ride, little girl?"

Esther turned and looked up through an open car window at a thin man in a white muscle shirt and a too large head with a purplish mole beside his nose. Tanned hairy arms wrapped the steering wheel; his hands were folded over the top of it. He was driving a silver Cadillac. He didn't look to Esther like someone who would be driving a silver Cadillac – he should have worn a suit to drive that car. An unpleasant, air conditioner smell wafted out the window and into the heat of the day's morning.

"No, thank you, sir."

The man chuckled. "No, thank you, sir?" He cleared his throat. "Say, you must be from away, what?"

"From away?"

"Yeah, from the mainland, you know."

"I'm from Montreal in the province of Quebec, and I'm not allowed to talk to strangers." Esther kept walking.

The silver car moved slowly along beside her. Esther picked up her step. The car kept her pace.

"Go away or I'm telling."

"Who're ya telling?"

Esther stopped dead. She was wondering the same thing.

109

"Well, just wanted to tell you that you're walking on the wrong side of the road. You always walk on the side facing the traffic." Esther stared at the mole on his face. The man stared back, then smiled real wide like he was biting into an overripe peach, exposing wide lips and small yellow tobacco stained teeth.

"Hey, are you that Girling kid that's been away all these years? Well I'll be damned. Yes sir, I bet you are. Shy one, are ya? Well, you tell your Mother that Lloyd Slader wanted to give you a ride. I'll be a monkey's uncle. I'll bet again that your birthday is August 29th, eh? Now isn't it?"

"How did you know that?"

"I've got one exact same age as you."

As he pulled away very slowly, almost teasing, Esther heard him say he'd have Francine give her a ring, and wondered why she would give her a ring.

Esther hadn't noticed that she was being watched by two girls, one tall, with big bones holding her upright, the other one perfectly tiny and delicate as lace with long fingers that no doubt played the scales on the piano perfectly. They both had thick long black hair tied in a single fat braid hanging down their backs. Esther was just a jump from the house appearing on the left where Gail and Sally Wright lived. Gail and Sally were Baptists. They had heard of Esther.

"You shouldn't be talking to Lloyd Slader, kid."

"Oh, why not?"

The sisters folded in half laughing then came back up. "Ask your mother."

"What's that supposed to mean?"

"We know who you are. You're the kid Girlings traded for a television."

"Pardon me? My name is Weinstein, Esther Weinstein."

"Maybe it used to be!"

Gail and Sally Wright doubled over again, laughing hard.

"Com'on. We've got to take you to Sunday School."

CHAPTER 29

Getting to Know You

A BELL RANG FROM A BLACK crank phone box that hung on the wall by the unused Girling front door, the same door that had no outside stairs. Each house had a three-digit telephone number and an operator sat in the telephone exchange building in front of a switchboard connecting calls just like in old movies Esther had seen.

The phone bell rang, two long and a short.

Luke called Esther to the telephone.

"Telephone, little sister."

"I'm not your sister." She picked up the receiver.

"Is this Esther?"

"Yes."

"This is Francine. My father saw you last Sunday up by Wright's house. He told me you might want to play. Do you wanna play?"

"Do I want to play? I don't know – I'll ask."

"You have to ask to play?"

"Well, I don't know. I haven't played with anyone yet."

"How about a bike ride? Yeah, we'll bike ride, come to my house, okay?"

"How will I know where to go?"

"Just get on the road and start riding toward Seal Cove, ride toward Frieda's house. What colour is your bike?"

"It's a blue three speed with coloured tassels on the handle grips."

"I'll meet you on the bridge."

"Francine, what colour is your bike?"

"Blue."

Esther and Francine met on the Seal Cove bridge, two short, dark haired girls with pixie cuts and blue bicycles. They laughed like old friends when they got up close to each other, but neither remembered they had met in the hospital ten years earlier.

"Hi!"

"God. We're both short."

111

"Yeah, aren't we just! Good things come in small packages. Remember that, Esther. We have to stop and show you to my mother. She made me promise."

"Why would she do that?"

"She told me the last time she saw you was in the North Head Hospital when we were born. She's curious, I guess."

Mrs. Slader gave each girl a quarter so they could stop along the way and buy a pop.

"You're mother's nice, Francine."

"I never thought about it. Come on, follow me, we'll ride over to my Dad's camp."

"You mean cottage?"

"Camp, cottage, what's the difference? If it's locked we won't be able to go inside, but you can see in through the window. I'm having my birthday party there. It's going to be a sleepover. Do you wanna come? Hey come to think of it, you don't have a choice. You have to come because it's your birthday too!"

Francine and Esther pedalled down the highway in the mighty heat without stopping until they turned off the road toward the water onto a short cut. The trail through the bushes came up to the back door of the camp. Overheated, they dropped their bikes carelessly, like boys do, and ran for the door.

"We can get a drink. Dad always has bottles of cola by the case to have with his rum."

One turn of the door handle and they were in.

"See, what'd I tell you? Go look over by the fridge, Esther."

Esther stopped dead. She was looking, but not over by the fridge. She looked into a doorway where Melba's brown eyes looked right back at her. Then Lloyd's face appeared, his elbow bent and his hand held one side of his head up. In the few seconds that passed, Francine made her way over to see what Esther was gawking at.

"Fucking A," Francine said, standing with her arm against the doorway. She had older brothers and knew all the swear words.

Lloyd said: "Jesus H. Christ. What the fuck are you doing here?"

"Question is, what in fuck are you doing here, with her?"

Francine had heard the raging fights her parents had late at night when her father came home full, smelling of cheap Avon. This was running through her mind as she grabbed Esther's arm and headed toward the door.

"Francine, wait," Lloyd hollered. "Don't tell your mother you saw me."

"And you never saw me either, Esther!" Melba shouted.

Both girls pedalled home in silence.

ESTHER SAT AT THE KITCHEN TABLE near dinnertime and watched Melba peel potatoes. She didn't say anything.

Melba had more suspicions of what Esther had or had not seen earlier that day, than Esther was able to comprehend. Esther didn't question her about the afternoon, but knew they were doing something very bad because they had no clothes on. Francine and Esther never spoke about it again either.

"Go get your fath'r down cellar."

"He's not my father," Esther said.

Melba wheeled around and shook the short, wooden-handled, paring knife in front of Esther's eyes. "I don't care who you think he is. I said, go and get him out of the cellar."

Gott in Heaven, Esther thought, *I didn't do anything. Please help me get away from here.*

GREY SLATTED WOODEN TRAP DOORS at the back of the house, next to the oil tank, lay flat open to each side. Looking down the stairs, Esther couldn't see much, but smelled damp mould and imagined at least a thousand spiders. She took two steps, crouched, and saw a dim light bulb hanging from an electrical wire. Underneath the light sat Russell Skunk on the split seat of a rickety wooden chair. The paint was almost peeled entirely off, and the back was missing. She thought Russell Skunk had an axe in his right hand. It was a hatchet! Esther didn't know the difference between the two. On the dirt floor in front of him was a stump, a well-used chopping stump.

"Your wife is calling you."

"Oh, you're a smart girl, com'ere."

Reluctantly, hesitantly, Esther moved forward. She didn't know why she didn't turn and run. It might have been because of the glint of the axe.

"Good girl. Sit here on my knee."

Russell Skunk wrapped his dirty fat arm around Esther's back and chest and pulled her close. "Did your other daddy kiss you like this?"

Esther pushed his arms off her as hard as she could and ran to the stairs, tripping on the first one on the way up. Her heart raced as she pulled down the door and stood on top of it trying to catch her breath. Then realizing he could come up at any minute, she raced into the house, into the bathroom, and brushed her teeth until they bled. He would never do that to her again. Esther opened the medicine cabinet and took a bottle of aspirin and put it in her shorts pocket. There was only one way out of this house. No one would believe what he had just done. The only person she knew was Francine, and after what happened earlier with Melba and Lloyd, she couldn't tell her.

Esther told Melba she wasn't hungry and went to her room. She took her Polaroid camera out of the trunk and took a picture of herself in the mirror then put the camera back. She wrote a note: YOU'LL ALL BE SORRY, and stood the picture up on the dresser and put the note in front of it. There. She had read some of Mummy's book *Valley of the Dolls*, and women in there took pills all the time. She remembered some of them even got sick and died. That's what Esther was counting on. Dying.

When it sounded like dinner was over downstairs, she went down and got a big plastic glass of water, the kind of glasses they had at the cottage. She didn't know how many pills were in the bottle. She just took them all, went into the cubbyhole closet, changed into her pyjamas and crawled in bed. Esther prayed: Dear Gott, please take me to Heaven to be with Daddy. Amen.

She dreamed about Mummy and Daddy. They were all watching horse racing on television.

Melba must have sent Floress to wake her up the next morning. She stood beside the bed shaking her arm. "How'd you take this picture, Esther?" Esther opened her eyes. She couldn't believe she was still there. "Give me that," she said and pulled it quickly from Floress' small hand. *Oh my Gott, the note!* Esther jumped up and grabbed it before she saw it.

"What's the matter with you? You don't look like your picture."

"Oh, I was just fooling around with my camera. Later on I'll take your picture, Floress, okay? Don't tell your mother about this stupid picture. I'll get my camera and come downstairs and take a picture of you and Stevie, just let me get dressed."

Floress went out the curtain door and Esther dived into the trunk for her camera and some scissors to cut up the note and the picture. She threw the pieces into the back of the cubbyhole to get rid of later. She was tired, but couldn't let them know what she'd done, so she got herself downstairs and took two beautiful pictures, one of Stevie, and the other of Floress.

"Where's your picture, Esther?"

"I didn't like it so I threw it out."

Later that morning, Esther felt a sharp chip with her tongue on one of her big front teeth. The unconscious grinding of teeth at 500 pounds per square inch will do that. Esther lost her innocent smile, the one that came so naturally on Montreal Island. Now her smile was broken, bitter, and hateful. It was her new Grand Manan Island smile, a Girling smile; it was hate at its smiliest.

Hate has a fearless memory.

Hate, like grief, is difficult to overcome even with faith, because first you must want to.

CHAPTER 30

Miller's Font

ESTHER HAD BEEN WALKING UP to the Harbour on Sunday mornings since the day Mrs. Kaye had pronounced her a heathen. It hadn't yet occurred to her to just not go. Besides, she was learning about this Jesus man, and how He loved all the little children, had them all in His hand. The whole congregation sang about it – the Bible told them so. She wondered who those kids really were that were in His hand. Were they the starving ones in Africa? Pastor John said the answers were all there in the Bible. *So,* she thought, *maybe it's a good thing?* Esther needed friends. She sat beside the Wright girls. They weren't mean to her any more, and they were allowed to play with her as long as she attended Sunday school at their church, Grand Harbour Baptist Church. This was the same church Melba sent the rest of the Girling kids to, and according to Melba, Esther wasn't going to be any different.

The small church was quite full in the summer time with tourists from away, filling in seats that were empty in the winter, keeping the church close and hot with body heat and odour. There were more adults than children, old people mostly, and every week they'd sing more songs of praise to the dead man Jesus. They seemed happy doing it; at least they all smiled at each other inside the Church.

"And it's no mystery," Pastor John said. "Folks, you can be there too, sitting with Jesus. All you have to do is stand up and be saved. Yes, I see some of you are thinking about it. Go ahead, stand with Jesus today."

Oy vey, Esther thought.

After a month of Sunday school lessons, Esther figured this might be an opportunity after all, an opportunity to stand up with Jesus and have Him straighten all this mess out. So the following week, after returning from her lessons in the basement to join the rest of the church, and to the surprise of the Wrights and dismay of several other hatted women in the church, when Pastor John asked who was going to stand up today, she thought, hum …

He asked again: "Who will stand up and be saved by Jesus today?"

Esther began plucking petals from the daisy she'd clipped from the flowerbed on the corner of the church when she entered.

He saves me, saves me not.

Saves me, saves me not.

Saves me, saves me not.

Saves me, saves me not.

Saves me ... Mozel Tov. And she bolted upright.

Amen, shouted the congregation, and more people stood up.

Pastor John had said Jesus could do anything.

Anything? Okay, then save me. Save me damn it so I can sit back down.

Many people stood up. Some of them stood up every week. And every week the congregation applauded, and they hugged their neighbours, and they sang. Hallelujah. He's got the whole world, in His hands. Praise the Lord. Amen.

At the end of that morning's sermon, Pastor John invited everyone to the baptismal of the new candidates at noon the following Sunday at Miller's pond. Esther gave Sally a questioning look, wondering what she'd just gotten herself into. Gail said flatly, congratulations. Gail was used to people standing up in church. She had been going to church and watching people stand up and down for her whole thirteen years.

The congregation took their smiles, chattering noisily out of the church. Esther trailed behind the Wrights as usual, walking down the gravel shoulder of the road.

"Are you going to Miller's Pond next Sunday, Gail?"

Gail laughed. "Land sakes no. We were dunked a long time ago."

"What do you mean dunked?"

"You know, dunked. Don't you know anything, Esther? The Pastor makes a speech telling everyone how you're being cleansed, washed like Jesus, no sins. And then, to make it work, he pushes your head under the water."

Esther shivered, horrified at the thought of someone pushing her head under water. She always had to pinch her nose closed before she jumped in Westminster Park pool. She looked down at her silver Mickey Mouse watch and wondered if it was waterproof.

"Will you and Sally go swimming with me after lunch?"

"I'll ask my parents and I'll call you later."

"Okay, I'll see if Floress wants to come. She can play with Sally."

"Good idea."

Gail and Sally went home for lunch and Esther walked back to Deer Curve on the wrong side of the road. By the time she got back to the Girlings, there was already a message waiting for her to meet the Wright girls back at the Pond Road at one-thirty.

It turned into a scorching hot afternoon. Esther doubled Floress on her bicycle to the Pond Road but left her bike there at the side of the road and walked with the other girls. Gail and Sally didn't have bikes, or a television set either for that matter. The walk was hot and dusty, two miles up a winding pulp road. Even on Sundays, those truckers thought they were pretty smart; they drove too fast, not even slowing down when they saw kids with towels on their shoulders walking along the edge of the road. Gail would corral the girls into the ditch each time a truck approached, and they held their towels over their heads until the dust settled back down.

It didn't matter that they were exhausted and dusty and thirsty. As soon as they saw the narrow dock sticking twenty feet or so out into the water ahead, they picked up speed, dropped their towels, ran the length of the dock and cannonballed right into the black pond water. Esther swam out far, farther and farther each time, trying to get to the other side, always trying to get to the other side. If she could just get to the other side, she thought, maybe Daddy would be there. Daddy would come and save her and take her to Heaven with him.

Flora had always said she had lots of blubber, just like Daddy; that's why we floated so easily. Mummy used to pack up like we were going on a trip, with towels, blankets, chairs, pail, shovel and sifter, and a blow-up duck. Daddy would wear it and sing "sitting in the water, doing what he otter!" Flora couldn't swim but you wouldn't guess. She just looked like she didn't feel like it right then. She'd make all the motions: put on her beach shoes and her bathing cap covered in mauve sequins; walk into the lake up to her big boobs like she was modelling down a runway; then she'd stop, cup her hands in the water and carefully splash her face and arms, and turn and walk right back out. After she did this, Sammy or Esther would have the messy job of rubbing the greasy orange suntan oil on her back and legs again.

CHAPTER 31

Liar Liar

"How much farther do we have to walk?"

"Not too far. Someone will pick us up."

Luke and Esther walked facing traffic and soon Stucky Girling stopped and offered them a ride.

"Who ya got with you there, Luke?"

"My sister, Esther."

"Oh yeah. I remember about her."

Luke boosted Esther from the bumper over the tailgate into the back of the truck.

"See, you don't have to hitchhike on the island. There's always someone that'll pick you up."

"How can he remember me, Luke?"

"You were born here, remember?"

"No. I don't remember being born, do you?"

Their hair blew into their eyes, stinging a bit, and a little chuckle bounced between them in the box of the truck for a few miles.

"Luke, where're we going?"

"Up to Pearl's at the Head for chips. My treat, little sister."

Luke put a gangly arm around her shoulder and patted it like one might pat a dog.

"Don't touch me! And I'm not your sister."

"Oooo, growly are you, Esther? I've waited for you to come home for a long time, you know."

"Why?"

"I've always known I had another sister."

"Luke, how do you know you're really my brother?"

"Cause I remember you, that's how. At the lake in the country, and I remember the big house in the city."

"Someone must have told you those things. You were never there."

119

"Oh, I was there all right, and Liona, and Mam. Maybe you just didn't know who we were. I suppose you were too little."

"Are you saying that SHE was in Montreal too?"

"She, you mean Mam? What do you think, we went on our own?"

"No. But I don't remember anyone."

"Esther, we stayed with you and Aunt Flora and Uncle Sammy. We all stayed with you. Maybe you were too young to remember."

"I don't look like any of you. I look like Daddy, everyone says so."

"That's because everyone that you knew in Montreal never saw any of us! You look just like Liona." Luke patted her on the head again as they pushed off the tailgate of the truck up at Pearl's.

"Hey, do you wanna a pop with your chips, Esther?"

"What's a pop?"

"You know, a coke, stupid."

"That's called a soft drink, you're meshuggener!"

"Hey, where'd you get the poon-tang Girling?" said a local young boy sitting over in the corner with nothing good on his mind.

"She's my sister, Esther. Leave her alone or I'll rearrange those pits on your face, got it? Stay away from her, she's just a kid."

While Luke was ordering, Esther stood behind him and heard the same boy say: "That's probably the one they sold for a TV set."

Pearl's restaurant up at the Head sold salty French fries, and gave away free gossip.

"These aren't chips; they're French fries."

"For Chrissake, down here they're chips. Keep your voice down. People are going to think you're some kind of a pill."

"A pill?"

"Yeah. A nut, a pill, crazy, get it?"

"Why would a soft drink be called pop here, and French fries be called chips?"

"Search me. Whatever you wanna call it, little sister."

"Don't call me that."

"Better get used to it!"

"Tell me something, Luke."

"Anything for you, little sister."

"Don't call me that, I said. Where did you get your television set from?"

"The one at the house you mean?"

"Yeah. Where did it come from?"

"Aunt Flora and Uncle Sammy sent it down. Why?"

"I was wondering why you have a huge floor model television set, but you don't have a bathtub that works?"

"I don't know. Just lucky I guess."

SUDDENLY IT DIDN'T MATTER WHETHER IT WAS TRUE, whether she was sold, or traded, or given away. It seemed everyone on that Island knew some version of a story about Esther and a television set. Maybe she wasn't worth a million dollars like Daddy had told her so many times; maybe her measure was the price of a television.

That night Esther opened her steamer trunk and climbed inside looking for her passport. She sat cross-legged on top of her past, and held the small navy cardboard booklet with "Passport" embossed in gold letters against her heart like a drowning person might clutch a life jacket. And as long as she held it there, unopened, she would remain Esther Weinstein. She didn't know what was on the pages inside. She'd never thought to look until now, but when she turned to the first page, she saw herself. Underneath the black and white photograph, in black type struck with uneven pressure and flying caps on an old manual typewriter, was spelled, Esther Lynn Girling, birthplace: Grand Manan, New Brunswick, Canada. Then she remembered the day Flora had picked her up early from school, and they went by taxi to a professional passport studio in Snowdon. Afterwards they had toasted ham sandwiches with mayonnaise on white bread from the grill in the Kresge store.

Esther took a blue ballpoint pen and, slowly at first, scratched over the Girling word until there was a hole in the page instead of a name.

Then she took out her writing scribbler and practised writing her name like she used to do at school. Penmanship had been important in class. Esther Lynn Weinstein, Esther Lynn Weinstein, over and over again, two columns per page, pages and pages; written longhand to perfection, for hours and hours, until every line in the scribbler was full. On the last line Esther wrote: "Daddy if you're in Heaven, please ask our Gott to save me. I want to be with you. Amen." Then she put it, and the passport into the bottom of the steamer trunk, got out, closed it, climbed on the bed, and curled into the corner like an abandoned kitten.

Seeds of doubt, chaos, anger and abandonment, depression and anxiety, pill-taking and suicide were planted in her short time on Grand Manan, and would follow Esther the rest of her life.

Esther didn't remember boarding the train at Windsor Station in Montreal, or packing the steamer trunk, or saying good-bye to anyone in the family.

She remembered the scraping sound of metal on metal, imagined sparks flying in the air; choking fumes worse than sitting in a smoke filled waiting room, porters in starched white jackets shuffling along with heavy grips and trunks, and the smell of shoe polish. She knew she must have gone to the island on a ferry, but didn't remember until now. Now it played back in her memory like a circus ride that makes you so sick to your stomach that you scream to a greasy haired young boy: "Let me off, please. Stop the ride! Please let me off I'm going to be sick." But the operator ignores you. He's sucking on a cigarette, one foot up, resting on a slatted wooden soft drink case. He will say he didn't hear you.

Mummy was the circus freak that looked like Jackie Kennedy. Come on folks. Step right up. Look at the woman who dares to dress like Jackie Kennedy. And, for no extra charge, take a peek at her travelling companion, the ten-year-old girl who thinks she's Esther Lynn Weinstein!

Part V

CHAPTER 32

End of Summer

MELBA STOOD AGAINST THE KITCHEN COUNTER reading Esther's letter out loud:

Dear Mr. Lee,

My name is Esther Weinstein. How are you? Can I call you Mr. Lee? I know you must be busy being Dracula and travelling around finding people to suck out their blood. I know some horrible people and you can suck their blood dry. I know they don't have hearts, but I'm pretty sure they must have some blood. They are evil people who say they are my mother and father but they really aren't. They kidnapped me from my real parents in Montreal at the beginning of the summer, and I can't run away until either they're dead or I'm older. Please Mr. Lee, I'm too young to kill them by myself and am not really experienced in these things like you are. Please write back and tell me if you can help me. They've already killed my French poodle Gigi.

yours truly,

Esther Weinstein

"Well what do you have to say for yourself missy?"

"You let Gigi die!"

"I didn't let her die. She ran onto the road."

"I told you she couldn't ever be loose. I told you she'd run up onto the road. I told you she didn't know about cars. I told you she was only used to sidewalks. You were supposed to look after her while I was at Sunday School."

"It was an accident, Esther. The fellow that hit her felt right bad. He even carried her down to the house."

"And do you feel *right bad* too?"

"How could you wanna kill my Mam?" Floress asked, concerned, but somehow gleefully curious at the same time.

"Eureka! My point exactly – YOUR MAM, not mine, got it stupid?"

124

Melba's Wash   125

"I thought you were sick in the head. Now I know you are," Stevie said. "You never shoulda brought her here, Mama."

"Esther, you may as well get it through your thick skull right now. Sammy is dead, Gigi was run over by a car, and Flora doesn't want a spoiled brat like you around anymore. No one's gonna save you. This is where you live so you may as well get used to it. Oh, and if I find any more of these letters missy, you'll get your ass tanned with the leather belt."

"GO FUCK YOURSELF, MELBA!"

Esther felt the burning slap of Melba's hand on her cheek. She burst into tears, headed for the stairs, and turned back and screamed at Melba.

"I hate you!"

Esther continued to write letters; they grew into quite a stack in her steamer trunk over the next three years.

CHAPTER 33

Fall

THE SEAL COVE SCHOOL BUS stopped on Deer Curve in the morning in front of the Girling house and picked up Paul, Luke, Stevie and Esther and took them to school in Grand Harbour. Floress would go to school the following year. Liona had finished school and was working in the fish factory.

Ellis was the bus driver. He wore a brush cut of sparse mousy brown hair on his perfectly round head that held a mouth that smiled less than the usual amount of teeth. This disgusted Esther. Ellis must've picked up on this right from day one and never again stopped the bus in front of the driveway to let them on or off; he coasted by the driveway in either direction as if he couldn't, as if it were impossible to stop in front of it. Esther would be the last one of the bunch to get on the bus, always holding back until the last minute, in case, in case of what? A better offer? It could be that Ellis figured Esther moved too slowly, and he never passed on an opportunity to prematurely pull the door of the bus shut and put the engine into gear causing a jerk. The folding metal door would either bang Esther or her school bag, knocking her off balance and back down the one step she'd managed to climb. This would cause an uproar of laughter from the Slader boys who claimed the back seat of the bus, while some of the other local smart alecks would react to the arrival of the Girlings by holding their fingers on their noses like clothes-pegs, and making sure any empty seats were immediately filled with book bags.

In the classroom Esther fidgeted in her too small one-piece desk, feeling like a baby strapped in a highchair. She wrote silly notes to friends she didn't have yet, stared tirelessly out the window at the mud flats in the harbour, and giggled to herself at her own jokes that played round and round in her mind. Esther had already covered the material in that class in the previous grade in Montreal; she was bored silly and should have been moved up a grade. No one thought of that. It was easier for the homeroom teacher to

126

simply categorize her as disruptive, and carry on with the rest of the good kids who paid attention.

Slowly Esther made a few school friends – kids became interested in some of her stories. Some of the kids in Esther's class had never been farther than North Head. Their interest lasted until another girl from away arrived. She was a year behind Esther, but Grades Five and Six were in one room. Liz Walker, the striking new girl, took their attention.

Esther had her first crush on a boy, Charlie Dell. Charlie sat one seat behind her, in the next row over toward the windows. They could just barely touch fingertips in the aisle between them to pass notes. They were notes of fascination with each other in the beginning: "are you really?"; "you didn't either"; "did you really?"; "you never?"; eventually making plans to meet and play after school, and on the weekends.

Charlie was from down Brown Point Road, an easy walk or bike ride from his house, along the seawall at low tide. The two went to the beach to play. The Anchorage Hotel had been there for so long that the whole surrounding area came to be called the Anchorage. The hotel was open only in the summer for tourists, so the sand beach and tall grasses and marshes reverted back to the locals after Labour Day, along with the fresh water pond, and Long Pond for bonfires and skating in the winter.

Eleven-year-olds with a crush on each other play much like monkeys, chasing and tripping and pushing for fun, tickling and poking and pulling hair for the affection they didn't yet understand. Esther and Charlie were driven by confused hormones to poke and tease each other into an exhausted giddiness that would topple them laughing onto the beach grass. They'd sit above the high tide mark, quiet for a while, looking at the water turn blacker as the sun went down, and watching the whitecaps move closer to shore and break into foam on the beach below them.

They went for long bike rides around the island, and spent time at the old Crocker house, probably because the sign in the yard said No Trespassing. The Crocker place looked like it might topple in a windstorm. Deep woods curtained the house on two sides. In the back were scattered outbuildings of grey-slatted worm-eaten wood with holes big enough to see through. In the front were thirty or forty old and gnarled apple trees.

Unfortunately, some nights, sure as fog, poachers drove their trucks into the Crocker yard with their headlights out, took up position and waited. Eventually, frozen in a jacklight, a buck or doe would be in position too, standing still as a steak on a grill. Esther would lie in bed those nights, willing the Mounties to come to Deer Curve and arrest the poachers. Then she cried, whether she heard the siren follow the gunshot or not.

The best eating apples were the Yellow Transparent, the most plentiful were small sour green cooking apples that lay on the ground covered with scars and scabs that the deer fed on. Esther would sometimes bicycle over to Crocker's on her own and sit with her back against one of those short, top-heavy canopied trees and read. She could disappear for hours inside a book of someone else's fiction. Or she might go there and write letters to Flora, then add them to the growing pile in her steamer trunk:

"Hi, wait till Daddy finds out what you've done.
Love Esther"
"Hi, I don't want you to send me any more American five dollar bills, when I try to spend them, people think I must have stolen them.
Esther"
"Hi, No, I don't want you to come and visit me. I want you to come and get me.
Esther"
"Hi, don't write me anymore unless you're coming to get me.
Love Esther"
"Hi. I hate you. Don't you miss me??
No love Esther"

Esther and Charlie inched baby-steps across the kitchen floor over broken shards of glass that had been there for thirty years. The tell-tale remains didn't add up to much: a rubber boot that had been sliced off at the ankle, a coverless damp curled Sears Roebuck catalogue, rusted mason jar lids, the sleeve of a man's shirt, bent rusty nails of all sizes, the blade from a very old ice skate, and an element lifter from the wood stove that wasn't there anymore. A charcoal black pipe, stuck into the kitchen wall above where the stove should have been sitting, vented the house with birds and bats.

This particular day, Esther and Charlie lingered in the orchard until almost dusk. Esther filled Charlie with stories of foot-long hot-dogs from the drive-in restaurant Miss Montreal, and drive-in theatres with a projection screen as big as a house, and downtown stores bigger than the fish factory, and downtown sidewalks so busy all you could see ahead was the coat of the person walking in front of you. It was dark by the time Charlie got home because it had become too dark to take the seawall; he had to bicycle home on the roads.

"You've missed your supper, Charles."

Hum, Charlie knew his mother was not too pleased with him.

"Where have you been?"

"Bike riding down around the Anchorage Beach with Esther."

"Esther? A girl? Esther who?"

"Esther Girling, she's new."

"Girling. Girling? She's not new."

"Yes she is, she's come from away, from Montreal."

"Well, I don't care if she came from New York City, I don't want you spending any more time with any of that bunch from Deer Curve."

"What're you talking about, Mum?"

"Never mind, just heed what I say Charles. I don't want you with any Girling girl, or boy either for that matter."

ESTHER WALKED INTO HER HOUSE, past her brothers and Floress, the only sister left in the house; Liona and Ross Mackie were living in Woodward's Cove. Esther headed straight for the bathroom to wash her hands of sea smells and old dirt. Stevie sang first: "Esther and Charlie up a tree, k i s s i n g, first came love, then came marriage, then came Esther with the baby-carriage."

"Where ya been Esther, grassing with Charlie?" Luke said, teasing.

"Esther's been grassin', Esther's been grassin'," Floress chanted, which sounded innocent enough coming from a six-year-old, but the snickering and carrying on and whispering of the older boys was not the least bit innocent sounding. In fact, they made it sound like something very bad, and very shameful. Esther didn't know what grassing was, but she knew she did roll in the grass.

"I've been playing."

"Yeah, well name it after me!" Stevie hollered.

Fall thankfully slid into winter where signs of play didn't stain Esther's clothes and sneakers.

CHAPTER 34

Winter

"GET YOUR ASS OUTDOORS and get some fresh air," Melba said. "It's a beautiful night." *That sounds somehow familiar*, Esther thought. *Maybe I really am a dog.*

They had gone out sledding. *They* had two five-foot-long sleek wooden sleds. The sleds had ropes for steering, and sharp steel runners to cut the snow like a new pair of downhill skis. *They* were Esther's brothers Stevie, Luke and Paul. Three boys and two sleds. The odd boy out held a broken hockey stick with one end swollen with black tape like a sore finger, the tape wrapped round and around, bulging. He held it to the back of the sled at the top of the driveway, and ran behind, pushing with all his might until he finally slipped and fell face forward on the snow, sending the sled down the driveway at an amazing speed. *They* steered recklessly down the driveway, through the yard, and only straightened up and quit fooling around down at the very end of the yard where they had to turn, guiding their sleds onto the narrow path that led through the bushes and down to the vegetable garden. You couldn't see them once they'd passed the barn and headed into the shadows at the edge of the woods. It was a game of who could slide the farthest down the garden path.

A yard light hung off the driveway side of the porch and Esther sat on the steps underneath, getting her fresh air like a good dog. She sat, a little jealous of their squeals, her tongue sometimes darting out to catch large snowflakes when she could stop thinking about herself for a second. She watched the boys drag their sleds back out from the shadows and up into the yard. They were headed for the porch and seemed finished playing. Esther almost asked them if she could try sliding. Instead, what fell from her mouth was: "Hey. Where did you get those sleds anyhow?"

"What's it to ya, you writing a book?"

"Just curious. They go really fast."

"Yup, we sharpened the runners."

"So, where'd you get them?"

"We got em for Christmas last year."

"From who?"

"Aunt Flora and Uncle Sammy stupid. Think the old man can afford anything like these? Practically everything in the place was sent or paid for by them."

The three boys walked past Esther dragging their snowy boots into the kitchen. Esther sat outside on the steps until someone shut off the yard light, then she went quietly inside, took off her jacket and overpants, walked to the edge of the kitchen, and peered in the living room. The three boys were sitting cross-legged on three sides of the heat register in the middle of the floor watching television and sipping hot chocolate from scratched orange or brown plastic mugs. Weinsteins had used the same hot/cold mugs at the cottage. The boys were fully absorbed with the television; free hands mindlessly picked ice balls from their grey socks and dropped them down the register grate.

Esther couldn't watch the television any more after finding out she'd been traded for the damned thing. She could never focus on the screen. She saw other people instead, other scenes playing out, old stories, on her memory channels that played on the other side of the glass.

And she saw those ice balls the boys had dropped down the register. They didn't melt, in fact they became harder and sharper like icicles and drove into Russell Skunk's round soft-looking head, making cavities like those photographed on early moonscape photographs. She imagined him still sitting on that broken chair in the cellar with an axe in his hand. As he tilted a mickey of rum to his chapped lips, the cavities drained the melted ice balls down the back of his head wetting the greasy collar of his green work shirt. Just at that moment, the thought of the smell of rum sent Esther to the bathroom to throw up.

"Have you made your list yet, Esther?"

"What list?"

"Your list to Santa Claus." Floress wondered how anyone could be so daft.

"No. I'm not making any stupid list."

"Why not?"

"Cause there's no such thing as Santa Claus. I've seen dozens of them in department stores; they're not real, they're fat men dressed in red suits."

"Well I asked for a coat last year and I got a brown one, so there."

"Let me see it, Floress."

Esther looked at it with recognition. "Nice little brown coat!"

Floress ran to the kitchen where Melba was kneading dough for white bread and rolls on the table. Esther followed her and the smell of yeast.

"Mam, Esther said there's no Santa. She's not gonna get anything right?"

"Right."

Melba's experienced hands, covered with white flour as if she were wearing gloves, rolled, punched down, turned, rolled, punched down, and turned sweet yeast smelling dough evenly and precisely on the kitchen table. She laboured at it, the force of her kneading bending the table in the middle as if it were breathing. Esther thought it appeared easy enough to do, and would have liked to try but would never have asked. Instead she stared at the white dust rise and settle back down again until Melba finally put the dough down and it sat on the table like a large mushroom cap. Then, with a sharp knife she sliced a piece of dough from the dusty mound and offered it to Esther.

"Wanna try some?"

"You never give me any dough," Floress said, whining.

"I always give you a piece, Floress."

"You don't either."

"Oh, here you go."

"Didn't Flora ever make bread, Esther?"

"No. We got our bread from the delicatessen. She said white bread wasn't any good for you. We only ate bagels, and rye and pumpernickel, egg challah, and black bread."

Esther liked the sweet taste of raw white bread dough.

"It tastes really good, mmm … Melba."

Esther never really knew what to call Melba because she still doubted she was her mother. Though it was times like this when Melba was wearing a soft, almost babyish smile, and perhaps offering Esther a lick of the beaters from a vanilla cake she happened to be making for dessert, that Esther thought briefly, sometimes I think I could like her.

But then Esther remembered a few nights before, when she was in her room, lying on her tummy, hanging over the hollow rail at the end of the bed in the street light, writing a letter to her cousin Beverley and saw Lloyd Slader's silver Cadillac coast down the driveway with its headlights out.

Esther sneaked downstairs, through the kitchen door and out to the porch to see what was going on. She stared through the porch window and saw Melba and Lloyd in his car; it was the white flesh of their faces that she could see. Esther fumbled along the wall with her hand and found the switch to the yard light. She stood there flicking it on and off, on and off, on and off, for what seemed a very long time, or at least until the passenger door opened and Melba came tearing around the car to the porch screaming: "You little Christer."

Esther had no idea that maybe Melba needed a friend, and that if a person were desperately unhappy enough, they might not be very choosy about picking him or her.

CHRISTMAS MORNING Esther refused to go downstairs. Floress had been awake for a while and came back upstairs and jumped on the bed. She kissed Esther on the cheek. "Merry Christmas. You gotta come down. Mam says we won't start without you."

"Don't pester me."

"You have some presents, I checked. Plllleeeease. Pretty please with sugar on it. For me?"

Merry fucking Christmas, Esther thought. But Floress' hound dog eyes and Esther's own curiosity about the whole Christmas thing finally got the best of her and she followed her little sister down the dusty stairs. Esther sat as far away from everyone in the room as she could. Or was it as far away from the television as she could get? She sat on the floor almost out by the telephone in the hall.

Russell Skunk, Melba, Paul, Luke, Stevie and Floress all looked at her.

"What are you looking at me for? Start. Do whatever it is you do already."

Esther watched. She counted that each person took three packages from under the tree. One present was a stupid plastic toy or silly game of some sort. The second was each a new pair of pyjamas wound around cardboard and wrapped in loud, crackly cellophane straight from Taiwan. The third presents were different for everyone, but they were all schlock, nothing but schlock as far as Esther was concerned. One, two, three and Christmas was over.

Everyone had opened their packages at the same time and crumpled piles of cheap wrapping paper lay in a heap on the linoleum floor. There were three presents left unopened under the tree. The sound of ancient Christmas carols sung by choirs played in mono from behind the test pattern on the television, almost pestering you to sing along. What a pile of shit! Where was God? She had stood up in the Baptist church and nothing had happened. She was still on Deer Curve and so were all the Girlings.

Esther got off her tush and headed back upstairs to her room, but not until she grabbed a grey work sock that was tied with coarse string to the banister – there was food in there. On the way downstairs earlier she had seen a store apple, an orange, and a bottle of soda through the worn spots and holes. She hadn't eaten an orange since, she couldn't say, but it was before she came to live with the Girlings.

"Hey, you didn't open your presents," Melba said.

"I didn't ask for anything," Esther said.

Christmases came and went, and Flora continued to send five dollar American bills every few months, but she never came back to get Esther.

CHAPTER 35

Some Spring

———————

ESTHER SEEMED TO FORGET EACH DAY once it had ended. She was in Grade Nine now but didn't remember much about the past few school years except for trips to the mainland to play with the basketball team. She remembered this because she was seasick on the ferry each time they went away. She didn't remember that her best friend Liz Walker lent her the money to go on one trip, Paul gave her some money he made from fishing for another, once Luke gave her half the money he made on his rabbit snares, and Liona crumpled a five in her hand another time and said: "Now don't spend it all in one place." The money was for food while they were away. For coke and French fries.

She spent a week studying music and drumming at Mount Allison University with the marching band but she only remembered learning how to kiss in the chapel on campus while she was there. She didn't know that one of the schoolteachers had paid for that trip out of her own purse.

One day in English class, hearing the name Montreal tweaked a spark of interest for Esther, and she listened to Mr. Reyd, who was an English professor from the States originally, talk about the American novelist Willa Cather who had summered and written short stories and novels in her cottage on Grand Manan for eighteen years. Esther found herself enchanted with this dead woman who wrote short stories, and like her was from away. She had lived in a cottage in Whale Cove with her girlfriend Edith Lewis. The local people referred to summerhouses as camps. Their stupidity continued to amaze Esther, because of course, Esther thought she knew everything, like Flora before her, and Victoria before her.

He said: "Miss Cather had her rye bread and bagels sent from a delicatessen in Montreal to the Island, and olive oil and garlic from New York City. She never settled for what was within reach at the local stores. She insisted on having the things she loved and was used to having."

135

ESTHER GRITTED HER FRONT TEETH unconsciously like she did in the night and imagined she could taste a thin rye seed from a heavy mound of dark pumpernickel rye bread. She looked at the blackboard and saw shelves, slanted shelves displaying all different shapes and shades of bread and bagels. It would have been Saturday morning; Flora would have sent her to the deli around the corner to buy fresh bagels for breakfast while she and Sammy had a little sleep-in. "Get whatever you want, honey, as long as it's fresh today."

"Some poppy-seed bagels please, Mr. Goldman."

"How many you vant today? Three?"

"Shure. And some sesame seed bagels too please."

"You vant three of those too?"

"Shure."

"How 'bout some coffee cake or some date strudel?"

"Okay, some date strudel."

"Good goyl, your Daddy vill be happy."

Mr. Reyd said: "Not many Islanders knew Miss Cather. Her friend, Miss Lewis, stayed with her at her cottage in the summers, so I suspect she was too busy to become social with the local people. She did, after all, write a dozen novels, and numerous essays and short stories in her lifetime. Many of those novels were worked on at some stage right here on the Island in the attic of her cottage."

ESTHER WROTE. No one knew that. Not since she was caught writing to Christopher Lee and told Melba she wouldn't write any more letters, but since then Esther lied when she had to. She wrote every night in bed.

Her room faced the road. There was a streetlight out there. It was the only streetlight from Girlings to the Harbour in one direction, and Girlings to the bridge over the Seal Cove Crick in the other. Esther would lie on the bed face down and pull herself close to the window. There was enough light to write by, and sometimes enough to read by if there was a clear sky and a full moon.

Sometimes Esther went over to Crocker's orchard and sat on their steps and wrote to that woman, the woman she used to call Mummy. She had written to Christopher Lee again, lots of times actually. She had written to her cousins Beverley and Ellen and told them how much fun she was having down at Old Orchard Beach and how Daddy and her played check-ers on her beach towel down at the ocean in the afternoon. And how after supper they strolled the Boardwalk and how Daddy bought her a Mogen David charm for her bracelet. She had written to Stanley and asked him if he still worked at the club. She also wrote to aunt Libby and uncle Abe and told them she was enjoying her vacation.

Esther sat inside her huge steamer trunk late one night and read all these letters she thought she must have written a hundred years ago, when she was a child. It was strange, because she didn't remember writing any of them.

But since she learned about Miss Cather, she mostly wrote about things she remembered doing with Flora and Sammy, and places they went together, the real memories. She wrote about meeting Buster Crabbe who was Tarzan, at the Catskills, and about the trophy he gave her for swimming the fastest race that day in the hotel pool. Esther thought that, if she wrote these memories down, they would stay with her forever, just in case she forgot how it used to be, like she forgot writing those other letters. Some things she made big notes to remember, like the day she was born. In Montreal with Mummy and Daddy, Esther's birthday had been celebrated on August 29. The Girlings, however, had insisted that she was born on August 28. Esther wondered why they pointed this out because she hadn't had a birthday cake since she was ten, on either of those days, so who cared anyway?

Willa Cather was from New York City. Esther was from Montreal. And Esther built bridges between them, between cities, between times, between life and death, between woman and girl, and went to her cottage as often as she liked to be with this woman who wrote stories a long time ago. Willa's best friend was Edith; Esther's best friend was Liz.

Could I live with a friend? Esther wondered. She decided yes, she'd like to live with Liz.

New York City and Montreal had the best boiled and wood-fire baked bagels in the world. They both had racetracks and stage shows and gambling and billboards and street lights downtown that never shut off, and old narrow houses built close to the sidewalks where the neighbours kibitzed for hours in the evening and then climbed tall iron staircases carrying small children to their apartments to go to bed.

The Islanders must have been proud to have Miss Cather on their Island, Esther thought. The principal of the high school wrote a pamphlet about her called "Willa Cather and Grand Manan." She did wonder though if anyone ever forgave her for being from away, because if you were from away, you could never really belong in the fullest sense of the word, and you weren't trusted when it came right down to it. Esther noticed there were none of Miss Cather's novels in the school library. How strange. She wondered if it was because she had her bread shipped from away.

CHAPTER 36

Another Summer

E STHER PACKED SARDINES at the Connors herring factory up at North Head when she was thirteen. They packed twenty-five cans to make a tray, four trays to a case, and the women were paid according to how many cases they could pack in a day. That of course depended on the size of the herring that came in the night before. There could be anywhere from two to twelve herring in a can. Once you packed a case, a man would punch a hole in your pay ticket, which hung on a wire above the stack of trays at the end of your worktable. He put the cases on a trolley to be rolled away into the steam room. Once they were steamed, the cans were filled with oil, covered, and then cooked again with the lids on.

Mostly married women and a few young, very young girls, like Esther, and Sharon the bootlegger's daughter, sat at tables across from each other alongside a moving conveyor belt that brought forth stinking freezing cold slippery herring from the holding tanks below. You used your hand and forearm to scoop the slimy fish onto the workspace between you and your table mate, cut their heads and tails off with a pair of scissors, and placed them alternately head to tail in a low flat tin can. The idea of all this for the workers was to make money; it was piecework after all. You had to be fast, very fast, or you'll have spent eight hours in the choking heat, and nauseating oily fish smell of the factory for almost no money at all.

The women were there to seriously make money, and prepared for it as soon as they got to work by wrapping all the fingers of the hand that wasn't their scissor hand with white bandage tape. They couldn't afford to lose time from work because of snipping off pieces of their own fingers and the resulting infections that invariably set in.

Esther did try. She soon had oozing blisters on her scissor hand, and jagged fingernails and open nicks from the tip of the scissors on the other hand. There was a way to hold the scissors at a certain angle and turn the fish a certain direction that was supposed to make it simple to do without cutting yourself too badly. Many of her fingernails landed in the cans. Esther just couldn't figure it out.

The twelve o'clock whistle sounded lunch. Lunch was in a stench-filled old school bus. Experienced women were fast to get to the trough to be among the first to wash in the tank of water and chemicals. Esther was always last to get cleaned up, and wondered whether her hands were cleaner before washing in the tank, or after. Just in case, she never touched her peanut butter sandwich. She held it carefully in the waxed paper it was wrapped in, let little bites get in between her lips, and tried to chew with her nose plugged. Even still, just holding the sandwich in her hand made the peanut butter taste like fish.

Melba had told her that she had to buy her own school clothes for the fall, and have her own money if she expected to travel to tournaments with the basketball team. And if she wanted a bra, she could order one herself from the Simpsons-Sears catalogue when she got her first pay envelope. Esther had been wearing her little Ladybug undershirts from the Lad and Lassie store since she arrived on the island however many years before. You could see through them. They were too tight. Oh, the price of a bra back then.

Once in a while Esther would squint her eyes in delight at what was coming on the belt, and gleefully haul in a catfish or a lumpfish or a sculpin onto her table. Then she'd scream like her arm was being ripped out of its socket and was being dragged away by the conveyor belt itself and the men in the factory would come running.

Esther would hold up the monster fish by the tail and giggle: "This one won't fit in the can, Mr. Connor."

Esther would laugh, and when the men turned away grumbling about what a jeezeless smartass she was, she'd wing the cold stiffening sculpin by the tail at their backs, just short of hitting them, of course. Sometimes Mr. Connor turned to her and yelled: "Keep it up and you'll be sent home, little girl."

That's when Esther would take aim a little sharper and throw another one at him.

"Oh please, Mr. Connor, take my pay ticket, make me chew off the heads and tails of the herring with my teeth, make me lick the floor with my tongue, but please, please don't send me home."

"You get the fuck outta here, you little Christer. And don't come back."

ESTHER RODE THE FACTORY BUS to North Head at seven o'clock in the morning for the next week like nothing had happened. She got off last at the factory and ducked around the back of the bus while the other women filed into the factory, already donning their plastic aprons and putting their hairnets on. Esther went to Miss Cather's cottage.

The year before, she had ridden her bicycle up to Whale Cove to find the cottage where Willa and Edith lived. She had never intended to go inside; she thought she would be able to look in the windows or sit on the veranda and satisfy her curiosity about the place and the women who had lived there. But the cottage was sealed and concealed with wild rose bushes and blackberry vines gone wild.

Esther scouted all sides, finally finding two wooden steps where thick honeysuckle vines veiled a small veranda. Esther tore her way through them, into complete and utter privacy, like being on her own stage, like being behind the glass of a television set, and acting out whatever scene she chose. Esther chose to be like Willa Cather, from away. Away from the Girlings, away from the stories she'd heard, away from the kids who had laughed at her. Each time she went there she brought tools she thought she might use to get into the cottage. During the year Paul's jackknife had disappeared from his dresser, along with strong scissors from the kitchen, and a hammer and flat screwdriver from the barn.

Now, suddenly with the prospect of whole days of her own to spend at the cottage, or at least until Melba found out about her being fired, she opened her chipped foam pillow slip and poured half the stuffing into another pillow case and tied up the ends of each pillow. She took one with her to Willa's, along with her transistor radio and a roll of toilet paper so she could make in the woods if she had to.

You could say she'd been suspended from the factory, kicked out, for what she thought was forever. Turned out it was only for the rest of that week. When Esther didn't show up at the factory the following Monday morning, the Mister in charge of the canners, phoned Melba to see where she was. Also, it happened that the Mister was her second cousin of the once removed kind, and Melba convinced him to take Esther back to work at the factory. Then it was Melba's turn: "Any more shenanigans from you, missy, and I'll send you to a home for girls." *Here we go again*, Esther thought. *Please, please, I'll do anything, but please don't send me to that home for wayward girls.*

Esther went back to the factory the following week, but refused to clip any heads or any tails. She bombarded anyone walking by with herring intended for the cans. And when she got bored of laughing like a seagull at the absurdity of it all, telling jokes, and generally being bad, she quieted down for short periods and scooped herring for Mrs. Stringer across from her so she could pack more sardines. Esther did get a few pay envelopes that summer, very small ones; as little as $2.20 one time. But even at that, she wasn't paid for any work she'd done herself. At the end of each day Mrs. Stringer had tagged a few of her trays with Esther's name so she was always paid a little something.

With the money in her first pay envelope, Esther didn't buy a bra. She bought batteries from Mason's store for the Mickey Mouse flashlight she'd discovered one night in the bottom of her trunk. Now she could go to the cottage at night. Flora had bought her that flashlight so she could find her way to the bathroom at night up at the cottage. It seemed to her that it had always been there on her night stand right next to the Mickey Mouse wind-up clock. Flora must have packed it in the trunk. Esther bawled and bawled long and hard at the thought of her Mummy packing the steamer trunk, and wondered why it was that she was so bad, what was so wrong with her, that even two mothers didn't want her. Esther would wonder this for her whole life.

CHAPTER 37

Victor Woods

AND MELBA WOULD WONDER why she met Victor, if he was only to die. She got the news after supper on a Sunday night. Melba was doing up the last of the dishes when the phone rang. It wasn't the box on the wall with the crank on the side that Girlings used to have; they now had a rotary phone. Still a party line though, two long and a short. That was exactly the length of time it took to shred Melba's last stitch of hope and send her reeling over into the deep end. Her last auspicious drop of hope was drowned by the ringing sound of two long and a short.

"Hello, this Wayne Bolton, you don't know me, but I'm a friend of Vic Woods, I'm calling from Halifax. He would have wanted me to call you. He told me about you. You see, I know how fond of you he was. Melba, he's dead. He died of a heart attack on Thursday. Melba, are you there?"

Why had she met him? She hadn't been fishing around for anyone at that point in her life. By then she was too busy and too tired of keeping house, making jam and bread and pickles, and doing the wash for the whole house in that old wringer washer, reaching in that cold water and bringing up sleeves and socks to send them through the wringer, watching for the buttons on all those boys' shirts so they didn't get caught and fly off. She was too exhausted from boning herring down at the fish shed in Seal Cove to fish for any man. She didn't even see Lloyd any more. She finally figured out that Lloyd was no better a man than Lucky had been a boy. Some men only wanted a piece of ass, any ass.

Esther watched Melba hang up the phone with one hand, as the damp cup towel dropped from her other hand to the floor causing dust balls to scatter along the edge of the floor where there should have been baseboard.

Esther had heard her words, "Oh NO!" followed by sounds that made Esther think of a cat drowning in the well. Although she had never heard a cat in a well that she knew of, she always thought she knew the sound. She remembered Flora for a minute. Huge tears dripped from Melba's lower eyelids, leaking steadily.

"What's wrong with you?" Esther asked, as if she gave a damn, because she didn't. She enjoyed watching Melba cry. Maybe it was the realization that Melba could be hurt, could feel pain and cry real tears. Standing there, Melba was reduced in Esther's mind to the image of a cat lying on the edge of the road that had just been run over by a car, and only partially recognizable at that.

Esther thought: *This is someone's mother?* She was further convinced that this woman could not possibly be her mother. Melba never cried. She never gave a hot damn when Esther cried and screamed and swore in words she had learned from her new brothers. She never gave a damn that Esther wanted her mummy and daddy back.

"A friend of mine passed away."

"Died, you mean? I didn't think you had any friends. Gee, that's too bad. Huh." And as Esther swung her young body around the knoll post into the shadow of the darkened staircase, she spat out: "You never cried for me, Melba."

Esther, oblivious to all but her own fourteen-year-old fears and hatred, had an angry face, and an angry body, filled with angry hateful words that spewed from her lips like a white foaming glass of beer dripping when she opened her angry mouth. She didn't know that Melba harboured her own despair, her own shattered dreams. Dreams of her own escape. Dreams of love, for surely what she felt for Vic was love, wasn't it?

Melba hooked the cup towel up from the floor with her scissor hand and forced it over her mouth. She ran to the toilet, dropped to her knees, and vomited the last strings of hope, dead. Dead like the pale curled dried dandelion stems lying all over the dooryard.

MONTHS BEFORE, Sylvia Price, who worked alongside Melba in the smoke sheds, had coaxed Melba to go with her to a dance one Saturday night up at the curling rink. Sylvia had kicked her old man out years before, and was starting to get fidgety. Russell was out on the boat, so what the hell, Melba figured she'd go. She hadn't been to a dance in a long while; Melba thought: *Jeepers creepers, those times were fun.*

Her hair was oily that afternoon, her forehead smooth like the grease from the oily fish she slit open up the belly with a sharp knife during the day, sitting on a old wooden barstool, her legs bent in brackets supporting her body. The stool itself was peeling with generations of fish scales. Melba's back ached, and her fingers were taped with white surgical tape. She boned smoked herring for ninety cents a case, slicing for hours and hours, underneath a dim bulb hanging from the rafters on a black dusty wire.

No matter how many sponge baths Melba took at the sink, she felt the fish scales on her skin, catching under torn fingernails as she scratched the hardened scales that pulled and grabbed at tiny patches of skin all over her body. She figured she probably just spread them around and planted them on other parts of her body with the small thin worn washcloth. When Melba finished her sponge bath, she splattered cheap perfumed talc all over her body, and on the tender places where the rough towel scratched her skin, and hoped she had masked the smell of her day.

YES, IT HAD BEEN SMOOCH FILLED, steal the feel of a titty, rub against the groin during the slow dances, fallen down drunk good time fun. The dance was the only social event for islanders who wanted to party. There was no movie theatre, and there were no nightclubs or pubs or restaurants that served liquor. That's how it was back then. It was no wonder they let their hair down, but it was incredible they made it home in the wee hours, driving the roads with cars full of mothers and fathers, around dark treed corners, through narrow bridges over the crick, and through thick fog patches in the coves, where there was no visibility, just sound, the sound of surf, and the sound of frogs and crickets arguing back and forth in the night. But luckily, after a long night of dancing and getting pretty full, most managed to catch a lucky star and follow it home without getting killed.

Sylvia and Melba drove to the dance that night in Sylvia's baby blue Vauxhall. Melba held her compact and fidgeted with tiny Avon lipstick samples.

"Which colour do'ya think, Syl?"

"Put on the one that's the longest. That way you can wear the same colour all night."

Melba chain-smoked, and rattled on and on about nothing much at all on the way. When they finally stopped at the curling rink out the dump road, Sylvia asked her: "What's the matter with you tonight, honey? You're jumpy as a flea."

"I dunno. I just feel funny, that's all."

"Maybe you're feeling lucky!"

"That'll be the day."

Instead of Russell Skunk holding up the bar like in the old days, Victor Woods sat there Saturday night. He looked up and met Melba's gaze at the opening door when she and Sylvia walked in.

This was the place and time of the moment in Melba's life that she was unable to understand, unable to avoid, and unable to ignore. Melba was needy. Melba needed to be loved, everyone does. Maybe somehow, she had felt it tugging at her, like a bass tugging on a fishing line. She was naive of her own truth, and had no clue that she really was fishing that night, that she, along with everyone else there was on an eternal pilgrimage, ultimately searching for the beloved. She didn't know that in between feeling and action lies morality. She just wanted some happiness, for crissake. That's what we all want. She needed validation for her sorry life. Of course, she didn't know that either.

Victor introduced himself as Vic from away. Of course, Melba knew right off he was from away. His wasn't a face that belonged to the island – he didn't look like anyone around, and no one around looked like him and he wasn't recognizable as being related to anyone. He didn't live in the house of anyone who had died, or moved away to the mainland. Melba had never seen him before. Of course, he was from away.

He was an insurance representative over from Halifax, boat insurance, a seasoned east coast traveller. He had been invited to the dance by Greg Roland, from up to the Head, after Vic missed the last ferry back to the mainland. Vic planned to stay the night with them up there in their big white two-storey house with black trim, on the hill above the Grand Manan wharf.

Melba and Sylvia walked through the door and Vic's eyes watched them enter. Almost as if someone had just whispered into his ear: "Hey, look who's coming in." Vic was friendly and curious by nature, and his over-smile actually dripped: "Hello there little lady, do I know you?"

Melba tittered: "You do now!"

Attraction and desire met that night. Melba walked carefully in her scuffed high-heels through the sawdust to the bar for a gin and tonic. You could see their eyes lock onto one another and know that something momentous and rare was taking place.

What Vic noticed first were Melba's deep brown eyes, surrounded by a girlish-looking tanned face, neck and arms, and short curly brown hair. Delicate features clung to small-framed bones held together with muscular tight skin. A shot of something, familiarity maybe, strong as a twenty-pound test fishing line, held their eyes locked. *What is happening to me?* Vic thought. He felt weak-kneed, and his stomach fluttery like bait on the end of that line, and excited, excited with desire he hadn't felt in years.

"You must be from away, are ya?"

"Yes, I missed the last ferry and had to stay over."

"Ahah, ahah, so you missed the boat, did'ja?"

Anyone who might have been watching the two of them would have witnessed them inexorably falling into a passionate love for one another, which neither of them understood, or knew how to stop, even if they had wanted to.

IN TIME, VIC NUZZLED HIS FACE AND TONGUE over Melba's neck. There were only sweet womanly smells of desire when they made love, and when he caressed her small, smooth, tanned body, he would feel no scales, and Melba would feel love. For the next few months they saw each other whenever it was possible, and they made it possible as often as they could.

As for Vic, he was, like most of us, painted with the human condition, content with cake at home with his family and wife on the weekends, but unable to give up the gift of a tightly wrapped candy bar that lasted through the week. Life tasted sweet and soothing, and it's difficult to give up things we love. We tend to want to hoard all of the wonderful gifts that are given to us. We don't always stop to think that the gift was taken by us, and not given at all.

It wasn't long before Vic started worrying that his wife would find out he was fooling around down on Grand Manan; lies began to swell up like day-old oatmeal sitting in a pot on the stove. Why was he making so many trips down to Grand Manan? Why was he missing the boat back to the mainland so often? Why wasn't he making any extra money on his expenses anymore?

In the summer Vic arranged with Richard Hart, a client from Grand Manan, to take Melba over to Digby once every two weeks, on Tuesdays. They would have most of the day and the night together. Richard would pick her up the next morning and take her back to the Island.

Melba would say she was going up to Herring Cove to do housekeeping for Kaye. Then it would happen to be too dark for old Melvin to drive her back down the island, so she'd have to stay over till morning. Melba always went home with a folded five-dollar bill stuffed in her bra, just to set the lie.

WHEN MELBA GOT UP THE MORNING after the phone call, she was sharp as a tack, or a cat. She was not crying anymore, and knew exactly what she was going to do. She clawed Esther as soon as she came down the stairs.

"You little bitch, to think I was gonna take you with me."

Melba's Wash   147

"Take me where?"

"Off this Peyton Place of an island and over to Dartmouth where Victor and I were gonna live."

"Yeah right. From what I've heard, Victor was quite married and had two kids."

"He was going to divorce them."

"Divorce his kids. You two would've made a perfect pair."

At this moment, Esther was on the receiving end of another strong stinging slap on the face.

"I hate your guts. You know that, Melba?"

"Do you now? Well, I wasn't gonna tell you this right yet. I was gonna give you a bit more time. But you know what? My guts are the only ones you have left, little girl."

Esther shoved Melba away from her. She was standing too close.

"What are you talking about?" Esther's body tensed.

"Flora died four months ago."

Esther held the same position, standing still, feet slightly apart, head back, she had braced for another slap, but not that one.

"Cat got y'ur tongue?"

"What did you say?"

"You heard me. She's dead."

"I don't believe you. How could you not tell me my mother died?"

"She wasn't your mother. I am."

"HOW COULD YOU NOT TELL ME MY MOTHER DIED?" Esther screeched.

She lunged at Melba's shoulders. "YOU BITCH!" They stumbled through the hallway and spilled onto the kitchen floor, Esther landing in a threatening position on top of Melba holding her arms down so she couldn't deflect the words that would come out.

Agonizing cat cries scratched the air, angry words filled with tears beat down hard, and horrific screams ricocheted off the walls and ceiling and floor like a black squash ball.

And finally, the wild tongue of a girl losing her mother, again, yelled: "Don't you ever say that again. You gave up your right to being my mother when you gave me away. This whole world could die and you still wouldn't be my mother."

FLORA HAD DEVELOPED DIABETES. She had never told Esther in her letters; she didn't want Esther to worry. She knew she had enough to deal with down there with that gang. She had gone into diabetic shock. Unfortunately it had happened on a weekend, and no one knew anything was wrong until she didn't show up for work at the gift shop on Monday morning.

Melba didn't go to the funeral; she didn't have the money. She didn't have any money until the estate was settled, that is. Then she had almost everything she had coveted, except for Sammy. She had Flora's money, china collectibles, diamond rings and other jewellery. Once the money was invested, there would be enough to last the rest of her life, and beyond.

Flora's landlord put everything valuable into storage until Melba sent him the money to have it shipped to her. Not to the Island, but to Dartmouth where Melba had planned on moving.

"All she left you is the big photograph of the three of you 'the royal family.' Your precious royal family. Royal family all right. Where's the royal family now?" Melba screamed. Then she grabbed Esther and shoved her against the wall, screeching even louder: "Everything she had is mine now, missy – all mine – do you hear me, Esther? All mine! Do you hear me?"

"You don't have my memories," Esther said firmly.

Esther stood dead still, now speechless. Involuntary unstoppable streams of tears dampened her jersey. She had heard what Melba just said, but she was thinking about all the hateful letters she wrote Mummy, and then, suddenly with great relief, remembered they were all in her steamer trunk. She hadn't mailed them.

"At least *she's* with Daddy," Esther said.

Silently Esther prayed.

Dear Gott in Heaven, please come and get me and take me up to Heaven with Mummy and Daddy. Amen.

CHAPTER 38

Willa Cather's Cottage

E STHER MOVED TOWARDS THE TELEPHONE blowing her nose, picked up the receiver and dialled Liz.

Oh My God, Esther thought, *what's happening? Not again. I've done this before, I'm calling, dialling my house, hello are you there? Daddy where are you? Mummy's crying. I want to come home. Where are you? Wait for me. I love you …*

"Lizzzzzz? CanIIIIcccccomeover?"

"Esther, what's wrong? Why are you crying?" Liz asked.

"Mummy's dead."

"Who's dead? I can't understand you."

"*Mummmmy*," Esther cried.

"Can you get to my house?"

I did before.

"Esther, come to my house. Come right now. I'll start out and meet you on the road. Are you coming?"

"Yes."

It was Sunday night and most girls weren't allowed out, but Esther was walking the roads. She waved rides by. *Go on, I don't want a ride.* She had forgotten where she was going, but wasn't without some direction. The bootlegger lived a mile or so up the road toward the harbour by the frog pond. It wasn't dark yet and Esther turned into his long rutted driveway. She hoped Sharon was home. She had worked up at the factory that summer too. Sharon was a good kid – she couldn't help it that her father was a bootlegger. Esther went around the back of the old house to Sharon's bedroom window and tapped on it. Sharon propped up the window.

"Esther, what're you doing here?"

"Can you spot me a bottle from your old man?"

"Jeezus, you look awful. Are you sure you want a bottle?"

"Very sure. Thanks, I won't forget this."

"Where'ya going, Esther?"

149

Esther didn't answer. She just took the bottle and started back up the driveway to the main road. She remembered where she was going when she saw Liz walking towards her on the other side of the road, and then she said to herself: *I'm going to see Liz.*

Liz was stunning, tall, with a thin layer of flesh covering her ribs and hips, and she wore her dark curly hair in a long shag. She had the unblemished white skin of the porcelain princess doll that had once sat on Esther's dresser in the city. Liz loved hearing Esther's stories; she wasn't positive she believed them all, but they were stories the other kids didn't have.

The two girls had spent the previous afternoon swimming at Miller's Pond, then had gone back to Liz's and taken a cool shower together. Liz's house was close to the shore and her bedroom window caught the ocean's breeze. They laid nude on top of the bedcovers underneath the window and dried in that breeze, while Esther told Liz about the Borscht Belt, the Catskill Mountain resort area in New York state, and how she had shaken hands with Jerry Lewis as he was on his way into the nightclub one evening. Esther was supposed to have stayed in the hotel room while Flora and Sammy were down in the nightclub, but instead, sneaked down the elevator to see what she could see. Esther had recognized Jerry Lewis from his movies. After a brief silence, Esther broke into the laughter like a hyena's cry.

"Liz, I've gone from drinking Shirley Temples with pink paper umbrellas in the Borscht Belt of New York state to scooping herring from the fish factory belt on Grand Manan. And I'm only fourteen. Who would've thunk?"

That was only the night before.

Liz sat waiting against the bridge in the harbour and soon saw Esther. walking towards her. Esther approached, crossed the road, then leaned back into the railing next to Liz and took a swig of gin. She wasn't crying anymore.

"Esther, you look like shit. What happened?"

"My mother's dead."

"Dead? Which mother?"

"Flora."

"Oh my God, Esther, I'm so sorry. She was going to come back and get you, wasn't she?"

"Uh huh."

"She always sent you American money, eh?" Liz asked.

"Yeah."

"What're you going to do, Esther?"

Melba's Wash   151

"Liz, I'm going to get drunk."

"Jayzus, I guess so. Where did you get the gin?"

"Sharon. Good kid that Sharon."

"I swiped a bottle from my mom, just in case," Liz said. "Where do you wanna go?"

"I'm going to the cottage."

"What cottage?"

"Willa and Edith's cottage."

"Esther, you just can't go break into someone's cottage just because you used to have one in another life a hundred years ago."

"I don't have to break in. I've been hanging out there for months."

"You mean it wasn't locked?"

"Not any more, it isn't. It's stupid anyway, to lock up a cottage."

Liz and Esther took a ride from one of the Slader boys to North Head, but got out on the corner by the Whistle Road and walked on the rest of the way to Whale Cove. Esther tilted her head back as they moseyed on and swigged gin in great mouthfuls she could barely swallow. Liz drank too, but her bottle of vodka had already been watered down by her mother. They sang and drank and drank and sang:

"We'll drink the drink the drink
to lady the pink, the pink, the pink
The Saviour of the HUman RA A ACE
She invented medicinal compound …"

Liz had told her mother they were both staying at a friend's for the night. She had seen her own mother drunk, many times. By the time the two of them got to the turnoff at Whale Cove, she knew she was going to have to stay with Esther that night, even if they had to spend the night together in the ditch. Tomorrow, she'd figure out what to do about her.

Liz knew there was something not right in that house on Deer Curve. She had only been there twice, but that was enough to smell something was not kosher in that house, just as sure as she could smell bad breath, or sour milk. Behind curtains on bedroom doorways perhaps. Down heat registers, some-where, Liz had felt it. The first time she was there was to pick Esther up to go away for basketball. Liz was a cheerleader, and her dad was waiting for them out in the car. Russell Skunk was in the house sitting at the table drunk. Liz stood on the mat at the back door. Russell mumbled that he was hungry.

Liz yelled for Esther to hurry up. When she finally got downstairs, Russell again said he was hungry. Esther told him she had his dinner ready and went to the counter and got the plate of pig's food that had been sitting there all day and put it on the table. "There you go, Russell," she said, and promptly pushed his drunken face into the plate. Liz was horrified. She had never seen this hateful side of Esther. Liz opened the door and grabbed Esther's shirt pulling her out of the house into the porch, hurrying to get into the car.

"Do you know where you're going, Esther?"

"Vell natch! Follow my flashlight, Liz."

"Where'd you get that?"

"In Disneyland."

"When were you in Disneyland?"

"Oh, I dunno, maybe I was six when we went there."

"Are you sure you know where you're going?"

"Sshure I'm sshure. You know what I miss, Liz?"

Liz nodded.

"I miss the smell of Cuban cigars."

"What are you talking about?"

"The men down at Daddy's club smoked Cuban cigars. Even in the day-time when there weren't many men in there, the cigar smell was still there. Heavy, it was in the carpet and the wood tables. Always there, Liz, never smelled any different."

"What made you think of that?"

"I dunno. I guess I was thinking about Daddy and that's what came to mind."

"What about Willa?"

"What about her?"

"Well, why are you interested in her? Does her cottage remind you of yours?"

"Not really. Ours was a lot nicer. But the cottage looks *away*. You know, look away, look away, look away Dixieland. And she was from away, Liz, like us. She and Edith lived at the cottage and ate bread and bagels from Montreal," Esther said, then sang: "Take me out to the deli, take me down to The Main, buy me some bagels and poppy seeds, I don't care if they stick in my teeth ..."

"Esther, only you could tell a joke when your mother just died. You're crazy."

"Yes. Meshuggeneh! That means crazy in Yiddish and having mothers and fathers who pretend to be mothers and fathers and then die on you

Melba's Wash   153

is crazy too. So I guess the joke is on me. And she died four months ago, Melba just told me."

"Oh my gosh. I'm so sorry, Esther. That was just awful of her."

"Yeah, we had a big fight."

"I bet you did. By the way, what's The Main?"

"The English in Montreal called Saint Lawrence Boulevard, The Main. Remind me when we're old and I'm rich again to take you to Schwartz's for a smoked meat sandwich on steamed rye bread. Yeah, I'll take you to Montreal for lunch."

"Okay, smarty pants."

Esther knew her way to the cottage in the dark, and Liz followed her from the Whale Cove Road onto a path in the woods that eventually led them along the side of a decrepit, rose-covered cottage. Around the front, the small veranda faced the Bay of Fundy to the northeast. On a clear day you could see away to Campobello Island, and Deer Island, and the Wolves – a long archipelago.

It hadn't been too awfully difficult to get inside the cottage. Esther had noticed there wasn't an inside pane of glass behind the storm window on one of the two windows that looked out over the veranda. It had been painted shut at one time but Esther slit what was left of the old paint easily. Salt breezes had already rotted most of it, and what Esther peeled from around the window with Paul's jackknife was mostly mould. The wing nuts holding the storm were rusted and eventually gave way underneath the force of Esther's hammering.

"You're not going to break in, are you?"

"Nope. Already taken care of that – last year." Esther laughed.

Esther removed the storm window like she had many times before and Liz followed her through and into what Esther figured must have been Edith's bedroom.

"What makes you think that?"

"I dunno. I think Willa must have slept up in the attic where she wrote. Better view of the Bay, better view of away. She always knew at the end of summer she'd be going away, going home."

Esther headed up the attic stairs on her hands and feet because it was so dark it was like having your head in a paper bag until she crawled from the last step onto the floor where suddenly clear moonlight illuminated most of the room. Then Esther shone her tiny flashlight back to light the way for Liz. Esther's chair, well, Willa's chair really, was in front of the window where she, they, had left it.

"Is this your pillow, Esther?"

"Yes, clever, eh? For those nights when I don't want to go home. Home, home on the range ... makes me want to puke thinking about it."

"Why don't you want to go home, Esther? Besides Melba I mean"

"Nighttime, Liz, nighttime. I hear footsteps on the stairs and I never know who it will be. Paul who feels me up with one hand over my mouth, or Russell Skunk who wants to stick his tongue down my throat."

"Have you told anyone?"

"No one cares."

"I care, Esther. I love you."

Liz and Esther sat together in the rocking chair, holding hands and looking into the blackness of the bay, silent for hours, long enough for Liz to repeat over and over in her mind what she knew her lips had to say.

"Esther, I'm moving back to the mainland. My dad bought a television sales and repair shop in Saint John."

Liz hugged Esther into her shoulder like a baby.

"Maybe I could go with you. I could live in your Dad's shop with the other televisions." A mixture of laughter and crying stung like a splinter in the small space between them as Liz held her friend.

"I've been trying to figure out all night what to do about you. You'll come live with me. I'll tell my mother I'm sick of moving and having no friends and I want you to come live with us. We've already moved seventeen times and I'm only fourteen. I know my dad, and he'll convince her it's a good idea after he figures out I won't pester them if I already have a friend when we land in a new city."

"Will I be able to bring my steamer trunk?"

"Why are you worried about your trunk?"

"I don't know. Because it came with me, I guess."

Liz woke briefly at some time during the night; they had moved from the rocking chair to the floor. Esther was puking her Girlings out. Liz had been sleeping beside Esther, and rolled her over so Esther was facing down, into the floor, facing away.

"I might love you, Esther, but you're not going to throw up all over me." Then Liz passed out.

If Liz and Esther had been awake at 7:10 the next morning, they would have heard the ship's whistle and would have seen the *Grand Manan IV* sail around Swallow Tail Lighthouse into the straight and head for mainland New Brunswick. Melba was on that ship.

Esther didn't find that out until two days later when she went back to the house on Deer Curve and found Stevie, in his pyjamas in the middle of the day, Floress too. Stevie's face was puffed and his eyes were swollen from crying. Like a bleating lamb he sobbed: "Maaa's, M'aaa's gone."

"Gone where?"

"She's gone on the boat up to the mainland," Floress said.

"Good riddance. Where's your father?"

"Out fishing we think," Floress said.

"Stevie, shut up for shit's sake. You're better off without her. You two look at each other. She left you here, alone, in your pyjamas. Don't cry for her – cry for yourselves."

Esther didn't know where the words were coming from. She had hoped she'd never wake up again after drinking that gin. When she had awoken in the late afternoon, her first thought had been: *Oh fuck, I'm still here.*

IT WAS UP TO LIZ'S PARENTS NOW. Liz really was going to see if Esther could come and live with them on the mainland. Her eighteen months on Grand Manan was the longest she'd ever lived in one place outside of her mother's womb. She was going to raise hell; she didn't want to leave the friends she'd made on the Island. She was sick of moving around.

Briiiiiiiing, briiiiiiiing, briiing.

"Hello."

"Esther, it's Liz. I talked to my parents and they said you could come live with us. In fact when I told them your mother had died, they said you can come and stay with us right now and move along with us to the mainland." A little tee-hee escaped into the receiver. "I didn't tell them which mother so go pack your stuff."

"You can't be serious?"

"I'm serious, Esther. They said you can come live with us."

"Who said, Liz?"

"My parents."

"I mean, what are their first names?"

"My mom and dad?"

"Yeah."

"Oh. Their names are Bella and Nelson."

"Liz, tell them thank you."

ESTHER HUNG UP AND DIALLED LIONA. She didn't notice that Stevie and Floress were standing behind her.

"Liona, you better get down here."

"What the frig. Where's the old lady?"

"I don't know, and I don't give a shit."

"Where's the old man?"

"I don't know and I give even less of a shit. I came back from a sleepover and found Floress and Stevie in their jammies bawling their heads off."

"Where the bloody hell could she have got to?"

"I don't know, but she's got money. She has whatever was left of Mummy's money. She won't be coming back, Liona."

"Well holy dyin', she finally told you about Aunt Flora?"

"Yeah. Well, you and Frieda better figure something out quick cause I'm not staying here. I'm not their mother."

"I'm not their mother either. Where the hell do you think you're headed to?"

"I'm moving to the mainland with my girlfriend and I'm NEVER, EVER COMING BACK."

Click.

LIONA HELD THE RECEIVER IN HER HAND but all she heard was the dial tone. She considered smashing the telephone to smithereens. Instead she went next door to her neighbour Elsie's, and asked for a ride down to Frieda's. Frieda didn't have a telephone.

Elsie was tickled pink; it gave her an excuse to take the car out for a ride. She loved driving her old Austin but felt "right foolish" simply taking it out for a spin like some people take their dogs for a walk, except on Sundays. Sunday drives were fine, just fine; everyone went for a drive on Sunday.

As the car stretched past Deer Curve, Liona's watchful eyes could tell there was something amiss at the house. For one thing, the yard light hadn't been turned off and it was two o'clock. For another, it was Monday and Melba's wash was not hanging on the clothesline.

Liona wondered how Melba and Esther could both take off like that and simply leave Stevie and Floress to fend for themselves. The old man was out on the boat, not that he'd be any consolation to those two kids. He'd be all liquored up, and he'd be some jeezus ugly when he found out Melba was gone.

Elsie's car pointed up the almost completely grassed-in driveway at Frieda's and ducked in under the clothesline as bed sheets flew up in the midday breeze. They would be pissy sheets from the night before; piss dried quickly on thin cotton sheets. Frieda had no washing machine of her own anymore, and only went up to Melba's once a week to do the wash, on Saturdays. So between Saturdays, bed sheets were turned end over end, and then reversed – top went to bottom and bottom went to top, then turned again until the last clean side had been slept on.

"Well, hello there. Ain't this a surprise, what?" Frieda said.

"Bye Elsie," Liona said, waving.

"That was real nice of her to give you a ride down here. What are you up to, Liona?"

"Melba's wash wasn't hanging out on the line when we drove by the house, Frieda."

"Boys oh boy, she must be some sick."

"She ain't sick. She ain't there."

"Well, where do you figure she's got to?"

"Haven't got a clue, but Esther called me and said she had left on the seven o'clock boat yesterday."

"Did she take the little ones with her?"

"Doesn't appear so. Esther said they're at the house."

"Is Esther up at the house?"

"If she is, she won't be there long. She's taking off with some friend of hers day after tomorrow to the mainland."

"Cripes, Liona. I was fourteen when Clover was born, and Mam was fourteen when I was born. Esther should be old enough to keep house for a while."

"If she were like you and me, she could. But she can't do much more now than when she first came back here, except screech and holler for bagels and bras, and dentists and money for trips away with the school, and lunch money for chocolate milk. She's real good at all that, Frieda."

"I remember Mam telling me how she'd sit at the top of the stairs banging her fists on the wall, and screaming blue murder how she had to go to the dentist for fillings for her dental caries. Dental caries if you please. I never heard such foolishness. None of the rest of us has ever been to the dentist for anything but to get them pulled and a plate put in. Poor little bugger just can't accept she's one of us."

"Well, it's getting on Liona, we should go check on those kids. Did Mam leave a note or anything?"

"I don't know. I didn't stop at the house on the way down. I wasn't going to get into it with Esther cause she sounded like a jeezus wild cat on the telephone. She won't be letting any grass grow under her feet though. I'll bet you a dollar to a doughnut she's taken off by the time we get up there."

"Oh probably, wouldn't surprise me none. Liona – I'm going to round up the wash, no sense in the kids sleeping on used sheets when I can put them through the wringer. Ask Clover to hunt down the rest of the kids, will you?"

Two of the kids each sent a bleached, cracked, wooden wagon rocking down the grassy driveway. Liona carried down the apple baskets of dirty clothes, and stood one in the back of each wagon. The middle boy and girl sat with their backs against the baskets and their dusty little bare feet cozied up to the front rail. Frieda's two oldest pulled the wagons alongside the road. The two youngest babies were stuffed into an old, very well used grey carriage that had some strips of vinyl still attached to its hood. They all walked, since there was no car, uphill to Deer Curve, like they did every Saturday to do the wash, except today was Monday, when Melba should have been doing her wash.

"Frieda, how come the old lady really sent Esther up to live with Aunt Flora and Uncle Sammy years ago? I've turned it around in my head six ways to Sunday and I can't figure it out for the life of me."

"Well, it seemed to make a bit of sense when I was thirteen. The way I remember it, Mam was too tired to look after her and she had to go down boning herring cause we had no money. Esther was only supposed to be gone for a few months. She was supposed to come back. Oh for heaven's sake, it doesn't make any sense now. Do you remember going up to the cottage to get her? You would've been seven or eight, I think"

"Yeah, I remember. Aunt Flora wanted me to stay up with them the rest of the summer and help with Esther, but I was afraid they'd keep me too."

"Yeah and Esther had already been with them, maybe six or seven months, and she didn't recognize any of us anymore. Or was it a year and six months? Anyway, she'd screech something mighty when Mam went near her. It was just like when Aunt Flora came down to get Amy, only Amy was older. Didn't matter though, neither of them wanted any part of their mothers. I was so mighty mad at Mam for not bringing her home. But at the same time, I had just found out that I was pregnant with Clover, so I thought, if I kept my mouth shut about Esther, Mam wouldn't make too much fuss over another baby coming. Funny how these things seem to make sense at the time. None of us ever talked about Esther after that trip. Liona, it was like she just never was."

Melba's Wash 159

"I've always been suspicious just because the old lady has always been so closed-mouthed about the whole thing. Wouldn't ever talk about it, or defend or deny any of the rumours. People have been talkin' for years who her father coulda' been, and if maybe that had something to do with why she was shipped away. And then there's all that talk of her being traded for a television set, and we DID get a television set from Uncle Sammy and Aunt Flora. Even if I could cotton on to the idea of giving one baby up because they couldn't afford to look after her – why'd mam go and have two more kids, Frieda?"

"Uh huh. You're right. It doesn't wash, does it? You know, I've always wondered why it was that Aunt Flora really brought her back here. Do you know, Liona?"

"That week she brought Esther down, I remember hearing her tell the old lady that she had a nervous breakdown or something. I guess Aunt Flora even took Esther to the shrink with her. I got the impression he's the one who told Aunt Flora to send Esther back."

"The shrink told her that?"

"I guess so."

"You know with Mam gone, there's going to be more talk about the Girlings."

"Did they ever stop talking? I'm sick to death of trying to explain or defend Mam. I'll take Stevie and Floress to live with me and Ross in the Cove until the old lady comes back, if she ever comes back, Frieda, and then I'll tell her to go straight to hell."

Part VI

CHAPTER 39

Saint John

IT WAS AN UNLIKELY SCENARIO for Esther to move away with Liz and her parents, yet as improbable as it may have seemed at the time, it was as easy as changing the channel on the television set. Or loading Esther's trunk in the back of their Plymouth station wagon as it turned out.

There were no first day jitters when they started school at Saint John High. There was no rush to make friends so they wouldn't sit alone in the cafeteria at lunch: They had each other. The kids at school assumed they were sisters from that first day, so Liz and Esther played it out. They sang in the school operetta "Down in the Valley," composed by Kurt Weill, and became cheerleaders both for the high school and the city triple A hockey team. Sunday nights they followed a pair of boys they had crushes on to the movies and sat behind them, giggling. Liz and Esther had a pyjama party that lasted eighteen months.

It lasted until Esther got home late one Saturday afternoon, after working a part-time shift washing dishes for a local dining room. When she approached Mr. Walker's storefront, she was stunned for a second to see that the televisions in the shop had no pictures, just interference. They did come back into focus while she stared at them through the window, though. It had happened that CTV had just gone on the air that day, and Nelson had turned off CBC and tuned all the televisions to the new channel. It was the interference that jarred Esther.

SHE WALKED AROUND THE HOUSE and up the back stairs to the kitchen. Opening the door, she felt interference in the house as well. The channel playing in the kitchen that afternoon was one of Bella talking about the new baby she was going to have. Esther looked around the kitchen and down the hall into the living room; the rooms suddenly appeared smaller, closing in on her.

"You don't have a whole lot of choice, Esther."

"Bella, I can't go back and live with Russell Skunk."

I'd rather die, Esther thought.

"I'm sorry, sweetheart. I just can't keep you anymore, not with the new baby coming. Believe me, I would if I could." A warm long body hug from Bella said she was sincere.

Oh please, Esther thought.

"I uh understand. You've been a ... I mean, good to let me live with you for this long."

Snot bubbles moved down Esther's face heading for her mouth. Liz handed her some Kleenex. Esther blew her brains out into the tissues and, when she was finished, her ears were plugged. Her memory was plugged too.

Oh Gott, where are you Daddy? Mummy? Come and get me and take me to Heaven.

"Esther, I don't know right now where you can go. But Nelson and I have talked about it and we think we should call Melba and ask her. She is ultimately responsible for you. You're not sixteen yet." Esther heard the words, but the interference in her head wouldn't allow her to respond.

She took the words upstairs to her and Liz's bedroom and put them underneath her pillow for the night. That night Liz pushed her single bed beside Esther's like they sometimes did. They hugged one another for as long as they could stay awake, then tossed and turned the rest of the night. They woke up holding hands.

BELLA TRACKED DOWN MELBA THROUGH FRIEDA, and called her over in Dartmouth.

"Mrs. Girling. Here's the deal, I'm putting Esther on a bus to Halifax at the end of the week and you'll let her stay with you until she finishes high school."

"I didn't hear any deal."

"Oh you want the deal? Well the deal is that if you take Esther like I've asked you to, I won't report you to child welfare for abandonment, not just of Esther, but the two little ones still over on the island. Other people have been taking care of Esther for a long time. It won't kill you to look after her until she finishes high school."

"Bella, ah, Mrs. Walker, you don't understand, Esther hates my guts."

"I can't do anything about that ... but quite frankly I understand."

THE LAST EIGHTEEN MONTHS WITH LIZ and her family would slide from Esther's memory like hot wax dripping off a candle, into forgotten pools for thirty years, until the next time Esther saw Liz on a local television station in Calgary.

She would only remember staring out the bus window at blurred green coniferous nothingness and listening to Karen Carpenter lament how she's leaving on a jet plane. Her voice carried a soft cry to the back of the bus causing salt tears to fall on a Native made fringed leather purse that Liz had given her for a going-away present. It had been Liz's, and now it was marked. Esther cried harder. In thirty years Esther would remember where it came from. For now, she couldn't bear to think about Liz and all the other people she loved that were gone from her life.

CHAPTER 40

Arriving Halifax

"You Esther?"

Esther thought to herself that she must look like an Esther or this peanut of a man approaching her was very intuitive.

"Yes, what's it to you?"

"I'm Cecil. Your mother's out in the car."

Esther stared at Cecil.

"Melba's your mother, isn't she?"

"That's questionable!"

"Better leave that shitless attitude here in the bus station before you step outside or you won't be staying at my place very long. I'm going to tell you right now before we even get to the car, I don't need any more crap. I've got two daughters of my own that have been running around like hellcats all summer. They're grounded to the house right now." Cecil grumbled to the car and got in. "A smart-ass that one, eh Melba?"

"Starting in already, are you Esther?"

"Hello to you too."

Esther looked in the rear view mirror. Cecil was watching her with his slitty pale green eyes. The lids were almost bare of eyelashes. Everything about Cecil was small. Small facial features, small framed body, small teeth and ears. *A small person – perfect for Melba*, Esther thought. *He's so small Melba could put him over her knee and spank him.* The thought caused her to look up and smile in the mirror.

"What's so funny?"

"Nothing. I didn't say anything."

"Well, I better tell you now. You're grounded to the house for the rest of the month. It wouldn't be fair to the other two if you weren't."

"You are meshugganeh!"

"Hey, don't talk to your mother like that."

"Oh, have we already established beyond a reasonable doubt that she is my mother?"

165

"Jeezus, Esther."

"Jeezus nothing, why would I be grounded for a month, I just fucking got here? I haven't done anything"

"Yeah, well let's keep it that way," Cecil stated flatly.

"So Melba, how did you end up here anyway?" Esther asked.

Melba told her that she answered an ad in the newspaper for a housekeeper. Later that night, in bed, Cecil asked Melba: "What's musheggeneh anyway?"

"Something she probably made up."

DRIVING ACROSS THE BRIDGE to Cecil's house in Dartmouth, Esther discovered that Melba hadn't wanted to go into the bus station with her hair in curlers. Esther thought: *Imagine that, Melba, too embarrassed to be seen in the bus station in curlers, but not embarrassed to live with Cecil and two of his kids, sleep in Cecil's bed, and make his meals.* He wore a suit in the daytime; he was a number cruncher. He lived in a 1300-square foot ranch style bungalow.

Cecil's daughters, Doris and Cheryl, shared their bedroom with Esther in the basement. The room was heated with electric heat. One September morning, the three girls woke up, each of them facing a different wall and got dressed for school. Before they left the room, Doris turned the thermostat up to eighty-five degrees Farenheit and said laughing: "Take that blast of heat daddy-o!" She pulled the bedroom door shut on the way out. The three of them headed up the basement stairs.

Esther thought this was the first day of school, but school had commenced a week earlier in Dartmouth. As it turned out, it wasn't Esther's first day at school either. Coffee and cigarettes and house rules and allegiances were on Doris' agenda, not school. The three girls headed for a coffee shop on Blossom Street, and pushed themselves into a red vinyl booth at the back of the restaurant. Doris ordered two coffees, and a hot chocolate for Cheryl.

"You do drink coffee, don't you, Esther?"

"Of course I do, but I prefer tea in the afternoon."

Doris laughed, thinking to herself that this was going to be easier than she had thought.

"Okay, here it is, I want everything straight right up front: you're Melba's kid, but you're living in my dad's house, and sharing my room. So what I say goes, got it?"

"Doris, did someone pee in your corn flakes? It's my room too. Why are you so mean? You know what, you sound like Dad."

Melba's Wash 167

"Cheryl, Cheryl, Cheryl, thank you to the peanut gallery. For one thing, I have to make sure she isn't going to rat on us for playing hooky and smoking and well, you know. Take today for instance. Aren't you supposed to be in school? Never mind, rhetorical question, piglet. But you get my point, don't you? Never mind, another rhetorical question, piglet."

"Doris, where's your mother?" Esther asked.

"She's shacked up with some hoser in Fredericton. She's got our two brothers up there with her. They're young still and can't leave their mother. Ark, ark! Wasn't there a song like that? Son of a bitch, I hate her."

"You coulda been their mother, eh Doris?" Cheryl rubbed her soft, eight-year-old hand along Doris' muscled forearm like she was stroking a cat. Doris was sixteen, and was only hanging around so that she knew Cheryl was all right. That's what Doris said.

"Your mother had a conniption when your friend Liz's mother called."

"Oh really?"

"Melba never mentioned she had a daughter in high school. She swore to my dad you wouldn't stay past Grade Twelve so you better not flunk out!" Doris said.

"How come she doesn't want you, Esther?" Cheryl asked.

"I don't know, must have looked at her the wrong way when I was born or something. The feeling's mutual. I hate her guts."

"I like Melba." Sweet Cheryl still had some of her child's eye of the world.

"Oh yeah, what do you like about her, Cheryl?"

"Uum. Her nail polish?"

Esther thought about that for a second and said: "I never knew her to wear nail polish. She used to wear fish scales. Tell me something, Doris. There's two empty bedrooms upstairs, and two more empty ones in the basement. Why are all three of us in one small bedroom?"

"Smart, Esther, but not clever. To save on the electric heat bill, of course! That and the fact they want the rooms empty in case they get a call from the mental hospital. They just got approved to take in mental patients for big room and board bucks by the government. You're not the first one by any chance, are you?"

"Let me think about that. Maybe I am. I could be. I've been a dog, a toilet, and a television set. Yes, I could easily be a mental patient."

"You are a nut case."

"Yes, I am. And I saw you crank up the heat before we left. What if your father goes down there and finds out?"

"He won't know which one of us did it, will he?" Doris said.

"No, I guess not."

"Exactly right, Esther."

"Doris, how did Melba end up at your house?"

"My dad put an ad in the newspaper for a housekeeper, and here she is!"

"She's a housekeeper, all right.. She sleeps with your father, Doris."

"Zingo!"

"Doris, I'm hungry."

"Of course you are Cheryl. It's lunch time already."

Doris walked over to the long grey Arborite counter and ordered fries and gravy for all three of them. They drank water.

"Thanks, Doris."

"Yes, thank you, Doris."

"Well, kiddies, piglet. Shall we go to school this afternoon, or make a whole bloody day of show and tell?"

"A whole bloody day of it, Doris."

"Don't say bloody, Cheryl."

"You did."

"You can say it when you're sixteen, okay?"

"Okay. I love you, Doris."

"Shut your gob, piglet."

"Doris, who has the plastic fetish at your house?" Esther asked.

"Again, my dad. If he could cut off our arms and legs and use us for floor mats, he would. Instead, he covered all the furniture with those god-awful maroon flowered throws. You can't even tell what's underneath. Actually, I don't remember myself what the couch really looks like. He's strategically placed those clear plastic runners in front of all the furniture. And leading to all tables from all furniture. And to the television from all furniture. And finally from the living room to the foyer, out to the main hall, and down the hall, past the bathroom and bedrooms. A few sticks short of a load, my dad."

"So I guess he doesn't want anybody making bodily contact with the furniture or that old gold shag carpet!"

"ZINGO again! I take it back. Maybe you're not a nut case after all! Listen up ladies and germs, I've decided you're not such a bad head, Esther, so here's the secret of the day. It's good to share, right piglet?"

"Right, Doris," Cheryl said.

Melba's Wash   169

"The key to the buffet is in the cookie jar on the kitchen counter. Oh, hang on sloopies, don't get too excited. There's never any cookies in it, just plastic bags."

"So what's so special in the buffet?" Esther asked.

"Just about everything you can think of: cough syrup, Band-Aids, Q-tips, aspirin, mouthwash, pickles, 'their jams and jellies,' dainty crackers, Cheese Whiz, tuna, peaches, and anything else that comes in a can that's worth eating. For two Band-Aids, tell me Cheryl, is the Spam in the buffet?"

"Nope, it's under the counter next to the sardines and the peanut butter," Cheryl said.

"Oh, you're a smart one. Two Band-Aids for you when we get home."

"Doris, what's the idea of locking up all that stuff? Can't you have any of it?" Esther asked.

"Zingo again."

"So, what if I want a Band-Aid, Doris?"

"You'll have to ask the warden."

"Holy Crap, sounds like fucking jail. Oh, sorry, Cheryl."

"You're catchin' on Esther. Oh, and Esther, watch the milk for lumps, it's the powdered shit. Cheryl calls them 'tumours.'"

"Well, now at least you've given me something to be thankful for."

"Yeah, what's that, Einstein?"

"I'm allergic to white milk."

"Well, la-de-dah-dah-dah. But if I were you, I wouldn't sit up all night waiting for a chocolate cow to be delivered to de front door in the morning, dah-ling!"

ESTHER LOST TWENTY POUNDS THE FIRST MONTH she lived with Melba and Cecil. She wasn't concerned about it at first. She had often thought she'd like to weigh an even hundred pounds. Only she thought she would have had to go on some whacko diet drinking twenty glasses of water and eating grapefruit eight times a day for three weeks. Esther had never entertained the idea she'd ever be staying in a sprawling rancher in Dartmouth, Nova Scotia, living in a basement room with two sort-of stepsisters, and they'd all be hungry.

By late fall, Doris found a job as a carhop at a drive-in restaurant on the main strip. The Skyline had a reputation, not just for the greasiest French fries and onion rings, but for the rough crowd that drove in around midnight after the late movie at the drive-in. They were greasy haired show-offs who would roll down the car window, and roll up their left sleeves showing off their stupid tattoos on their forearms before they ordered. Like it meant something. Like it would change the food and maybe make it taste better.

If you could smile and listen to their mostly filthy, foolish mouths, and laugh like you actually thought their liquored jokes were funny, they left good tips on those trays hanging off the car windows. And once in a while they might turn the car headlights on for service after the carhop had taken away their tray. If this happened, you might get a joint, or a hit of acid, a ride home, or all of the above.

Most people's daughters weren't allowed to go to the Skyline, never mind work there. But for Doris, it was perfect – all the food she could eat during her shift, and she always left the parking lot at night with French fries for Cheryl and Esther. ·

CHAPTER 41

The Prat Family

BY THE END OF NOVEMBER, Esther had met a boy, Alec Prat. Alec was from a Roman Catholic family of five kids, and had been named after his great-uncle who was Monsignor Alec. He could actually trace his heritage back to England and his family had their own coat of arms; for what purpose she didn't know, but there was something impressive about this to her. Alec was related to many priests, bishops, and nuns. Well, really, one priest, one bishop, and one nun. In any case, there were a hell of a lot of religious people.

Esther fell in love with Alec's mother first, Mrs. Sally Prat. Alec was the oldest boy; there were four brothers younger than him. Esther would make that a half dozen, and be a daughter for Mrs. Prat. Mrs. Prat cooked three times a day; she cleaned up the dishes three times a day; she did laundry and ironed; she swept floors; she made peanut butter and banana sandwiches for the kids to take to school for lunch every day; and she made a fresh pot of tea for anyone who stopped by. She loved when people came by, probably because she could allow herself to rest and have a cup of that tea herself.

She never saw a paycheque of any kind; she did, however, always have a smile on her face. The mat outside the Prat home said welcome in six different languages, and even the dust made you feel at home when you settled into their living room. But it was the smells, the smell of splattered oil from popcorn the night before, or fat burning on the element from bacon cooking after church on Sunday morning, or the sweetness of apple pie, or warm pineapple upside-down cake, or the comforting smell of yeast from homemade bread, that lured you to the breakfast nook in the kitchen where they sat every night like spokes of a wheel, held together by the strength of not only God, but the whole family, and generations that had come before. Mr. Prat said grace before each meal, and either out of well practised habit, or hunger, so quickly, at first the only recognizable words Esther understood were the last ones: "inthenameoftheFatherandtheSonandtheHolyGhostAmen."

171

Alec had told his mother how they locked up food over at Esther's, and that was why her clothes had begun to hang on her as if they were borrowed from someone two sizes bigger than she was. Soon Esther went home with Alec every day after school where she now had her own seat at suppertime around the breakfast nook, where she gave up the fresh mouth Mummy said she had, stopped swearing, and learned to say grace when her turn came.

One Saturday Mr. Prat asked Alec and Esther to go with him and the boys to get a Christmas tree. Mr. Prat was nice, and Esther trusted him. This was a new experience for her. Mrs. Prat packed sandwiches and cookies and thermoses filled with hot chocolate and marshmallows for everyone. It was exciting, and Esther discovered it was their family ritual.

She sat in the front of the Chevy truck with two of the little ones; Alec and his other brothers sat in the back. It was an hour drive to Spruce River Road where they turned off the highway for about ten minutes. Then they saw cars and trucks everywhere! The snow was so deep that they didn't walk into the woods very far, and spent a lot of time pulling each other out of snow sinkholes. Sometimes their boots were left in their footprints and Mr. Prat would come and help dig them out. Esther was wearing an old pair of Alec's boots that were too big, so she was stuck a lot! Melba wouldn't buy her winter boots. She said Esther had to work for them. She did work, but at fifty cents an hour, it would be spring before she saved enough money to buy boots.

Her feet were cold and her socks were wet, but she didn't care because she was having too much fun.

Mr. Prat called all of them over to the spot where he was standing.

"How about this one, kids? Mother would sure be pleased to have a blue spruce this year."

"It's quite tall," Esther said.

He chuckled and assured her that by the time he and Alec trimmed the top and bottom, it would be just right.

Mr. Prat asked: "What about you little ones, what do you say?"

"I'm cold."

"My feet are wet."

"Can we have the hot chocolate soon?"

Esther smiled at this big man up to his knees in snow and said: "Yes, it's perfect."

He let Alec cut the tree down so he could show off, Esther thought, *but he really was a good woodsman.* They all turned around, grabbed a branch and started walking back to the road. Yes, they had to stop three times to pull someone out of the snow, but eventually made it back to the truck to have their lunch and hot chocolate.

Dear God thank you for a fun day, Esther thought.

By Christmas, Esther had fallen in love with Alec. At least she thought she was in love. She said the words. Alec said the words. They are only words, after all. Those three words are the easiest words in the English language to slide off one's tongue.

Maybe what they really meant is that they could now have sex. Alec loved Esther as much or perhaps more than any eighteen-year-old boy; she was his first love, and the Prats had all but officially adopted Esther. She didn't think about birth control. Back then you had to have your parents' permission to take birth control pills, and Esther didn't want to have anything to do with Melba. She thought they'd only had sex two, maybe three times. It wasn't even fun. She had thought sex was supposed to be fun, although she didn't know where she got that idea. It seemed to make Alec happy for weeks; it made Esther sore.

ESTHER STOPPED HAVING HER PERIOD and found herself a doctor who confirmed she was pregnant.

Shy gentle Alec, his head always bent a tiny bit forward, would lift it up dramatically to throw his long brown bangs to the side, and out of his soft pale brown eyes. Esther told him right away about the baby and he was happy, really happy. "Then we'll just get married earlier than we planned." They told his parents that same night. They were just as excited.

Around the kitchen nook, Mr. and Mrs. Prat planned just about everything for the wedding except the flowers. They would get married at their church and have the reception at their house, with a few friends, a lot of relatives, and lots of party sandwiches.

Before school finished for the year, Esther stood facing the mirror wearing just bikini underwear, and turned to each side, looking for a swollen profile.

"Does my stomach look any bigger, Cheryl?"

"No. You asked me that this morning."

"I know, but I had a big supper at Alec's tonight."

"Sorry, looks the same to me."

"The book the doctor gave me says the baby is this big." She holds her fingers out to show Cheryl.

"Really? But where is it?"

Esther picked up her summer pink lipstick from the dresser and drew the outline of a little baby on her belly.

"Here, Cheryl."

"Hey, cool. Can we show Doris when she comes home?"

"Sure!"

BY MAY ESTHER WAS THREE MONTHS PREGNANT. One Wednesday morning Esther had phys. ed. next class but decided to go home. She felt nauseous. She lay in bed downstairs for an hour and it was past lunchtime when she walked up the basement stairs into the kitchen. Melba found her squatting in front of the fridge looking for something to eat.

"Soda crackers and weak tea used to help me."

"You scared the shit out of me, Melba. Well, so you know, you guessed I suppose, saves me telling you anyway."

"What're you going to do, Esther? You know you can't stay here once you start to show. Cecil won't have you influencing the girls."

"Now there's a laugh if I ever heard one."

"What do you mean by that?"

"I mean, do you think I got pregnant by studying biology down in our bedroom?"

"Watch your tone of voice, missy."

"Oh for shit's sake, it was Doris who showed me how to sneak out of the house at night."

"What're you talking about?"

"I'm talking about coming upstairs in the evening and having a bath and fluff and powder and going downstairs and getting dressed again and climbing out the window above the dryer."

"You sneaky little bitch."

"Takes one to know one eh? Well, don't worry, I'll be leaving soon. I'm getting married."

"You're only seventeen, that's not old enough to get married. You need *my* permission. What if I don't give it to you?"

"You're just priceless. I don't fucking care about anyone's permission. If I don't have your so-called permission we'll simply get married in Calgary after my eighteenth birthday."

"Calgary?"

"Yes Calgary, we're moving in August. Alec's been accepted into an engineering program at the University of Calgary."

"Why would he have applied in Calgary instead of Dalhousie?"

"To get out of the Maritimes for one thing. He applied to several colleges and universities. Calgary's the farthest one from here, and there's lots of jobs out west."

"How're you two figuring on supporting yourselves and a baby in Calgary?"

"Since when do you care anyway? But for the record, Mr. Prat is giving us his old Pontiac to drive out there and Alec is approved for a Canada Student Loan, and we'll both find part-time jobs. Lots of people do it. So are you going to sign the papers?"

Melba bent over the kitchen table and laid her Melba Girling down in blue ballpoint ink above the black type that read "parental consent." As she pushed the pen in loops to the right, she said: "Don't forget, I'm doing this for you, you know."

MELBA INSISTED THAT CECIL WALK ESTHER down the aisle at her wedding. Cecil, of all the people on her do-not-like list. Melba said it would be proper. Melba wasn't married to Cecil, so how could she talk about what's proper? The whole conversation made Esther laugh.

She could hear Melba's voice saying: "I'm doing this for you, you know" when she told Melba they set the date for the wedding on the fourteenth of July, and then got married one week earlier. It seemed the only way Esther could assure herself that Melba wouldn't show up. She didn't want her or Cecil anywhere near St. Agnes Church or Mr. and Mrs. Prat.

The night before the wedding Esther climbed out the window above the dryer as usual. She had already packed a few things and arranged that she would get them from Doris a few days later. Doris bear-hugged her before she climbed onto the dryer, and Cheryl blew a kiss for luck as Esther crawled out the window. She caught it: "Thanks, sweetie."

Alec and Esther spent the night in adjacent rooms at the Prats' home. A thin wall of plaster board separated her sleeping bag from his bed. They'd never made love in a bed. That would come the following night – this is what Esther was thinking. Alec, on the other hand, on the other side of the wall, was culling through his trunk, remembering the long hours he spent gluing and fitting together the thousands of plastic pieces that made the Cutty Sark clipper he caressingly wiped dust from with his fingertips. He could have been dusting nineteen years of growing up in the Prat house from his now, much larger shoulders.

Part VII

CHAPTER 42

Glass Walls

FIVE MONTHS LATER, the Prats got news from Calgary of the birth of their first grandchild, a boy, David Prat. Mr. Prat didn't say mazel tov, he said: "Holy blue cripes, a fourth generation Prat boy." He danced Mrs. Prat around the kitchen until she made him stop. "That's enough, Mr. Prat."

"Oh, I almost forgot to tell you. Alec said they bought a television with the money you gave him. Alec loves his television."

Esther always wondered about David being christened. She always thought of him as her little Jewish boy, but that could never be because he was a descendant of Catholics, including his father. In her mind, Esther lived between a Christian and Jewish upbringing. She lived this duality her whole life.

Finally Alec set a date with a priest, and each chose their closest friends as godparents. The grandparents back on the east coast were disappointed they couldn't be present, and Esther was furious that their extra money bought a damned TV. He didn't know he had married one, and a flush. He didn't know her story and perhaps he never would. Esther was not ready to tell him her own secrets and lies.

"Great! I'm driving over to my dad's place to tell him the news," Mr. Prat said. "This is way too big to put into the telephone receiver, Mother."

"Don't you two get into the sauce," Mrs. Prat said. "It's barely noon."

"Wouldn't think of it, Mother!"

Alec and Esther's third-floor apartment in Calgary was small, and warmed softly with hot water heating. The sun shone during the day through the kitchen window; the blue gingham curtains she sewed were never drawn.

In the bathroom, she turned on the taps and filled the deep, old-fashioned claw-foot tub. David and Esther were having a bath. She lay back and he faced her, lying belly down, belly to belly, against his mother just like he used to before he was born. But now he was on the outside, and didn't see that he lay on a raw-looking vertical incision that still looked like

178

Melba's Wash

a zipper along the seam that Dr. Chan had opened and lifted him from. Esther felt the tickling, itchy, tightening, sensation of healing along the line from David's birth and wondered if he could feel it too. One day she'd show him where he came from.

Esther covered David's small fuzzy back and tiny white tush with a face cloth. As she poured water over the cloth to warm him, David arched his body, head and legs rose, and his arms flapped like a baby seal. He floated along his mother's chest and docked in between her breasts. She kissed the top of his bald head.

Esther and Alec lived on his student loan, and on nights and weekends, they worked opposite shifts at a pizza restaurant. Alec cooked and Esther waited tables. On nice days Esther and David went for walks to the playground while Alec was at school.

It didn't take long for the tiny apartment to fill with a larger crib and baby toys and a playpen. Esther and Alec searched for a bigger place to live. They found one in a newer three-storey apartment building with lots of babies who lived on the same floor. Often, either in the morning or afternoon before nap time, mothers opened their apartment doors and let four little boys play, crawl, toddle or run the length of the hallway chasing balls or big plastic trucks, or each other. The mothers took turns watching them.

Esther and Alec stayed there until they had saved a down payment for a house of their own. They found that house out in the country. Three years later, David's baby sister was born. She was named Rachel, and had a full head of hair, and a tiny fuzzy body. They had a rich man's family – a boy and a girl.

Esther was unhappy. How many times would she have to move? How much money would she have to spend replicating her childhood home? She was a grown woman and still wanted her mummy and daddy. She went for counselling and that didn't help. She went to a psychiatrist and he gave her anti-depressants, and anti-anxiety medication. This road would spread before her for most of her life. No one understood her, especially Alec. She was happy with bagels and lox and cream cheese, and serving up childhood recipes from her Jewish cookbook *A Treasure For My Daughter*.

When David started school, they moved back to the city so he wouldn't have to take a school bus. They thought he was just too young for that.

Esther and Rachel walked David to school, and this worked for a few years until Esther found a newer, quieter place to live on the other side of the city and talked Alec into another move into a newer house with nice neighbours with a swimming pool. They seemed happy there.

Esther worked as a secretary at a community college; Alec worked long hours for an international engineering firm. David went to cubs and both children took swimming and skating lessons. Esther was busy: up at 5:30 making lunches; taking the kids to babysitters, working all day, picking kids up at the end of the day, and going home to make supper for the family; squeezing in homework, laundry, grocery shopping, and the kid's activities. Oy vey.

When David was seven, Alec was promoted and given his first field project, in Vancouver. He worked two weeks out and four days home for a couple of years. Esther found it exhausting taking care of the children and the house while working full time. When Alec came home one weekend, Esther had found another place to live.

A condo, with a dishwasher, caretakers to look after all the yards, do all the shovelling, and best of all it came with a fitness centre – an Olympic pool and squash courts. Esther had been on a quest for the perfect place to live. She should have known that perfect didn't exist, and neither did her childhood home. Alec was furious; he just couldn't make her happy. He swore he wouldn't move again, but that changed as the kids got older and they all needed storage for their bicycles, skis, and tools, and Esther was still bitching that she wanted a dining room.

By the time the children were in their early teens, Esther still wanted a dining room and Alec decided they wanted a garage. So they moved again. They bought another house that appeared to have everything they both wanted. David played football and baseball. Rachel took modelling and piano lessons, and also played baseball. Many nights they ate dinner at ten o'clock at night. They were all busy. Esther was never content, and she knew Alec wasn't either. He didn't know she was a television and a toilet and a bathroom. He knew from nothing except he needed his laundry done and wanted sex.

ALEC LOVED HIS JOB WORKING IN THE FIELD. He also worked in Toronto, the Northwest Territory, and even had a stint in Halifax close to his parents. The summer he was there, Esther took all her vacation time so she and the children could fly back to visit with her in-laws, and see Alec.

Between projects Alec came home and worked at the head office. Esther wanted to move the family with him to each new city, but Alec made more money being on his own and collecting a "living out" allowance that allowed Esther to shop, have nice vehicles, and go for family ski trips in Banff and Lake Louise in the wintertime, and Disneyland in the summer.

Each time Alec left for work on a Sunday, Esther felt abandoned. When he started working in the Northwest Territory and only came home once a month, she became depressed and took leave from work. She started taking anti-depressants and anti-anxiety medication to help get her through her days. She felt like this for more than fifteen years. He didn't know how deeply she was hurt by the loss of her Daddy and Flora and Mummy's poodle Gigi and the loss of her best friend Liz, and her parents. He didn't know she had lived with them. Their story was mostly Esther's story, one she had only partially told her psychologist.

THEIR STORY MOVED AS QUICKLY AS THE YEARS, until Esther wanted Alec to come back to Calgary and find an office job instead of working in the field. Esther was actually surprised that Alec wanted a divorce, and what Alec wanted was not negotiable. She didn't know how unhappy Alec was. Now Esther really was abandoned. Again. She fell deeper into depression, said to herself, *Gott in Heaven, I'm coming home*, and swallowed all her medication.

David found her in her study and called an ambulance. Rachel called her father and he flew home. Esther spent a few days outside the nurse's station locked inside a glass room. She didn't realize why. She knocked on the glass, and pounded on the glass wanting her own pyjamas, her own pillow, and a pencil and paper to write on. She MUST have a pencil and paper. She needed to write this story. She felt like she was going crazy. No one would listen to her. If they would just give her a pencil and paper then she would stop yelling and pounding on the glass. But they wouldn't. So she screamed. And it was nighttime, and finally nurses came into the room. Three of them. And they told her she had to calm down because she was keeping people awake. They held her down gently and gave her a shot. They explained to her that they could not give her the things she asked for because they didn't want her to hurt herself. Esther laughed and yelled: "I've been hurting my whole life!" The nurses left knowing that Esther would soon be sleeping.

She started in again in the morning. A new shift of nurses were on, but they were ready for her. She now had "meds" and the nurse watched that she swallowed round white pills four times a day. On the third day she was moved to a regular room on the psychiatric ward. Esther saw a psychiatrist in his office on the same floor. He prescribed a new anti-depressant along with more anti-anxiety medication.

Alec went to see Esther. Her face was swollen from crying. His face was taut and hard. He had no time for this and gave her her own pillow, some pyjamas, and a scribbler. He told her if she wanted to write, she had to get a pencil from the nurse at the front desk. Esther told him to go to hell. He left for good, back to his routine.

Esther went to the nurses' station and asked for a pencil and a cigarette and a lighter, then went outside into a small fenced courtyard to have a smoke. She felt better. She talked to another patient and asked what she had to do to get out of there. Tammy, about Esther's age, told her: "Don't stay in your room all the time. Come out and interact with the others. Eat all your meals. Eat your snacks. Write, colour, read, do anything so they see you're focusing on things other than yourself, and, shower and get dressed before you go to see your psychiatrist in the mornings. That's a biggie. You've got to convince him you're not suicidal. Be as alert as you can be and be ready to go home when he decides you can go."

Esther returned the lighter to the desk.

It was eight days before Esther was discharged. She left with more pre-scriptions than she had before, and was set up for therapy at the hospi-tal twice a week for two months. Esther went for private therapy with a psychologist, for many years, where she learned the word No. This, she believed, led to her divorce.

She was on a drug journey that would overtake her, but didn't realize this yet. Her concentration was minimal and she had a difficult time hold-ing her thoughts together. She didn't remember what she did from one day to the next. She didn't journal anymore. She ate too much, slept too much, took pills, and put on weight. She was lost somewhere inside her mind and didn't wake up for ten years when suddenly she started investigating the side effects of long term use of the drugs she was taking and decided to cut back on all her medication. She didn't tell her doctor that she was doing this; she continued to get refills on her prescriptions and hoarded away the pills. She was addicted to them, and simply couldn't be without a backup supply, just in case. Just in case of what, she didn't know yet.

Esther continued to move around from apartment to apartment, to British Columbia and back to Calgary, then finally seemed to settle in High River, Alberta where Rachel was living, just thirty minutes south of Calgary. She lived in the one apartment for two years, and was beginning to feel pretty good after spending eighteen months cutting back on her medica-tion. She made angel food cake with seven minute frosting for Rachel's

Melba's Wash 183

birthday and could actually follow the recipe. Esther delighted in this small effort, but huge accomplishment. Over these ten years she had forgotten how to cook even simple things.

Without a sponsor, she had given up trying to gain acceptance at the synagogue, so she went to church and yoga and spent time with her daughter and grandson.

Until the flood.

Part VIII

CHAPTER 43

High River Flood

ESTHER WENT TO BED a bit anxious on June 19, 2013. She had a coun-selling session at 9 a.m. the next morning. Counselling, counselling, counselling, for extreme anxiety and depression. Years ago she threw out most of her cache of medication, and only had a small amount of extra now. She thought: *When will it ever be over? Will I ever feel well again? Maybe when I'm dead.* Esther wouldn't tell her this. She hadn't met this woman yet so she wasn't expecting much from the first visit. She took a Valium before bed in the hope that she would sleep. It was raining too hard outside for the sounds to be soothing.

It was pouring again in the morning. Once Esther left the street she lived on and drove onto Central Avenue, she saw water running through the streets downtown, exactly where she needed to go. She could see the building just across the railroad tracks, but couldn't drive there. Police cars, with their lights flashing, blocked the track crossing. She was lucky enough to be able to do a U-turn, right in front of them, and went home.

Esther drove into her parking spot at the back of the apartment building where she lived. She went in and called several times to cancel her appoint-ment, but there was no answer. She thought about all the water downtown and decided there must have been a broken water main.

By 11 a.m., there was no cell phone reception and no power. She went through the apartment collecting candles and getting ready for the night just in case. She had a queer feeling that if there was no cell phone service, something else must be wrong and checked her medications, anti-depres-sants and Valium, to be sure she had enough. Enough for what? She didn't know, but someone addicted to Valium has to know where her next pill is.

Her windows and balcony faced the back alley and the parking lot, and oh my dear God, the water had started to rush down the alley. She watched a large truck loaded with people in the back; they seemed to be holding bags and packsacks and were tossed about as they drove away. Esther felt sorry for them because it was still pouring rain.

At 5:30 p.m. she saw the bizarre scene of a front-end loader bouncing down the alley with the bucket full of people! She also noticed the water had risen half way up the tires on her car. Esther was completely befuddled. The alley was at a higher elevation than the street in front. She left her apartment and walked down a flight of stairs to look out the front door. She started to hyperventilate watching the muddy water pull cars down the street. They all seemed to follow the same path, and one by one the cars smashed into one another against two trees in a neighbour's front yard near the end of the block.

She went back upstairs and tried her cell phone again, still hoping she could find her daughter, son-in-law and grandson. She tried again several times through the evening.

Esther obviously wasn't going anywhere so she put on her pyjamas and housecoat. She lit a candle in the bathroom, which had no window, and one on the stove that seemed like a safe place for now. Her cat never jumped on the counters. She opened a can of Alphagetti and ate it cold out of the can. Not too bad. Esther read for a short time, tried her daughter again, and took another Valium.

It was cloudy and pouring rain, the light was quickly waning. Flashlight in hand, she went downstairs again about 7:30 p.m. and shone the light down into the basement. There was at least a foot of water, but there weren't any more cars floating by. There were Sea-Doos! They were driving up and down the street. One spotted her standing in the doorway and turned around, dipping and splashing right up to the top step into the building. The fellow made hand motions to open the security door. Esther stuck her head out. By then, there were two men and two Sea-Doos.

"Go grab a bag and come with us."

"I'm fine. I'm on the second floor," she told one of them.

"Here, I've got a lifejacket for you, just come out and get on behind me."

Seconds passed and she thought: *I'm in my pyjamas, and there are candles burning in the house.* She decides to tell him this.

"And I need my medication. And I have a cat. Do I have to go?"

"Complete evacuation isn't mandatory yet, but it will be by morning."

"No! I'm not going. Besides, I'm terrified of those machines you're on."

"Then I need your name, Ma'am."

Esther told him, and they sped off. She didn't have time to ask them what was going on. But one of them did say that the street was eight feet deep with water. Her apartment building had become an island.

Esther went upstairs. She'd be all right. She lived on the second floor, for Heaven's sake. There was no way the water would come up that high. She wanted to check the apartments on the rest of the second floor, and the third floor, but it was too dark in the stairwells. Esther assumed that everyone was still upstairs. She just couldn't figure it out; there were still cars down in the parking lot. Then she thought about the big truck and the front-end loader she saw this morning; maybe those people were from her building.

Nervously Esther went back into her apartment, turned the deadbolt, and put the safety chain on. Then it suddenly hit her: If there was no electricity, the security locks on the front door of the building wouldn't be working. She hauled a kitchen chair and put it under the doorknob like she'd seen in movies, took two more Valium and went to bed.

It seemed nothing was going to knock her out, so she watched searchlights and red flashing lights pass her window, reflecting on the walls all night. Later she would learn that helicopters were out all night searching for people. Some were rescued from rooftops of houses and garages.

Esther finally achieved a few hours sleep once daylight came. She woke up to sounds of a commotion in the hallway. It was her neighbour, Len. She quickly got dressed, dismantled the barricade at the door, and hurried out into the hall.

"Hello! I thought I was the only person left in the building."

Len said: "You probably are. What are you still doing here, Esther? They evacuated yesterday."

"Well, how did the tenants know?"

"Search and Rescue came about 4 a.m. and announced on their megaphones a State of Emergency, and for everyone to leave the building before they couldn't get out."

She let out a soft chuckle. "4 a.m.? I wear ear plugs and I took a sleeping pill last night." She thought sleeping pill sounded better than Valium, but who cared now?

Len and his girlfriend had come back in his 4x4 truck to get some clothes and shaving gear.

"You'd better get ready to leave, Esther. The whole town is under an evacuation order. The military has moved in and all roads in and out of High River are either flooded or closed so looters can't come into the town."

Esther needed coffee and her medication. She really needed them. Did she say that out loud? She didn't know how long she was packing for, so she packed for two days. She took all her medication, two pairs of panties, socks, and her goose down pillow. She stuffed them into a backpack, and spent the rest of the time putting bowls of water and food and more litter out for Jazzi, her cat. She didn't realize until later that she forgot the pyjamas she had just taken off, and all her toiletries.

Esther kissed Jazzi and told him to be good and Mummy would be home soon. She thought she'd be home soon. She locked the apartment door behind her. Len was waiting.

"I don't know if my car will start. There was a lot of water in the parking lot last night."

"It doesn't matter," he said. "If it doesn't start, we'll go in my truck."

As they were walking out, Esther asked Len where they were going.

"I've been thinking about that. Maybe the fire station would be good. They'll know what's going on. Esther, I took a zigzag way here on the high spots, so follow me and don't worry, I'll get you there."

"Len, it started!"

"Okay, let's go."

What a ride, they went through alleys and up on lawns in between flooded streets, but they did make it to the fire hall. Esther thanked him and he waved, driving off before someone had time to ask him where he was going.

She sat in the fire station parking lot and smoked a cigarette. A handsome young fireman opened her car door and extended a hand for Esther to get out. She felt like she was in a movie.

"What about my car?"

"I'll find a place to park it and get the keys back to you in a little while," he said.

"Okay, thanks."

"You'll be here for a while; the bus isn't leaving until sometime after lunch."

"The bus to where? What about my cat?" she shouted.

"Esther, is it?" he asked.

She nodded.

"You'll be briefed inside, Esther. Don't worry, you'll be fine."

A nurse came up to Esther and took her arm. They went into the station to an area that was set up as a triage station. She wasn't rushed, but Esther felt like she was on fast-forward in her own movie. Her pulse was racing and she was hyperventilating.

"I need a Valium!"

"I see. What other medication do you need to take this morning?"

"My anti-depressant."

"Do you have your medication with you, Esther?"

Esther found her pills in her backpack and the nurse brought her two small cone shaped paper cups of water.

"Not very classy, eh Esther! Red Cross is delivering supplies and food and cases of water any time now."

"When can I go home?"

"We don't have that information yet, dear. We'll update you if there is any news."

"Do you have cell phone service?"

"Sorry sweetie, all cell phone use has been restricted by the carriers for emergency channels' use only."

Esther could only pray that her family was somewhere safe. She kept praying while the nurse took her temperature and blood pressure and then took her to another section of the fire station. She offered Esther a blanket and a soft drink; she took both.

A Red Cross van showed up and firemen unloaded dozens of cases of water and many boxes. Esther hadn't really thought about all the people working there. Dear Lord, they had probably been here since yesterday. She watched them fill a long table with cups, coffee and tea, water, salads, sandwiches, fruit, juice and desserts. Hamburgers and hot dogs went straight to waiting barbeques. It wasn't long before everyone filled their paper plates.

Along with the food came news that all the rain they had been having caused excessive and premature run-off from the Rocky Mountains. Dams and levies had been compromised and the Highwood River had flooded 90 percent of the town of High River. A total evacuation of 32,000 people was still underway. Police and Canadian Armed Forces were going door to door looking for people still in their homes. Many people south of the city were also being evacuated. Farmers' houses sat in fields of water, and secondary roads near the Sheep and Highwood Rivers were flooded, as was the Trans-Canada Highway south to Lethbridge. This was very bad. Esther took another Valium.

The bus arrived. Esther was extremely anxious about where she was going and for how long. With half the bus full, they left for the small town of Vulcan. A town east of High River, where there's a *Star Trek* museum. The drive was about an hour, an hour to pray for her daughter Rachel, her husband Jeff, and her only grandchild Sean, who was five. She also prayed there would be cell phone service in Vulcan.

They arrived at the Vulcan community centre where volunteers were friendly and efficient, filling out long forms: name, address, age, next of kin, health concerns, phone numbers, medication requirements, drug allergies, food allergies, pets at home. Once they had arrived, they had to be accounted for. And Esther, continually interrupting asking the same questions about cell service, how could she reach her daughter, how long would they be there, and what about her cat in the apartment?

Esther was tired.

Then people on medication were channelled to the side where they registered their medication requirements with a local pharmacist who would no doubt be up half the night filling prescriptions urgent for people with heart conditions and other serious illnesses. Everyone would get a months supply by 9 a.m. Then they were escorted to the gymnasium, which was a sight right out of a disaster movie – their own.

There were hundreds of red, Red Cross cots, each with a red and white blanket folded neatly on the end. It was a sea of red. Along two walls were piles of clothes on the floor or tables. Signs above them read men, women, children, footwear, pillows, and extra blankets. Tables were filled with every toiletry from disposable razors to diaper cream. The volume of donations new and used was astounding. Esther was shocked at the organization of what she saw in such a short time. The realization was setting in; they were going to be there for a while. She put her backpack on a cot against the far wall and went outside for a cigarette. No, two cigarettes. She exchanged stories with other smokers and found out that the food was delicious. Who would've thunk!

Twenty Hutterite colonies donated food from their stocks and were working sixteen-hour days cooking, cleaning, and organizing at just two of the many shelters. The women were so kind and caring; faces of all ages always had a smile. It had taken just one phone call for the cooking and feeding of 700 people in these two shelters to begin. *God Bless all these people caring for so many strangers*, Esther thought.

That night the overhead lights were turned off, and dimmer lights throughout the room came on. This helped relax Esther. It was 9 p.m. Parents wiped hands and faces of the children, put them in pyjamas, and lay down on the floor with them on top of piles of sleeping bags. Esther didn't hear a child cry. Exhaustion overcame the room of a few hundred strangers, and they slept.

In the morning Esther stood in the line-up for her medication. After lunch she went outside for her cigarette and once more checked her phone. She couldn't believe it – she had a message from Rachel who was just leaving the shelter in Nanton, a town a half hour south of High River. She was so happy to know they were all right. They had been trying to find her too. Because of the registration when Esther arrived, they were able to. *Thank you, God.* They were safe, and on their way to pick her up! Esther sucked back as many cigarettes as she could because that would be the end of her smoking for a while; she didn't smoke around her grandson. Esther checked out at the registration table; the women were very happy for her.

Esther saw their truck pull up in front of the centre and Rachel jumped out and ran to her with tears pouring down her face. She blubbered, and they hugged as if they'd been apart for months.

"I was afraid you were one of the missing women, Mom."

"And I was afraid for all of you."

Two women and a man were killed the day of the flood. Two days without cell service had let their minds wander to the worst possible scenarios.

Rachel apologized that Esther couldn't stay where they were staying, but had arranged for her to stay with her sister-in-law Sharon and her family in Calgary, which was an hour north of High River.

Rachel, Jeff, Sean, and even their Siamese cat had been rescued by boat. Then that boat broke down, and they all had to transfer to another boat. Like Esther, they were taken to a shelter in Nanton, but stayed only one night because it was too busy and crowded for Sean to settle down.

No one was allowed back into High River for thirty-nine days. The R.C.M.P. and the military barricaded and patrolled all entrances.

Esther didn't realize yet that she was homeless.

Now, safe in the city of Calgary, every day she telephoned animal rescue numbers, all of them were too busy to rescue Jazzi. Finally on the ninth day Esther connected with a Town of High River employee who happily got a cage and went to her apartment and rescued Jazzi who was pretty confused and scared, but happy to be picked up. Esther knew she had locked her apartment, but the military had in fact checked every door looking for people to rescue, and had left the doors unlocked when they left. Jazzi was taken by van to be boarded at no charge, in Cayley, another small town about an hour south of High River, at Cyndi's Pet Palace. Oh, Esther hoped he was all right. She'd seen cat crates stacked high against walls in the newspaper. She

Melba's Wash

wished she could go and see him but her car was somewhere in High River and she couldn't get back into the town to get it.

Esther stayed with Rachel's sister-in-law for about three weeks, and then another sister-in-law, a bit more than two weeks. She stayed until the highway barricades came down and the military left, and she could finally go home.

Esther's niece drove her out to get her car, which was in a car lot next to the fire station, and miraculously it started. Later, it would be written off by the insurance company; the water had been too deep inside the car. But in the meantime, they drove out and picked up Jazzi. He was a bit matted, a bit thinner, a bit skittish, but he had survived.

CHAPTER 44

Squatting

D AVID HAD FLOWN HOME FROM WORKING IN HAITI, to help wherever he could. He had been staying with friends in north Calgary. Esther called him and told him she had just picked Jazzi up from the shelter and was going home. She hadn't seen David in eleven months, and it was a wonderful reunion.

David moved in with her that very day. He slept on the couch, and Esther had her bed. For the first two weeks there was no electricity, but the toilet worked so they were in business. Esther's car hadn't been towed away yet, so he volunteered, always with a smile, to make a Tim Hortons run every morning for coffees and bagels. Tim's was one of the few stores open in High River.

There were Salvation Army trailers set up in a big muddy parking lot not far away. One of them served a big lunch between 11 a.m. and 2 in the afternoon on weekdays. But there were trailers and tents with clothes and food as well, so they picked up canned foods like stew and soup and Alphagetti and beans that didn't need heating because there was still no electricity in the apartment building. There was a strict drinking water ban so David schlepped cases of water up the apartment stairs for them. They showered at Rachel's as soon as they got their new hot water tank installed. Eventually, electricity came on in the apartment, but all the fridges from the apartment building, and beds and televisions and couches and chairs and freezers from surrounding houses, were out on the street waiting to be taken to the landfill. David and Esther had a welcome diversion when the cable and internet service was restored. Such a small thing, but it sure made them happy. Now they were three steps up from tenting!

Esther loved spending all this time with David, but in her mind she was always worrying where she was going to live. Her income was dwindling and the rent had just risen to $1,000 a month. She had been looking for some place cheaper before the flood. But now, like so many other High River residents, there was simply no place to go.

The town brought in ATCO trailers and made a makeshift tin city, but these were only for families. University campuses in the province sheltered people because it was summer, but no pets were allowed there.

Parts of Calgary were also flooded along the Bow River, so there were many displaced people there as well. What was available to rent was way out of Esther's price range.

One night Esther's sister Liona called to see if they were all right. She told her Frieda had just moved from mainland New Brunswick back to Grand Manan. She also said the apartment beside her was for rent for $500 a month, and wondered if Esther might consider moving home. That was half the rent she paid in High River! Esther had to consider it.

Esther talked to her landlord and was told it could be six months to a year before all the repairs to the building were done, and that as repairs were done in the basement, like new boilers and electrical, the restoration and renovation crews would be moving to the second floor. All the floors had been damaged by rescue teams searching for occupants. Esther was welcome to stay a bit longer, but the building really was not healthy to live in. She had to make a decision; they couldn't keep squatting in the apartment!

Esther's counselling appointment on June 20th had been to help her sort out her accommodations, and deal with the anxiety of facing another move. She didn't want to move. Now Esther was left to her own decision making, which hadn't turned out well in the past. Since Alec and Esther divorced twelve years ago, she'd lived in four different apartments in Calgary, in British Columbia, and finally High River, where she had seemed to be settling down to stay. But now what should she do? She didn't trust herself.

Esther talked it over with Rachel and David; they just wanted her to be happy. Did she imagine some encouragement to move where the rent was much cheaper? Rachel said she would fly her back to see them once a year, then the next year she and Sean would visit her. David wasn't working yet so he had time to drive her to New Brunswick in a U-Haul truck.

They just had no idea how deep and far back Esther's losses began. They began in the womb: her mother, father, her other mother, and their father. Yes, Esther should have been able to cope with these, but she'd never gotten over any of them. There was something wrong with her. She couldn't be fixed.

Esther decided to move east; she didn't know what else to do. She phoned U-Haul, picked a date, and David agreed to drive her and Jazzi across the country to the little island in the Bay of Fundy where she was born, the place she said she'd never return to when she was fourteen. But as

Liona said: "Where else can you walk the beaches, and watch sunrise and sunsets that are on postcards and pay $500 a month rent?" So okay, Esther decided she would try it for a year.

CHAPTER 45

Grand Manan Island

THE DRIVE WAS MORE THAN 5,000 KILOMETRES. Jazzi did pretty well; he cried for an hour or so in the mornings, then settled down in his carrier for the rest of the day. Esther was so exhausted when they pulled over each night, she slept well even though the beds weren't comfortable.

They arrived at the ferry terminal in Black's Harbour, New Brunswick, on the seventh day and caught the next available ferry to Grand Manan. About and hour and a half later they unloaded the truck and put the furniture back together. They went to bed exhausted and Esther woke up with a scream in the middle of the night. The head of her IKEA bed had fallen down. Her own head was practically on the floor and her feet were raised in the air.

"David! David! I can't get up. I can't see."

In his sleepiness he answered, "Turn the light on."

She laughed and hollered: "I can't. The bed fell down and I can't get up."

Finally he woke up enough to come from the couch to the bedroom and turn the light on. Esther saw his goofy, middle of the night smile.

"What the heck? I thought I heard something. Okay, get up and I'll fix it."

"I can't get up! I need help."

"Of course."

By this time they were getting kind of silly. He pulled his mother up and she was finally vertical.

"You go in the living room and I'll fix the bed."

"Don't be silly. It's the middle of the night. We'll fix it in the morning."

"Mom," he said. "I'm up. It *is* morning. It's 3:30 in the morning. I'll fix the bed. No problem."

Esther wasn't going to argue with her son in the middle of the night and win, so she tried to be of some help, and left to look for the box that said "coffee machine – open first." Ideally, it was the last box in the truck and the first one out. Ideally. She did find it and made them each a coffee, black, with sugar. They had no milk, which was tomorrow's job, or today's really. Yes, get

197

groceries before they had to take that honking truck back that they had both come to despise climbing in and out of.

"Got time for coffee and a smoke, David?"

"Hey, sounds good. I'm almost done."

Now he was 100 percent awake, after working with IKEA tools and screws and bolts and nuts.

"Hey, why did you make your bed fall down?"

And they both had a big belly laugh. They stayed up about ten more minutes then David crawled back on the couch and Esther went back to bed. She was so nervous to move or roll over, for fear the bed would fall down again, that she hardly slept. David slept until noon and didn't even wake up when Frieda came over with milk for coffee.

David stayed a month. He had no place to live in High River either, so he wasn't in any hurry to fly back to sleep on another couch somewhere. They did the tourist thing for a while: lighthouses, the boardwalk, historic smoke sheds, all the different beaches, and they ate fish chowder, dulse, and of course lots of lobster and scallops.

David found Esther another car online and made arrangements to see it. She bought it for cheap and then spent the rest of her money on repairs for three different breakdowns.

Esther was upset about the car, but David, the eternal optimist, said: "We have beds, we don't sleep on the dirt. We have a roof that doesn't leak. For God's sake we have a coffee maker that makes coffee in less than ten seconds, and there's a grocery store full of food on the island."

Finally Esther interjected: "We don't have a washer and dryer."

"In Haiti we washed clothes on a rock in a tub of water and wrung them out by hand and hung them on a makeshift clothesline!"

"Okay, okay, I'm thankful for that red piece of metal in the driveway already."

"As long as it gets me to the airport in Saint John when I go back to Calgary." Esther was laughing so hard she almost peed herself.

"Hey! And gets me back here too!"

"Of course, of course."

The brat was still laughing.

AFTER DAVID LEFT, Esther fell into a deep depression. One day she stopped by her sister Liona's restaurant and she rattled off a dozen things Esther could be doing or volunteering for. Esther didn't want to hear any of it. When she pulled in the driveway at home, there was a blue and red for sale sign in the yard. Esther was furious. The landlord should have told her the building was going up for sale before she moved across the country. Esther couldn't face another move. She wasn't even fully unpacked.

Over the years Esther had stayed in contact with Frieda. She could tell by her letters that there was a connection between them, a bond that felt strong. Maybe because Frieda loved her and looked after her when she was a baby. Liona loved Esther too, but she was busy with her restaurant and didn't have the time to visit like Frieda had. Frieda was retired.

After David left, Frieda invited Esther to church with her every Sunday, and for dinner Sunday nights. The pastor introduced her to the congregation and Esther felt a bit awkward for the first three Sundays because she didn't know any of the hymns, so she just stood there. But each week he and a parishioner, Claudia, came to where Esther and Frieda sat at the front and clasped their hands and welcomed them. Esther felt uncomfortable, until unexpectedly, she just didn't anymore. She watched people sing and noticed they had something in common, something she'd noticed right away that Frieda had. They had God. Esther could see it by the glow on their faces when they smiled.

Esther began to smile, and wondered if someday she would glow too. She thought not.

There was no one under the age of fifty, and those people had attended this tiny church their whole life. Pastor Ward had been there fourteen years, and everything during the mass happened with a familiar sync, but not rote or boring. It was a light and cheerful community. About once a month the pastor stopped by for a visit at Frieda's, then he visited with Esther right next door. She adored his glowing face.

Frieda and Esther loved each other right from the day they met again. Frieda's words, actions, and strengths were straight from God, and she glowed. She had a past; they all did, but she was a woman of God, and Esther was so proud of her.

They shared countless meals, made up recipes for inexpensive ones, and made blackberry jelly in the fall. Frieda shared her little books called *My Daily Bread* and they went every Thursday to Thrifty's, a little second hand shop to scrounge for bargains; they never left empty handed. Tuesdays Frieda went to Bible Study, and Esther cleaned her apartment and made dinner for her when she came home. Esther lived for Sundays and spending time with Frieda.

After a few weeks, on a Wednesday, Pastor Ward came to visit. Frieda wasn't home so Esther spent more time with him. Esther told him about growing up in Montreal with a Jewish family, and although she felt so welcome and happy going to church, a part of her was torn in half, and Esther didn't know how to fix herself. He said a prayer for her and hugged her in a very loving, Christian way. He was a good man of God, and she felt privileged to have met him.

CHAPTER 46

Good Riddance

B Y SPRING, CHURCHILL'S BLACK DOG had gotten a hold of Esther. Except for Sundays. Sundays she forced herself to get dressed and go to church with Frieda. The rest of the week, she woke up in the morning, had coffee and cigarettes, then went back to bed on the couch until eleven or twelve o'clock, drifting in and out of sleep. She would see Frieda walk past the picture window, either taking or picking up her laundry from the utility room next to Esther's apartment. Sometimes she watched her cup her hands around her face, blocking out the sun, and look in to see if Esther was up. Often Esther did get up and let her in. Frieda was always happy; God made her this way. Esther would make her coffee and they'd smoke a couple of cigarettes and then Frieda would leave. Esther didn't blame her, Esther was as miserable as she looked.

One morning, Esther was on the couch as usual when Frieda knocked on the door. Esther assumed the worst. The duplex they lived in was still for sale, and she thought maybe she had gotten a call from the landlord saying they'd have to vacate. Just the thought of having to move sent her closer to the edge. Maybe the edge was home.

Frieda just smiled and said that God would provide another place for them to live. Esther didn't have her confidence.

But she had just gotten a call from the nursing home where Melba lived in St. Stephen, New Brunswick. Melba had passed away in her sleep. She was ninety-three, and had dementia. Part of Esther was angry. How could she be so fortunate as to just fall asleep and not wake up? No pills, no psychiatric units, just bloody well fall asleep.

Liona didn't go, but Frieda left the next day to pick up Floress and together they went to the nursing home on the mainland to get Melba's personal belongings. They donated clothes and blankets to the home for anyone who might need them, and left with just her purse. They arrived at the crematorium in time to say their goodbyes and pick out an urn. Her ashes would be sent to Cal's Funeral Home on the island.

201

Frieda and Floress arrived back late that night on the last ferry. Esther saw her car lights turn into the driveway around 11:15 p.m. It was too late to go over, so she set her alarm for 8 a.m. so she wouldn't sleep in.

That night Esther thought about the last time she corresponded with Melba, thirty years ago. After a year of psychotherapy, Esther wrote her a letter and told her she was glad she gave her away to Mummy and Daddy, but would never forgive her for taking her back. And she didn't forgive her for leaving Stevie and Floress with no mother when they were seven and eight years old. She left them to be abused and raped by their father and brother. On the top of that page she wrote: It doesn't matter now – they're both dead.

Frieda had written her when Russell died of appendicitis and Paul of cancer. Good riddance is what Esther thought about that.

Esther implored her to tell her who her real father was, because she could never believe she belonged to the likes of Russell Skunk.

The day Esther mailed the letter, she curled her hair, put on makeup, dressed like she was going to a dinner party, and drove to the nearest mailbox. She pulled down the handle and dropped the letter in, then opened it again, just to be sure the envelope did indeed go down the chute.

Esther went home, changed her clothes, and got on with her day. She felt empowered; of course that was supposed to be the point of the whole exercise.

A little more than two weeks later Esther got her letter back, inside the same envelope. Melba had simply written Esther's address on a piece of paper and taped it on the front. The chutzpah! She sent her own letter back.

She denied Esther's abuse, scribbled over her words, and then wrote between the lines "troublemaker" and "liar." Between the lines again, she wrote: "I had to take you back, Flora didn't want you because you were a spoiled brat." And: "It's not my fault you'd rather live with a gangster. I bet you didn't know that someone came up from New York and shot him! Yes, your precious daddy. And I have all the IOUs he had in his office, over $50,000 I'm going to collect." All over Esther's letter where she saw what she didn't like, or wouldn't admit, she scribbled out Esther's words, and replaced them with nasty words of her own. She did include a small piece of paper telling Esther she had caused her another angina attack. "As for who your father is, just look at your sister, Liona – you look just like her. You all belong to Russell Skunk."

Well, that was a lie, because Frieda found her real father when she was fifty-two. He had been married when she was born. And the baby that Frieda heard crying in the house up in Janeville when she was just a baby herself, was Robert, who was dropped off at the church when he was an infant. It took him sixty years, but he eventually found all of his siblings, and Melba too.

Then on the back of the piece of paper, she added that Esther was being taken out of her will, and she had investments from Flora's jewellery and other valuables until 2022.

How could Melba take all these precious things that Sammy had bought Flora and turn them into investments all the while calling Daddy a gangster? Esther told herself it didn't matter who she thought he was. Esther knew who he was.

Oh my Gott in Himmel, why didn't good memories remain as vivid and real as the bad memories? Esther didn't know if she had these memories all in fifteen minutes, or off and on all night. She awoke a complete mess, and didn't know which she needed first – coffee, cigarettes, or Valium. She opted for the Valium and went next door with a cup of coffee in hand and talked to Floress while Frieda talked to Liona on the telephone.

Frieda relayed the news for the day. Melba died intestate, there was no registered will. Liona had hired a lawyer as soon as she had gotten the call that Melba had died. It was going to be a lot of work for Liona to have the courts release enough money to pay for her cremation, and other funeral expenses. It took three weeks for this to happen.

Frieda called Liona the night before the funeral service to make sure flowers had been ordered. Liona announced that, if Frieda, Floress and Esther wanted flowers, they could chip in and buy them. This was 8:30 at night and the service was at 10 a.m. the following morning. Frieda was so angry she could barely speak, but she got on the phone, called the right people, and they picked up two flower arrangements at 9:30 in the morning. She told the owner of the flower shop to put them on Liona Green's account, for their mother's service.

The service took fourteen minutes, and that included a hymn played on a guitar by a Pastor they'd never seen before. There were no refreshments, dainty little party sandwiches, or desserts. They all simply left.

Liona went back to work at her restaurant. Frieda, Floress and Esther went to the grocery store to look for something for supper, something easy, but good. Fish chowder they decided – just fish, potatoes, onions, butter and milk. Back at Frieda's, they all helped chopping onions and peeling potatoes. They just had to add the fish when they were ready to eat.

Floress went to the bathroom, then stopped in the bedroom where she'd been sleeping and came out, slowly waving Melba's purse.

"Hey, I almost forgot I had this."

She couldn't just dump the contents on the kitchen table, no. She reached in and took out one item at a time.

There was a cheap beige, vinyl wallet that matched the colour of the purse, a chequebook, a panty liner, a small crumpled package of Kleenex, some Certs, a package of gum, some rubber bands, and a lipstick and mirror.

Her wedding rings from Cecil were on a safety pin attached to the lining of the purse. Floress left what she thought would be important to Esther to near last.

"Here Esther, I know this wasn't Mam's ring, so it must have been Aunt Flora's."

Esther could see that ring, along with Flora's other rings and her watch in a green flowered bone china dish sitting on her dresser. Frieda had brought Esther that dish a couple of months before. She knew it wasn't Melba's, but Melba had given it to her some years back.

"I've never known what to put in it, so I never put anything in it. Now that you're here, you should have it," Frieda had said.

It was a wide, thick gold ring. The setting resembled a tied knot covered in diamonds. Esther picked it up and stared at it, tears falling down her cheeks that dried before she even noticed she was crying.

"This was Mummy's every day ring. She wore it every day of life, and at night she put it in the green dish along with her wedding rings and her first watch from Daddy. Melba must have thought this was the least valuable piece of jewellery, and just had to keep something for herself. That's why it wasn't sold with the other pieces and put into the investment funds."

Both Frieda and Floress said it wasn't Melba's in the first place. It was Flora's, so now it belonged to Esther. She thanked them for saying that, and let them both try it on. But like Cinderella, it only fit Esther's finger. She was very happy that the ring had come back to her. Flora and Sammy would have wanted to see this moment.

There was one more thing in a small zippered pocket. Floress reached in and took out what appeared to be a small folded piece of black fabric inside a piece of waxed paper. As she unfolded it, Esther shouted: "Oh my Gott, surely this is a sign from Heaven." Floress and Frieda looked confused.

"What are you talking about?"

Esther finished unfolding the fabric, knowing full well what it was. But why had Melba taken it from Flora?

Frieda asked: "What is it?"

"It's called a yarmulke. It's Daddy's yarmulke!"

Esther put it on her head.

"What's it for?" Floress asked.

"It's tradition that Jewish men cover their head as a sign of respect for God, who is around and above us."

"Why would Mam keep that?" Floress asked.

"She coveted everything of Mummy's, including Daddy."

"Frieda, you know you don't belong to Russell Skunk. Now I'm going to prove I don't belong to him either."

"You don't have to prove it – you look just like Sammy. How are you going to prove it anyway?"

"DNA testing." Ever so gently she showed both her sisters the hairs that had collected around the band of the yarmulke.

"Doesn't that cost a lot of money?" Frieda asked.

"Yes it does, as much as $2,000 a hair. We're each going to get around $10,000 from Melba's estate, and I have a diamond necklace that Mummy gave me the night before she left me on the island. She had said: 'You're too young now, but when you grow up and ever desperately need money, you can sell it.' You know I just remembered her telling me that. I did have it appraised for insurance some years ago, and it's worth over $10,000."

"Were you ever tempted to sell it, Esther?" Floress asked.

"Floress, I've needed money many times, but I never thought about selling the necklace. Not until this very moment. To prove Daddy is my father, I will."

Floress said: "It sure would have been a whole lot easier if Mam would have just told you the truth."

"Yes, but by keeping Daddy's yarmulke, maybe that was her way of telling the truth without having to admit anything. I have really always known the truth. There has never been any doubt in my mind. Sammy is my father. I've just wanted someone to affirm it is so."

"Esther," Frieda said. "If there's never been any doubt for you, then why do you think you have to spend $20,000 to prove it?"

"I'm tired of living surrounded by a Girling cloud of evil. It makes me sick to think I could have come from his gene pool. Sorry Floress."

Frieda said: "Esther, you just said you have always known Sammy is your father, maybe God has the only truth, my dear little sister."

"You could be right, Frieda. Everyone used to say: 'It's funny, she looks just like him.' Why was it funny?"

"Well, Esther," Frieda said, "his family knew that Flora wasn't your mother, so what else could they think? You were Melba's kid. Melba's kid who looked like Sammy. So it's funny. It's loaded. Maybe his family guessed right from the beginning who you belonged to, and kept their mouths shut so they wouldn't make trouble."

"I feel like I have to prove it."

"To whom?"

"To myself."

Frieda said: "What if the hair is too old and it can't be proven? What are you going to do?"

"I don't know."

"Esther, I know this isn't the greatest time, but Betty called and left a message while we were out this morning."

"She's sold the duplex?"

"Yes, I guess she has. We have to be out in sixty days, the new owners are doing renovations. Don't worry, my beautiful little sister, we'll find another place!"

CHAPTER 47

Dark Harbour

E STHER WASN'T SURE what to do with herself.
In the afternoons she went through boxes she had moved here and hadn't opened yet. She found linens, blankets, clothes, shoes, knick-knacks, and scarves she had no need for anymore. On Thursdays she went with Frieda to Thrifty's and put bags of these items in the donation pile, but still came home with something – like a small clear plastic angel that glowed in the dark which she placed her on the kitchen table.

As the weather warmed, she went for walks on the sand beach across the road, and past the old fish sheds. She found a spot between two large rock outcroppings and the shoreline where she could sit and pray, beyond sight of other beachcombers for rocks, seashells, and sea glass. Sometimes she forgot how to pray and fell asleep. One day Esther tried to remember the number of times she'd moved during the time Alec and she were married, and since then. Esther lost track at eighteen. She realized she had been trying to replace her childhood home in Montreal. Even though she had her own children, she still missed the royal family.

The duplex Frieda and she lived in had been sold, and again, like in High River, where would she go? Her anxiety was through the roof. How could she not worry? She didn't know how to not worry. She did know she shouldn't take any more Valium, because she couldn't think straight when she did.

Oh hell, Esther popped two in her mouth.

She didn't have the faith Frieda had. Esther became more frightened and anxious as days passed. She continued to clean her apartment of everything that wasn't necessary, and took more belongings to Thrifty's.

She found her jewellery, and cleaned her diamond necklace. Twenty-two diamonds sparkled alive; it was stunning. Esther started wearing it under her hooded sweatshirts! No one would know. She wasn't ready to sell it, so instead waited for Melba's money to be released by the courts. After no legal will was produced, it was deemed she did in fact die intestate and her small estate, made up of Mummy's valuables was divided equally among the six

207

living siblings. They each received a cheque for $10,642.35 minus legal fees. Now she could start DNA testing without selling her necklace, at least not yet. Esther did research about testing Daddy's hair and it appeared to be very difficult for an accurate determination to be made with degraded hair. The laboratory required hair with the root attached, and even then the success rate was low. With tweezers she pulled short hairs from around the band of the yarmulke and placed them on a black scarf, looking for the largest root under a microscope she had borrowed from the high school. She found nothing usable and decided to have the hair tested only if she had to.

Esther discovered she could have a sibling-to-sibling match done to see if they had the same x chromosomes. This would determine if they had different fathers, or if Dear Gott, she was a Girling. She asked Floress if she'd be willing to do a cheek swab to send with Esther's to be tested. Floress was willing. Esther ordered a DNA collection kit and when it arrived she went over to her house. Floress was beautiful, with dark naturally curly hair and double eyelashes, she was also the sibling who most resembled Russell Skunk. She was a nurse, so Esther asked her to do the buccal swabs. Floress wondered how long it would take for the results. Esther told her three to five business days after they received the kit back.

"What are you going to do if we match, Esther?"

"I don't know, hon."

Esther knew she would get the results by email before they arrived in the Queen's mail. She didn't tell anyone else that she was having this done, and was a nervous wreck checking her email and popping pills every day. On the third day she called David and Rachel and ended the conversation with how much she loved them. On the fourth day she invited Floress and Frieda and Liona for fish chowder dinner and hugged them close when they left. Later that night Esther drove to the gas station and filled up the gas tank.

Day five she went to her secret spot on the beach and confessed all the sins she could remember from the age of five, when she hit a girl who lived down the street. Esther asked Gott, or God, or Jesus, whoever was listening, to forgive her.

Day six the report was in her inbox.

Esther's eyes scanned quickly over numbers and words didn't understand until she reached the place she had been terrified to see:

Both siblings have uncommon x chromosomes.
The same father is excluded.

Melba's Wash 209

This was enough information for her. She thanked Gott that she didn't belong to Russell Skunk.

It took fifteen or so minutes to drive to the Dark Harbour Road turnoff. Esther thought of the last person who drove off the three hundred foot cliff, and got hung up on some trees. She hung strapped in her seatbelt upside down for two days. She was rescued, but had permanent brain damage and lived in a nursing home.

Esther didn't speed at first, and didn't wear her seatbelt either. In the distance, the spot she needed to turn loomed. She pressed down hard on the gas pedal and crossed the centre line with a feeling of complete calm control.

The car flew for a few seconds before it began to descend and clear the trees. The front of the car began to drop, then flipped over and Esther was in the backseat. The window was open.

Esther was finally on her way home.

Home to be with Gott in Himmel.

Home to be with the royal family.

Epilogue

I NOW KNOW THAT A PHOTOGRAPH does not always capture the truth; that sometimes a photograph cements a lie to history. Or many lies.

BEFORE THE CAR HITS THE GROUND, I imagine I see them in the photograph of us taken in the lobby of the Catskills Hotel. I am wearing a short sleeve aqua print dress with a crinoline and belted at the waist, and over it, a new white angora cardigan trimmed on the cuffs and up the front with sequins. I talked Mummy into buying it for me a few minutes before we posed for our photograph. She didn't think I needed it, so that's why her smile isn't real.

I am standing in front of Daddy with my hands joined loosely in front of me, and my feet in ballet style second position. He is wearing a white shirt, striped tie, and a monogrammed white hankie barely sticks up from his jacket pocket. His suit is charcoal grey and his matching shoes have just been shined.

Mummy is wearing a stunning bronze cocktail dress and her sable mink stole. Her coloured auburn hair is perfectly teased and backcombed, stiff with hairspray. She is standing shoe to shiny shoe beside Daddy, leaning into his right shoulder; her arms wrap his at the elbow. Her wedding rings sparkle. Daddy's hand hangs between us, with nowhere to go. His left hand is solid and warm on my shoulder.

Written on the back of the photograph in Mummy's handwriting is:

"the royal family" 1959
Flora, Sammy, and Esther

Acknowledgements

Thank you to Sara Murphy for kick-starting my career.

Thanks to Aritha Van Herk for her guidance at the University of Calgary.

Thank you to Editor Julie Roorda and General Editor Michael Mirolla at Guernica Editions for their patience and keen insights while I recuperated from two major surgeries during the final presentation of this work.

Thank you to Karen McLaughlin for our life long friendship and childhood escapes to Willa Cather's cabin on Grand Manan Island.

Thank you to William R Coombes for his support, determination and belief in me.

Thank you to my family members, Michael, Cheri-Lynn and Phil for their relentless encouragement and support.

There are many people who in one way or another contribute to an author on the journey from idea to published work. When I consider all the writers I have met, my studies at College and University, writers groups, poetry readings, books read and discussions over cups of coffee, it is a long a list. I am grateful to every one, and thank you for your brave contributions to our vibrant literary community, your often passionate and humorous role modelling and stimulation.

About the Author

Born into an impoverished New Brunswick family, Reesa Steinman Brotherton was taken to Montreal, raised Jewish, then at age 10, sent back to her family of origin. A "dark horse" among Canadian authors, she received a Certificate of Creative Writing from Humber College and also from the University of Calgary. After a lengthy time away, she moved back to High River, Alberta to be near her children and grandchildren.

Printed in July 2019
by Gauvin Press,
Gatineau, Québec